GUARD KATE

*A Kate Killoy Mystery - Suspense
for the Dog Lover*

Peggy Gaffney

Kanine Books

Sandy,
Thank you for all
your help, I couldn't
do it without you.
Merry Christmas!

Peggy Gaffney

*This is dedicated to my son Sean and my
Samoyed dogs Dillon and Quinn.*

CONTENTS

THE KATE KILLOY
MYSTERY SERIES

CAST OF CHARACTERS

Family

Kate Killoy Foyle – *Dog Breeder/Trainer, Knitting Designer, with a talent for solving mysteries, K-9 partner 'Dillon', owner of a dozen Samoyed dogs.*

Harry Foyle – *Kate's husband and owner of a successful cyber security company and former math geek for the FBI.*

Tom Killoy – *Kate's brother, CEO of Killoy and Killoy Forensic Accountants the family business, boyfriend of Gwyn.*

Will Killoy – *Kate's brother, finishing his degree at MIT and about to join the family business, an extremely talented chef.*

Seamus Killoy – *Kate's brother, twin, senior in high school, talented cyber researcher, works part time for Harry, girlfriend Satu.*

Tim Killoy – *Kate's brother, twin, senior in high school, athletic superstar*

Claire Killoy – *Kate's mother who is a math professor*

at Yale

Ann Killoy – *Kate's grandmother*

Agnes Forester – *Kate's 2nd. Cousin, former supermodel, President of Forester's Bank in NYC, engaged to Sean Connelly*

Sybil Forester – *Kate's great-aunt, Agnes' grandmother, engaged to Bill Salverson*

Maeve Killoy Donovan – *Kate's great-aunt, former MI-5, married to Padraig Donovan*

Kate's team

Satu Mituzani - *Senior in high school, talented cyber researcher, works part time for Harry, Seamus' girlfriend.*

Dani DeFelice – *CT State Trooper, K-9 partner Bouvier des Flandres 'Jake'*

Sal Mondigliani – *Retired police chief, manager of Kate's boarding kennel, works with Kate to train dogs, including police dogs. Constant companion Ret. K-9 officer Samoyed 'Liam', Dillon's sire who has developed a bond with the retired cop.*

Sean Connelly – *CT Sate Trooper, K-9 partner Golden Retriever 'Patrick', engaged to Agnes.*

Sgt. Gurka – *CT State Trooper, K-9 partner, GSD 'Teddy'*

Lt. Leon Holmwood *a CT State Trooper*

Special Agent Deshi Xiang – *FBI based in Washington DC office, friend of Kate and Harry.*

Malcolm Bullock – *Agent in Charge FBI Washington DC office, Des' boss, friend of Kate and Harry.*

Sgt. George Braxton – *Bolton Landing, NY Police Dept., Gwyn's cousin, old friend of Kate's*

Dr. Gwyn Braxton – *CT Forensic Pathologist, George's cousin, Tom's girlfriend, childhood friend of Kate.*

Involved in the case

Bill Salverson – *Inventor of the Salverson Defense Shield, engaged to Sybil*
Ellie Bullock – *Malcolm's wife*
Richard Carsley – *Friend of Kate and Agnes, bank president in NYC Congresswoman Jannah Mastalski*
Joel – *Mastalski's assistant.*
Congressman Roosevelt Heller
Howard – *Heller's 'fixer'*
Congressional Chairman James
General Cutter – *In charge of testing the Salverson Defense Shield*
Corporal Pavlo Turchin/ Konstantine Lazar
Annabelle Harrington Heller/Anna Chesnokov
Charlie Salverson – *Claims to be Bill's brother*
Karl and Anna – FBI agents

Others

Mr. Edwards – *In charge of project to assemble Kate and Harry's manufactured house.*
Bert – *Crane operator on house project*
Jimmy Buchanan – *Fence construction man, former classmate of Tom's*
Fr. Joe – *Kate and Harry's parish priest*
Roberto – *Son of one of Kate's professional knitters*
Carisa Amaya – Jr. handler who worked with Agnes'

greyhound Thorin

CHAPTER 1

Wednesday afternoon

There were two problems with the line of fuzzy white dogs along the fence. The first was that two of them were neither white nor fuzzy. The second was that unless they fell from the sky, it was impossible for these non-fuzzy nor white visitors to have gotten into the pen without Kate knowing.

A sharp bark from Quinn, Kate Killoy's youngest Samoyed, broke through her astonishment. She walked forward, her hands reaching out to give pats and snuggles to each dog in turn. When she arrived at the two large greyhound bitches which she'd know since they were born, she snuggled them, while at the same time checking to see if the bitches were injured, or if their coats showed any sign of

1

rough travels. Nothing. From the tips of their whip-like tails to their long-pointed noses, they were sleek and ready for the show ring. They were even wearing decorative snoods over their heads and heavy, elaborate, decorative collars. So if Thorin and Twisp were here, where was Agnes?

She walked into the kitchen and called, "Agnes?"

Nothing. Opening the front door she repeated the call. Still, nothing. Pulling out her phone she called Agnes' number. It went to voicemail. Odd. She called her grandmother whose house was at the end of the driveway.

"Hi Gran, is Agnes with you? Her girls are in my exercise yard."

"No, she's not. Maybe she's visiting Ellen."

"I'll check." Ending the call she stood there. This wasn't like Agnes. Agnes Forester, former super-model, did not go anywhere without a fanfare. Kate began to feel uneasy.

Looking out the kitchen window, she saw no sign of her cousin's car. Wait, she thought. Security. Maybe Agnes came when she was listening to the news while cleaning the kennels. Taking her phone back out of her pocket, she pulled up the security app and hit the code to show anyone who'd entered or exited the property in the last four hours. The only entry was Mrs. Sager who picked up her Basset Hound, Howard. So how did a former supermodel recently turned bank president, sneak two large greyhounds onto her property, which had cameras and alarms everywhere; without that system letting out a peep? Plus, why hadn't she heard barking from her dogs? Granted, they are trained to obey Agnes as well as her, but still...

As the kettle she had turned on when she came in, clicked off, Kate reached for a clean mug and a teabag. Then she keyed in Agnes' phone number again and waited. Voicemail. As she disconnected, her phone rang, the display showing Sean Connelly, Agnes' fiancé.

"Sean," she said as she answered, "just the person I need to talk to."

"Great!" he replied. "Can you tell me where Agnes is?"

"I was calling you with the same question. She somehow managed to sneak the girls into my dog yard when I was cleaning the boarding kennel. None of my alarms went off, so I don't know how she got past the security. Harry's going to have ten fits. We were told nobody could get by this security after what happened at the wedding."

'I found a note on my kitchen table saying she

was called out of town and would be back soon. She said that you had the girls."

"Did you call Sybil?" Agnes still lived with her grandmother who had bred greyhound show dogs for close to fifty years.

"Sybil got the same note I did."

"Harry is due back from the city in about an hour. He had to go into New York to wrap up two of the cases he finished right before the wedding. He may have an idea on how she got in here and out again or where she is now. But short of adding an invisibility cloak to her million-dollar wardrobe, I can't figure it out. Look, I'll go talk to my knitters before they go home. Maybe they saw something. You're coming over tomorrow when they deliver the crane to put our house on its foundation this weekend. While you're here arranging the traffic control for all the huge flatbeds, we can talk. Hopefully, Agnes the Invisible will report in by that time."

She put away her phone and stared out the window at the dogs. They showed no sign of stress or upset of any kind. She wished she could say the same for herself. This was not Agnes' style. She liked dramatic entrances, coming through a door with a swirl and a pause until she was sure every eye was focused on her. If there was one thing that Agnes wasn't, that was subtle. Low key wasn't part of her vocabulary.

Checking the clock, she saw it was almost time for her knitters to leave for the day so Kate finished her tea, put on her parka, and trotted across the parking lot while huddling inside her coat to fight the cold. She ran up the staircase outside the barn and pulled open the door to her knitting studio. Walking into a blast of warmth, she tossed her parka on the coat rack, she pushed her way through the inner door. The swish, swish of the knitting machines competed with the laughing chatter of her knitters. Several kids were squatting at the low table in the back of the room playing a game. The school bus picked up and dropped off the children of her employees so that they didn't have to go home to an empty house. Kate had built an area where they could do homework, play with their younger siblings or rock the babies in the nursery room.

Kate had decided right from the beginning when setting up her business that she would employ minority women or single parents who had a hard time fitting both a family and job into a normal work situation. Here, they could work happily surrounded by their families. This created happy employees who worked hard. She also paid well and provided health insurance which meant that there was a waiting list of people wanting to work here. Her studio manager, Ellen, ran training classes as part of the town's evening education program. Those who completed the classes were eligible to take on part-time work when the studio was under pressure to complete a big job. If they worked out, they would slowly be added to the workforce.

Kate and Ellen were hard at work developing plans to build an extension on the barn which would give them an additional workroom and could house specialty equipment, like lace-knitting and automated machines, used for special orders.

Smiles greeted Kate as she walked into the group gathered around Ellen. Her manager had laid out the sketches Kate had drawn of the possible expansion. Everyone had suggestions for what should be included. Kate had just begun answering their questions when Roberto, Concetta's eleven-year-old son, asked if he could come to visit the big brown dogs sometimes.

"Oh, you saw the greyhounds."

"Yea. I saw you put them in with your Sammies.

They certainly look different. But they seem nice, just big."

"They are nice. Both are females, and they are very gentle especially considering their size. I didn't see you watching them."

"Oh, I had just dashed out to put my backpack in the car when I finished my homework. I didn't want to forget it. I noticed because you were wearing your old red jacket. It showed up when you went out into the woods after you were done."

Not wanting to cause any alarm, she chatted with two of the new knitters who were still learning the way the business ran, but after gathering no more information about possible sightings of Agnes, she pulled on her parka and headed back to her house. She had just entered the kitchen when her phone rang with a call from her grandmother.

"Kate, I've got an emergency here. Sybil is on her way over. Apparently, a close friend of hers and a long-time friend of her late brother-in-law, Paul has died, and she's really upset. It's not like Sybil to be this emotional, so I think there is something much more wrong. Could you come to talk to her? Apparently, his death was unusual."

"Of course, I'm on my way. Harry will be back soon, so I'll leave him a note."

She tore off a sheet of her work pad and scribbled the information that she was at her grandmother's and set it in the middle of the kitchen table, put her parka back on, and headed for the front door, then stopped. Roberto had said he'd seen her in the dog yard wearing her old red parka. She opened the coat closet door and looked inside. Both the red parka and the knitted hat that matched were gone as well--Agnes was doing it again, disguising herself as Kate.

The security ding on her phone told her that Sybil Forester had arrived at the property. Kate went out and locked the door. She plunged down the front steps and began running up the driveway in the direction of her grandmother's home.

The looming hole in the ground was impossible to pass without being impressed. It was huge. The finished foundation for their home appeared even larger in the half-light of dusk. Dark came early this close to the shortest day of the year. She felt excitement grip both her in anticipation of the arrival of the sections of their factory-built home on Friday. The crane which would put all the pieces in place was due tomorrow and then before dawn on Friday, trucks carrying the sections of the first and second floors would get here. Somehow, the attic was carried flat on top of the second-floor sections. She was curious about how they could carry another floor of the house hidden. Friday she guessed she would find out when they put that together.

Mounting the front porch steps, Kate let herself in and heard sobs coming from the kitchen. Sybil was at the kitchen table crying with Gran holding her sister-in-law in her arms. She looked up as Kate came in and nodded. Kate slipped into the chair across from them and reached for Sybil's hand.

"How can I help, Sybil? Tell me what happened and what I can do."

"You can find his killer and bring him to justice."

Startled, she asked, "Whose killer? What happened. I'll be glad to help and so will Harry and Tom, but we need to know who was killed."

"Bill was murdered. My...." A wracking sob stopped her.

"Bill who?" Kate asked gently, trying to ease her great-aunt's grief, so she could catch her breath.

"Bill Salverson. He is...he was my best friend. He's been on the board at the bank for over twenty years."

"Bill Salverson the dog show judge? Didn't he do hounds and terriers? I remember showing Twisp under him for Agnes. Lovely man. He came to

Thanksgiving here several times."

"He was a lovely, wonderful man. A lovely, caring man who didn't deserve to be smashed to death."

"Sybil, please, tell me what happened." Now Gran was crying along with Sybil. Kate didn't want to be pulled into their heartbreak. She got up and made a fresh pot of tea after putting a new box of tissues on the table. Once the tea was poured and fixed the way the women wanted it, they both were able to pull themselves together enough to sip their tea and talk.

"About an hour ago," Sybil began, "a state policeman contacted me. It seems Bill had listed my name as the person to call in case of an emergency. Late yesterday afternoon, Bill was driving home from the city on I-84 when a large truck pulled up beside his car and began moving into his lane. Apparently, people in other cars noticed the move. The first time it happened, Bill braked and the truck moved ahead of him. Traffic behind the truck then began clogging up when the truck slowed to ten miles-per-hour under the speed limit. Bill waited for the traffic behind him to pass, and then he moved into the middle lane to pass the truck. After driving for a while, Bill moved back into the right-hand lane, so he could prepare to exit. The truck moved up on the left side of Bill's car again, but this time, Bill didn't have the time to get out of the way. Drivers told the police that the truck purposely swung to the right, plowing into Bill's car and kept pushing until it broke through the guardrail and rolled down the hill. The truck then swung back onto the highway and a minute later took the exit and disappeared.

"Two of the cars following got the license number of the truck and others called the police, but by the time they got to Bill's car, he was dead. Kate, it was murder. I don't know why, but someone murdered him. I've been trying to call Agnes to tell her, but her phone goes to voicemail."

"Sean told me that she was away," Kate said. She left the bitches here but I didn't see her."

Sybil looked at her. "We've got to talk to Agnes. She might know who did this. Bill called her the night before last asking her to meet with him yesterday afternoon."

"Did he say why he wanted to talk to Agnes?"

"He didn't tell me, but after he spoke to Agnes, she seemed upset and worried. She said it was just business, but she seemed apprehensive. I almost asked to go with her, but yesterday was my morning to volunteer at the public library. When she came home yesterday, she was very quiet. She got a phone call late, just as I was going to bed. I didn't hear what she said but I looked down from the stair landing and saw her staring at the phone as though it had bitten her. When I woke this morning, she and the girls were gone."

Kate's phone dinged showing that Harry had pulled into the driveway. She scrambled to her feet and moved around to Sybil. Reaching down, she hugged her.

"Harry just came home. Sybil, I promise you, we will find Bill's killer. I think you should stay with Gram tonight."

Without adding what was beating on her brain, she quickly left and ran down the hill to meet her husband as he got out of his car. She wrapped her arms around him and held on tight. Visions of her past horrors came flooding back. She looked up, with tears beginning to fall, as she fought the gasps she had held in check.

"Harry," she choked out, "Bill Salverson is dead. Murdered. And I think someone is trying to kill Agnes."

CHAPTER 2

Wednesday evening.

Harry wrapped his arms around her and half-walked, half-carried her onto the porch and into the house. He gently seated her at the kitchen table and turned on the tea kettle. Then, checking the clock, he reached into the freezer and pulled out a paper canister labeled 'pea soup' and put it into the microwave to thaw and reheat. He heard the kettle click indicating it had boiled and quickly made a mug of tea.

With tea in hand, he rounded the table and set it on the table in front of Kate then moved his warmed hands to her shoulders, massaging the knots until a sigh had him pulling her up against him and wrapping his arms around her.

"Are you ready to tell me what happened today

that has you so upset? What's happened to Agnes?"

Kate dropped her hands from her face and reached for the tea. Then she drew a shuttering breath and resting her head against him, began telling him. She began with finding the two greyhound bitches in the pen with her Sams. Harry just listened. When she finally got to the part with Bill Salverson being pushed off the highway to his death, he wrapped her shoulders in a hug. She told him her suspicions about the threat to Agnes and the fear that she had fled for her life. He eased himself into the chair beside her and while still holding her with one arm, he pulled out his phone and dialed Sean, putting the call on speaker.

"Sean, there was a vehicle crash involving a truck pushing a car off I 84 yesterday. Can you find out whose in charge and get every drop of information they've got?"

"Probably," Sean answered.

"The victim was Bill Salverson."

"Sybil's friend?"

"Yea."

"Agnes was supposed to meet with him yesterday afternoon."

"Yeah, she said something about that."

"I think she might have. Wait. Does this have

anything to do with her note saying she had to go somewhere? With her not answering her phone?"

"Possibly. From what Kate got out of Sybil, Agnes got a call last night which upset her. Today, she parks her greyhounds with Kate and disappears disguised in some of Kate's clothes."

"She's disguised as Kate--again? Let me get that information and I'll be at your place as soon as I can. We've got to find her. If she's running and on her own, she is probably in danger."

"That's what we thought. Get us all the information you can and find out who's in charge. We'll be waiting for you."

The microwave dinged while he was talking to Sean. When he disconnected, Harry stood, kissed the top of Kate's head, and went to get bowls for the soup. This was a new recipe Will wanted them to try. He was trying to cut down on the amount of salt usually found in soup recipes by substituting different herbs and spices. The cardboard containers he used, he got at a restaurant supply house and were really convenient for reheating. Plus it meant no pan to wash.

Kate's fear for Agnes still consumed her but the smell of the thick pea soup with chunks of ham distracted her momentarily. It had her picking up a spoon and eating. The soup was delicious. Harry placed a small bowl with crackers next to her plate. It was just the thing to give her enough energy to free her mind, so she could begin a search for answers.

All the dogs had been let in. Both Dillon and Quinn wedged their heads into her lap as she fought off her fear and upset trying to guess where her cousin was. Agnes was out there alone. Kate imagined her loneliness. She felt pressure on her shoulder. Turning her head, she recognized Twisp's beautiful head resting there, snuggled as close to Kate as she could get. Kate reached up with her left hand and stroked the long muzzle. "You miss her, don't you. You probably know your mom is in trouble and scared and you want to be with her. I know exactly what you feel."

As Kate stroked the bitch's sleek neck, her hand felt the edge of her decorative collar. When she looked, she saw a puppy had been chewing the edge. She gazed down at Quinn, the obvious suspect. "These collars are too beautiful for Quinn's puppy teeth to destroy," she told the bitches. "I've got collars you can wear while you're here. Just think of it as dressing up in blue jeans while your visit Aunt Kate rather than your usual Chanel. She unbuckled both collars and taking the two bitches with her, she went into the whelping room and pulled two broad buckle collars from the drawer under the counter and put them on the girls. Then she pulled a plastic baggie from a box she kept in the same drawer and carefully put the fancy collars inside placing them alongside the decorated collars her dogs would wear at Christmas time. She sent the girls back to play with her Sams and looking again at the beautifully decorated fancy collars, she smiled. They were so Agnes in their style.

After she and Harry finished eating, they headed out to feed the boarding dogs. Most were regulars. Harvey, the Saint Bernard, always spent this week with them while his owners would visit some of their children in California prior to Christmas. They referred to it as Harvey's annual vacation. Harry greeted the huge dog with enthusiasm. "Hey there, Harvey old boy. Do you need a snuggle?"

"Towel." Kate called as she undid the latch on the run across the way that held two Cairns, Grahame and Gavan.

"Oh, right, I keep forgetting you are the slime king." Harry pulled down the hand towel that was pushed through the chain link in the door, and quickly wiped the drool from the dog's smiling face before snuggling him. Then he reached over to yank the rope that would lift the door allowing the big dog into the outside run. "Outside now. Go pee before bedtime."

Kate laughed as she quickly cleaned the runs on her side of the aisle and placed the dinner dishes on the rolling collection cart. They worked their way down the opposite sides of the aisle, greeting each dog, with pats and snuggles, and scooping poop. Kate bounced a tennis ball for Mack, an Irish Setter who jumped high to catch it and then dashed out the door as she opened it.

She looked over to see Harry romancing Sally, a shy English Cocker Spaniel bitch. He was murmuring quietly to her, encouraging her to go out using snuggles and coaxing. This was Sally's first time away from her family, so she needed more attention than the dogs who viewed this as their vacation home.

Once all the dogs had been let out and their runs cleaned and hosed down, Kate went to the bin where biscuits were kept and grabbed one fistful passing it to Harry. She then grabbed another and pulled the main door control for each side of the aisle, and all the dogs flooded in. Shoulder to shoulder. They walked down the aisle saying good night to the dogs as they passed out treats. The whole process hadn't taken long but the familiar routine had Kate feeling more relaxed. She had almost reached the office door when she suddenly froze, hearing a sound that was out of place. Reaching out to stop him, she asked Harry, "What was that?"

"What?"

"I heard something."

They stood for a minute but heard nothing. Harry shook his head and turned toward the office when a faint musical sound came from the other end of aisle. Kate rushed back toward her feeding station, but stopped and straightened. She held up her hand and took a few steps forward, her gaze sweeping the area. Then she turned to Harry and frowned.

"Call Agnes."

He pulled out his phone and keyed in her number. A faint musical tune began and Kate dove for the feed bin. Pulling off the lid she pushed her hands into the heavy kibble. It took force plus a lot of wiggling to get her fingers deep enough, but by the third time Harry had called the phone, Kate's fingers had located where it hid and contacted the smooth surface. Harry used his hands to clear the weight of the kibble off her arms to allow her to free the phone.

Agnes being Agnes, had placed it inside two plastic bags to keep its beautiful cover undamaged.

"Well, this means we won't be able to trace her phone to find her," Harry muttered, frustrated.

Kate turned and looked at him and said, "More importantly, it means the killer can't use her phone to find her."

Harry glanced up startled and then nodded in agreement.

They walked back toward the house, and had almost reached the kitchen when the phone rang again. Harry pulled it from the bags expecting it to be Sean calling. He wasn't. In fact, it was a number neither of them knew. Kate told Harry to answer the call and as he did, she pulled out her phone and pointed for him to push the speaker button on Agnes' phone at the same time she hit a button on her phone to record the call.

Kate lifted her voice to make it more like Agnes and said, "What..."

A distorted voice said, "Bitch, don't speak. Listen. Do not try to hide. Hand over what he gave you, now. If you don't hand over the files Salverson gave you, they are all going to die--your ugly dogs, your beautiful cousin, and even your grandmother. I know where they are, and they will die if we don't get it by Monday morning. They will die and it will be your fault. Salverson was warned but didn't believe me, and he paid the price. Don't you be stupid and make the same mistake." The call ended.

Kate froze. Her life had been threatened in the past, but she'd survived. This time though, it was different. Harry reached for her when he realized she wasn't moving. He went to take her hand but saw she was holding it over her stomach. He stopped and as he understood the gesture, went cold--the baby.

Since the day he'd literally bumped into her and fallen head over heels in love with her, Kate's life had been in danger multiple times, and he'd fought constantly to keep her safe. She never went looking for trouble, it came looking for her. Even during their wedding and on their honeymoon. He cursed and swore, "Kate. I promise you I won't let anyone, and I mean anyone, hurt you or our baby. We will catch this bastard and you will be safe."

A shudder ran through her, but after a minute, she looked up into his beautiful green eyes and nodded. Taking a breath as a shiver ran through her, she moved her hand from her belly and placed it in Harry's. Then they went inside to feed their dogs.

Dillon knew instantly that something was

wrong. They filled the dogs' dishes and handed them out, but when all the dogs were told to eat, Dillon took only a few bites and stopped. Raising his head he stared at Kate and Harry. Kate wanted to reassure him that everything was okay. But it wasn't.

Harry stepped forward and reached out to rub his head. "Eat hearty, Big Guy. You're going to need all your strength. We've got a job to guard Kate" After a few seconds, Dillon lowered his head and finished his food. Quinn who had been watching, sighed and finished what was in front of him. There'd be no sneaking his dad's meal today. Once the bowls were collected, Kate took a fistful of biscuits to the door and Harry followed with more.

Kate always began this ritual with the oldest dogs. It came under the heading of another lesson in patience for her pups. They learned quickly not to try to cut the line. When she got to Liam,he leaned in and brushed his head against her leg. One hand now free of treats, meant she could place her hand on his head scrub it hard with her fingertips. She called it 'brain scrambling' when she was young. The dogs loved it. After a few seconds of that, he happily took the biscuit and exited to follow his father Rory across the yard.

Dillon had relaxed at the sight of his father racing across the yard. He did his show pose and took the biscuit and ran, followed quickly by his half-sister Shelagh and his son Quinn.

Kate's phone dinged, and she saw Sean pulling into the driveway. Harry went to the front door to greet him as Kate wiped down the counter and rinsed out the dog dishes. The repetitive tasks helped calm her.

Sean walked in and went straight to Kate hugged her. They'd been neighbors and close friends all their lives. "I drove by Sybil's but there were no lights on," he said.

"She's spending the night at Gram's, and is very cut up by what's happened. I've noticed recently Bill's name coming up more and more in her chats with Gram. I think something has been going on between them recently. He came to our wedding as her plus one."

"Well I know Agnes is... was fond of him." He turned to Harry, "These are the details from the crash. There were a bunch of witnesses because it was rush hour when it happened. It got reported immediately since so many people have phones in their cars. They even got the license number but the state units had zero luck locating it. All I can think of was that the plates were clamped on and the side panel ads, were just covering for something else. In five minutes, one man with a screw driver and a box cutter could change the look of the semi and have it back on the road, unnoticed.

Harry placed Agnes' phone on the table and told Sean about finding it hidden in the dog kibble. "On our way back into the house, it rang with an unknown number. I pulled it from the bag and put the caller on speaker while Kate recorded the call." They listened, and Sean glanced at Kate as his face drained of color. He looked from Kate to Harry and saw his friend's anger. When he looked back at Kate, his eyes caught the unconscious movement of her hand and his expression turned to horror.

"My God Kate, you're pregnant." He grabbed Harry's arm. "She needs to be guarded. Too many killers have gone after her. She needs constant protection."

Kate and Harry stared at him shocked that he knew she was expecting.

"How..." Kate asked.

"I have older sisters, who have been popping babies out one after another for years. I can detect whose pregnant before they even know after all this practice."

Harry couldn't help grinning at Kate with pride.

Picking up the papers Sean had brought, he began them. "The driver was probably hired for the hit. Whoever is behind this has resources. I'll get a trace on the phone call, but I suspect a burner. I didn't find the number in Agnes' call records and according to Sybil, he's called before. Plus we have another major problem." Harry said. He looked at them for a second until the name of the problem sank in. "The house."

CHAPTER 3

Wednesday night

S ilence filled the room. Kate quietly picked up the now abandoned report and began reading while the men talked.

Harry shook his head, "Talk about a nightmare. We're probably going to have half the town here on Friday. Anybody could walk in with a gun in his pocket and in minutes kill them all. It's not as though we can make it private. There's got to be another answer. This killer could be someone we know. "

"That crowd is both a curse and an advantage. There will be hundreds of people and most will be surrounding Kate," Sean mused, "What she really needs is someone armed and looking dangerous with her all the time. Someone the killer wouldn't want to mess with who could be at her side constantly, looking like a guard."

They stared at one another and then said in unison, "Dani."

Sean grabbed his phone and hit a single key. "Gurka, we've got an emergency."

Twenty minutes later, Sgt. Gurka who headed the K-9 Division at the Bethany barracks, Trooper Danielle DeFelice and her K-9 partner Jake, a Bouvier des Flandres, and Lt. Leon Holmwood, who was in charge of Bill Salverson's murder had joined them around Kate's kitchen table.

Harry finished passing around cups of coffee and for Kate and Lt. Holmwood, tea. Kate had thawed some of her brother Will's muffins and put them in the middle of the table. Ideas and plans were tossed around, thrown out, then tossed around again. Two hours later they were still at it. The forces of law sat at one end of the table talking, with Kate, sitting at the other end. She got her laptop off the counter where it had been charging, and began doing some research on Bill Salverson. Beginning with Google images she typed in his name. Hundreds of photos appeared. Apparently, Bill was more famous than she'd realized. Shots of him getting awards from the former two presidents, speaking to Congress, in the field with a bunch of generals, if the stars on the shoulders of their fatigues were any clue, and with the directors of the FBI and the CIA. Kate only knew him as a dog show judge and a friend of Agnes' late uncle Paul. He would come to Thanksgiving or other large family gatherings.

The second page seemed to show his more social side. He was featured in groups of people wearing gowns and tuxedos. It was here that she saw him with Sybil. It was strange seeing her still lovely great-aunt, with all these A-listers while on Bill's arm. In some photos, she also saw Paul and Agnes with them all smiling at the camera. Agnes was someone who wanted to know your every secret but apparently did not believe that people should know hers because Kate had no idea about this relationship. Kate flipped through a few more pages of photos, but by page six, felt as though she might be missing something. She went back to the first page and was about to begin again when Harry pulled her attention away from the computer by asking if she agreed.

"Agreed to what?" she asked.

"You haven't been paying attention.?"

"Sorry, I was doing some cursory research on Bill Salverson's know associates."

"I'm sorry Mrs. Foyle, but the investigation

should be left in the hands of trained state troopers, not the public," Trooper Holmwood said.

Gurka looked down embarrassed keeping his gaze to the table, and Sean reached out to grab Holmwood's arm as he began to speak, but it was Dani's peal of laughter that threw drew the men's attention.

"Kate," she asked. "Do these idiots do this every time someone threatens to shoot you? I don't know how you stand it. I would have Jake bite them but it might get him in trouble with the boss," she said and glanced at Gurka. Do you want me to let Dillon in?"

"Don't bother, Dani. If it becomes a problem, I'll sic the FBI on him. Both the AIC for New York and Washington owe me. Harry, what did I miss when I was wasting police time investigating Salverson's murder? Did you come up with a plan for Friday? Oh, don't forget I've got the Christmas Pageant rehearsal tomorrow afternoon. That at least is in the barn so it's not an exposed position."

"Right. I'll add it to the schedule. Dani has been assigned to you until we get a handle on this killer. Lt. Holmwood will be heading up the State Police investigation. Sgt. Gurka will make sure Roger is filled in before he starts working the kennel tomorrow, and he'll have his k-9 officer with him. Sean will have his Golden, Patrick, as well. Needless to say, Dillon and Liam will be shadowing you all weekend. I'll talk to Jerry about plugging in a camera on the new X-Pen that will go in behind the barn. He wants to look at the blueprints to make a plan for securing the new house. I think Roger already has the app for security here and I just added it to Sean and Dani's phones."

"Sounds great. Have you figured out how Agnes got in and out without being detected?"

"No. That's something else I need to discuss with Jerry. He swore there were no holes after the fiasco surrounding the wedding."

"Well, if all else fails, we can ask Agnes when she appears."

Kate's laptop beeped. It was an email from Sal. "Whoops," Kate muttered.

"What?" everyone asked.

"Nothing. I forgot to upload my blog post which is scheduled for today and Sal is yelling at me."

"Oh, no. We've got to tell Sal what's going on. He'll kill us if we don't," Dani said.'

Gurka looked uncomfortable but squared his shoulders. "I'll call him tonight. When it comes to Sal, I'd rather have him on my side than on my case."

"Sal?" Holmwood asked.

"Former Police Chief Salvatore Modigliani," Dani said. "Sal is a force to be reckoned with. You want him with you. He and Kate run the K-9 training for most of the departments in southern New England."

Harry checked the list again. "Dani, you'll spend the days with Kate and at night will stay at Ann's and provide protection to Sybil Forester, Agnes' grandmother. Sybil is there now and Kate will convince Ann that it would be smart to have a trooper plus Jake in residence at night. Agnes' bitches can spend the night there as well if she wants, but her house isn't fenced. But It might be a comfort for Sybil who raised ten generations of greyhounds including Twisp and Thorin. It would be good if we could have someone with Ann and Sybil during the day. You gentlemen could work on that. Kate and I have one more thing to share with you, Holmwood.

"Agnes Forester has been a longtime family friend of Bill Salverson. Ms. Forester is the well-known former supermodel and is now president of Forester's Bank. She met with Salverson the afternoon of the day he died. Apparently, Salverson gave Agnes something. He entrusted her with something important. Whatever it was, it got him killed. The person behind Salverson's death phoned Agnes last night. We know this because her grandmother, Sybil, heard her answer the call and saw that Agnes was very upset by it.

"Agnes has disappeared. We assume she went under her own power. She left notes for her fiance, Sean Connelly here, and her grandmother saying she was called away and would be in touch. She somehow managed to leave her two greyhound bitches in the yard here with my wife who is her cousin. We have no idea where Agnes is . She is in hiding--hopefully successfully.

" This evening we were feeding our boarding kennel dogs when Kate heard a sound. It was a phone ringing. Kate guessed that it might be Agnes' phone and by calling her number, we located it. This means that we can not trace Agnes by using her phone. But it also means, as my wife was quick to point out, that the killer can't as well. As we brought the phone into the house, it rang with a call from an unknown number. We answered the phone, putting it on speaker, and recorded it."

Harry stopped talking and pushed the button on Kate's phone. The room filled with the voice of the man behind Salverson's death. Holmwood, Gurka, and Dani all stared at Kate.

"Dani, I hope you realize what you are taking

on," Kate said. "I won't hold it against you if you choose not to guard me. It's not as though I haven't been down this road before, but I'd hoped... Well, you guess what I hoped. I have a rehearsal of my search team tomorrow to get ready for the Christmas pageant and then, of course, Friday the house arrives and half of the town will be dropping by to look. We've been describing it as a circus."

"Well, my mamma always told me that I was a clown. So, yes Kate, you can count on me and Jake to be part of your team. I'd also like to make a suggestion, that just occurred to me. I think it's time for Ann and Sybil to have a family reunion."

Kate smiled and high-fived Dani. Gurka chuckled and Sean and Harry burst out laughing.

Holmwood looked at them as though they'd lost their minds.

Harry picked up his phone and quickly dialed. When it went through, he hit speakerphone. "Harry, dear. How is my favorite new great-nephew? Ann tells me that you are flying in your house on Friday, swinging it into place with a monster crane. It sounds fabulous."

"Maeve, my love. I hope you and Padrig are still doing well. I'm calling to invite you to come to watch the great extravaganza. But I have an additional request. I'd like you to come armed to the teeth. You see Bill Salverson has been murdered, Agnes has been threatened and has ghosted herself leaving us with no idea where she is, and the murderer has now threatened the lives of Kate and your sister Sybil as well as Agnes' bitches. We're setting up protection, but Dani pointed out that you would be very upset if you weren't invited to the party."

They heard a clunk of a phone being dropped and muttering in the background. Then came the sound of it being picked up. "Harry," Padraig said. "She's gone to pack. Let me speak to Kate. "

"I'm here Padraig."

"Nobody is going to harm our girls again. Do you understand?"

"Yes. I love you too. I'll see you tomorrow."

Harry disconnected the call and moved to sit next to Kate and hold her. "That takes care of Sybil's protection, so we've got a basic crew in hand."

Gurka leaned over and patted Holmwood on the shoulder. "You'll love Maeve. We all do. Former MI-5. I'd lay good money that she can still outshoot anyone in this room. A classy couple she and Padrig."

Holmwood looked around the table with a slightly glazed look as Gurka talked to him, "Well

34

I guess we've got a team. And it looks as though everybody knows his assignment."

Kate gave an unladylike snort and looked at the people in front of her. "And I suppose I'm to pray that this bozo doesn't get a clear shot at me?"

"No, Sweetheart. Your job is to photograph everything and everyone while wearing your wedding present from Sadie. I know it's uncomfortable but better safe than sorry. You and Dani will have Dillon and Jake sniff out the crowd for bad actors. Oh, and in your spare time, your job is to figure out who Bill's killer is." He kept looking her straight in the eyes until she finally nodded.

They said goodbye to their guests and after giving the dogs a final chance to go out, they headed to bed. Kate changed into her pajamas and crawled into bed with her laptop. "I think that what I need to do is see if I can track down Agnes. I'll check with some of her old friends and with some bank contacts, I know about. I'll check the Greyhound feed online and see if there is a mention of her. However, if she is disguised as me, she might be hiding anywhere. The threat mentions Monday. That tells me that something is happening on Tuesday or Wednesday. If it involves something that Bill would be active in, I should look into military tests or meetings of some sort."

Harry leaned over and kissed her. "I love the way your mind works. I guess that's why they pay you the big bucks." He closed her laptop, took it from her, rolled off the bed, and walked out of the room. A minute later he returned, with a couple of crackers. "Leftovers," he said. He was followed by Dillon, Liam, and Quinn. They settled into their usual spots after shoving their heads over the edge of the bed to get hugged by Kate. They finally circled and found their favorite spots as near to Kate as possible and fell asleep.

Harry came into the room. "The lights are now off, everyone is bedded down and I put your laptop on the counter where it's charging."

Kate grabbed the crackers to munch on while Harry quickly shed his clothes and crawled into bed next to her. He could tell Kate was still tense with worry from not knowing where Agnes was hiding or that she was safe. Knowing that the next few days were going to be insane, Harry did his best to distract her for the next half hour until they both relaxed. And finally, they slept.

CHAPTER 4

Thursday early morning

She was going to throw up. Her eyes popped open but that was the only part of her body she dared to move. Of all the possible inconvenient times, morning sickness chose this morning to hit her for the first time. And hit it did, as soon as she woke up and went to move.

Harry was still asleep. Shifting the blankets slowly one at a time while trying not to jostle anything, she managed to ease her legs over the edge of the bed. But that's when she discovered it was the actual act of becoming vertical which was the major trigger for her queasy stomach. She barely made it to the bathroom before she barfed.

The dogs, of course, followed her into the bathroom as they were worried about her. They pushed against her and licked at her cheeks as she tried to hold them away from her retching and calm her stomach. Finally, she flushed the toilet and rocked back to sit on the floor and hug these creatures who loved her in spite of the incredibly awful smell in the room.

When she was able to stand, all she wanted was to crawl back into bed. But checking the time, she realized that she had too much to do. So after one more hug for each dog, she sent them out and closed the bathroom door, took a shower, and got dressed.

Kate stood in the kitchen trying to decide what she could face for breakfast when she found herself lifted to one side. Harry reached over her shoulder, took down a box, and handed her a few saltines.

"I'll make breakfast," he said gently easing her into her chair. "Do you feel up to bacon and eggs or do you want your oatmeal?'

"Oatmeal, I think." Harry seemed to have figured out why she hadn't been in bed when he woke that morning. She nibbled on the crackers and began to feel more like herself.

"How did you know about the saltines?"

"I downloaded a bunch of books onto my Kindle including one entitled, What to Expect When You're Expecting."

Kate shook her head. Knowing her husband, she

bet he now knew more about her pregnancy than she did. To him, it was simply a new problem to be solved. Not with mathematics this time, but with information nonetheless. She ate a few more of the crackers, then had her tea, took her vitamins, and after a few minutes, cautiously began eating the bowl of oatmeal Harry had handed her. By the time she was half-finished, she was feeling fine.

Harry placed a schedule on the table. "Dani will be here later this morning. She's going to put her things in her room at Ann's and then start following you everywhere. We'll give the dogs their morning snacks and then do the boarders. Your friend Jimmy will be here later this morning with the chain link panels for the new exercise yard. Jerry will get the camera in thereafter the yard is finished."

""Roberto said that he saw me, meaning Agnes, heading out into the woods after the greyhounds were put into the kennel. I think that she put the dogs in the yard, and stayed out of my sight until I went into the house. Then she hid her phone, went out the far kennel door, and walked out into the woods. Our only camera in the woods is on the main trail. If we have two cameras on the back of the barn, with one watching the dogs and the other pointed at all the entrances into the woods, we'd have better coverage."

"Jerry always keeps extra cameras in his van, so I don't think that will be a problem."

"Working together, they let out the boarding dogs and cleaned the runs. By the time that was done, most of the knitters had arrived, so they went up to the studio. Kate let Harry explain all the extra security for the weekend, the parking changes, and the fact that everyone would be encouraged to take photos from the big front window since that would give wonderful overhead shots. He only asked that they upload copies of all their photos to the Dropbox file he was posting on the bulletin board. Kate had met with Ellen in her office and explained that there was someone who had threatened both her and Sybil who was now staying with Ann. She explained that she wanted Ellen to be aware of the extra security that would be around but Kate didn't think that the knitters needed their fun disrupted.

Harry told them that the new exercise yard would be going in below their back window and that security cameras would be installed so that Kate could keep an eye on the dogs even as she is handling all the house stuff. "I want to thank you in advance for all the wonderful photos you will take to make sure our twenty-first-century version of a house raising will be recorded." Finally, they left and headed back for tea and coffee before the fencing arrived.

When they got back inside, Kate made tea and Harry toasted a couple of slices of homemade bread. She brought Dillon in so that he could be with her all day. They had just finished their snack when both their phones dinged letting them know that the dog run fencing had arrived. At the sound of a truck horn, Kate grabbed her parka, dashed out the back door, and headed for the barn, leaving Harry to follow. Jimmy was getting out of his truck and lowering the tailgate to allow for the kennel panels to be removed when she reached him.

"Jimmy, right on time. If you back around the side of the barn, it will be easier to unload. I had a load of gravel put down to give a clean surface inside the cinder block base wall. The panels will rest atop the blocks. I also had piping attached where the fencing will connect to the barn."

He backed the truck into position next to the cinder block knee-walls. "I love the setup. Most of the time I have to build in escape barriers when I set the panels up. Of course, with all your years of experience with Sams, you can almost think like one."

"I rarely think of their escapes as running away,

but rather like making social calls to all the neighbors. They are people dogs, and none of them has ever met a stranger. The only time I have had them react negatively to a person was when someone was trying to kill me. Thank God, they can sniff those people out and dispense with them efficiently."

"I heard about the wedding. Dillon and young Quinn were quite the heroes."

"It was my brothers' idea to include them in the wedding. Something for which I shall be eternally grateful."

"The Killoy family is famous for entertaining this town with drama and it has for three generations now. I hear that Tom has a girlfriend now, a feisty little thing with purple hair."

"Gwyn Braxton, Dr. Braxton actually." Kate laughed. "They met over a couple of dead bodies."

"Are you telling tales about Tom?" Harry asked as he walked up. He reached out to shake hands with the man chatting with Kate. "Hi, I'm Harry Foyle, Kate's husband."

"Jimmy Buchanan," came the reply. "Believe me, we all look for interesting stories about Tom. He was the valedictorian in our class in high school and has put the rest of us to shame with his exploits.

Those of us who've known him since elementary school, never tire of stories about Super Tom."

"Super Tom. I like that."

"Don't tell Gwyn. She'll never give him any peace." Kate said laughing.

Kate reached up to grab the end of one of the chain-link panels, only to find herself being lifted off the ground and set to one side. Harry told her, "You are management and tell us where they go. We are labor and will put them wherever you want." The extra stare from her husband was all the reminder she needed that she was carrying their child.

"Fine. Begin with the panel which attaches to that pipe over there on the far side. I'll attach the clamps which will hold them in place as we go. Once that one is set, the rest will follow nose-to-tail like elephants in the circus."

"Are you putting this in for your classes?"

"Well, we will need it for my dogs while they bring in the sections of the new house. My guys can't have sections of the house flying over their heads. Plus the workers need to be in the exercise yard and that means the gate will be open. This way, my dogs will break the new yard in and when the classes start again after New Years Day, I'll have a place for students to exercise their dogs or just let them play off lead. It's a win-win." Barely thirty minutes later, Jimmy was pulling out of the driveway and Kate was admiring her new exercise yard as Sean drove in followed by Dani.

Harry and Kate met them in the parking lot. Kate told Harry, "Dillon and I are going to take Dani up to my grandmother's. I'll get her settled and I'll talk with Sybil. They climbed into Dani's car and headed up the hill to get her protection unit and friend settled in. Then would come the hard part, explaining the threats against them and the plan they had for doing something about it

Ann and Sybil were sitting at the table along with Tom and Gwyn when they walked in. Kate had only just introduced Dani when her phone notification went off, and she saw that more backup had arrived. "I need to talk to you all, about Agnes and what is happening, but first I should tell you that you're about to have even more company."

Seconds later, the front door burst open and Maeve raced into the room going directly to her sister, Sybil. "Kate told us about Bill. Sybil, I can't express enough how sorry I am. He was such a wonderful man who loved you dearly." Kate was startled by that comment but realized she shouldn't have been after seeing all the photos of Bill and Sybil together. "Have you heard from Agnes?"

Kate interrupted. "Maeve, I'm glad you made it so quickly. I was just going to go over all we know so far. I don't know if you remember Dani from the wedding. She's going to be with me for the weekend, but bunking here with Ann. Oh, and the Bouvier with her is Jake."

"Hi Dani, I do remember you. I also remember Jake going after that mobster last month. It will be good having you both here."

Padraig walked in and after kissing Sybil's cheek, reached out to hug Kate and whispered, "We'll keep you safe, Katie, and Sybil too. Don't you worry?"

Kate hugged Padraig and they all settled at the table. Knowing that there wasn't much time until the crane arrived, Kate began to fill everyone in on what was happening. She explained about Agnes going into hiding disguised as Kate after sneaking her bitches into the Samoyed yard. Then she told me about how she and Harry had found her phone hidden in the boarding kennel and the threat they got when they answered an unidentified incoming call. Placing her phone on the table, she played the recording.

"Oh no. This person is pure evil." Sybil gasped.

"You won't get an argument from me." Kate told her, "However, it one respect this is good. If he is hunting us, trying to smoke Agnes out of hiding by killing off those she loves, he's not going after her. His focus here gives her safety."

"But that puts you, Sybil, and the bitches right in his cross-hairs." Maeve interrupted.

Dani added, "In addition to the threat, the number of people wandering around as they put the house together tomorrow will make a possible assassin hard to identify. Many visitors will be strangers. Hopefully most unarmed. Kate will have Dillon with her and I'll be at her side with Jake. These dogs have a talent for sniffing out trouble. Sean and Roger will be here as well with their dogs, so that will give more firepower."

Silence filled the room and Gwyn stood, quietly walking around the table hugging everyone and finally ending with Kate. "I've known you since we were kids, and I owe you more than I could ever repay," she said looking at Tom, "so know this. I will fight to keep you safe. I may be small, but I'm a crack shot and in my role as part of the coroner's office, I'm law enforcement and licensed to carry a gun. Barring dead bodies turning up, I will be at your side all weekend."

"Thanks, Gwyn. The one piece of information I did get from this is at least it gives us a time-line. Whatever this person is after is something that must be delivered somewhere by Monday. Where it's to be taken or what he wants, I don't know, only that it must be by Monday."

Padraig looked around the table and then asked the obvious question, "I wonder what happens on Tuesday?"

CHAPTER 5

Thursday, late morning

K ate's phone dinged, and she looked at the screen. A sedan was entering the driveway followed slowly through the turn by a semi-trailer truck with a crane on the back. "Well, it looks as though the show is beginning."

Everyone took coats from the closet and headed out as the truck moved at a slow walk. It maneuvered its way through the turn between Kate's tiny house and the large colonial where she had grown up. The massive truck straightened to continue toward them until the trailer was just past the new house's foundation. With a screech of brakes and the engine turned off.

They all filed down the hill toward the big machine. The driver set heavy boards at the back of the trailer and scrambled up. Once on the flatbed, he climbed the side of the crane and made himself comfortable in the cabin of the machine, started the huge and extremely noisy engine and the tank treads began slowly moving forward. It followed the direction of the long crane arm which extended past the foundation and almost past Kate's house.

Kate jumped when arms encircled her from the rear but relaxed when she heard her husband's voice whisper, "Ready or not, here we go."

Mr. Edwards stood near the top end of the crane arm directing the driver with a pair of colorful flags. When the last link of the treads met the driveway, the arm of the crane began to rise. Everyone moved down the hill to get the full effect of the machine in action. Kate hadn't realized she had pulled her phone from her pocket to record the event without even thinking. The driver swiveled the cab of the crane so that the arm now extended almost straight up, but faced toward the foundation. Then when they'd all gotten used to the overwhelming noise, it stopped and the silence was even more deafening.

"Well folks, are you ready to get your house?" the jovial site manager asked.

Harry went forward to shake his hand and

introduce Mr. Edwards to Kate, explaining that family and friends had gathered to witness the event.

Padraig asked, "How does this house go together?"

Edwards said, "If you have your blueprints handy, everybody can follow me into your little house, and I will show you how this massive puzzle will be put together. Bert here is a master at this type of construction."

Sean, who'd been waiting next to Harry, stepped forward to introduce himself to Edwards. He explained he would be the trooper who'd be in charge of traffic control tomorrow. They chatted about the details as everyone moved further down the driveway to Kate's porch and then inside. Since Kate's kitchen table seated twelve, there was plenty of room.

"Mr. Edwards, that's quite a fancy toy you've got there," Kate said.

"Well, Bert here can pick up a house section and put it down as if it were light as a feather. You'll see. With boxes as large as they are for your house, you need someone with his skills. If you have your plans handy, I show you the order in which we'll be installing your sections, and we can go over the schedule."

Harry grinned. "I love the fact that not only is

the frame built, but the insides are finished, with the flooring, ceilings, doors, and windows. It's even painted inside. The fixtures, counters, including the tubs, showers, toilets, and sinks in the bathrooms come all installed. The counters, sinks, and built-in stoves and banquet in the kitchen are all in place. Even the bookshelves are in the library. All we need to be done is connecting plumbing and electricity, finish the siding outside, brick the fireplaces and finish building the porch. Once they connect it to this house, it will be done. Kate and I are hoping to celebrate Christmas there.

"Christmas?" The shout came from almost everyone except Kate, Bert, and Mr. Edwards."

Edwards chuckled, "Mr. Foyle has made it worth our while to make sure that it happens, and you can depend on that it will."

It was Tom who broke the shocked silence. "So, what will we see tomorrow? Which section will be first?"

Edwards pulled a grease pencil out of his pocket and after folding back several pages of the blueprint, he came to the first-floor layout. He drew a line across the center from right to left stopping at the end wall of the living room. "The first to go in will be the first floor rear. That will include the back of the kitchen up to this oven on the wall, and across past the powder room, the dining room, minus the bump-out section which will go in on Saturday, to the back of the living room wall including the firebox and chimney flue liner. The brickwork for the fireplace will be finished once the pieces are in place. It would have been too much weight to add all those bricks prior to installation."

Gwyn pointed and ask in astonishment, "All that will be picked up in one piece by that crane outside?"

Bert chuckled, "And laid down gently on the foundation exactly in place. All it takes is my baby out there and three guys handling the guide ropes."

Edwards pointed to the next section. "Once the back is in place, it's much easier to fit the other pieces. This front will include the front of the kitchen, the library which I must say turned out really nice, and the front of the living room. This door in the end wall will lead to the master suite, which will go in on Saturday. Once the first floor is in place, temporary lolly column supports will be fitted underneath until the finished columns are installed.

It's a big expanse to hold up with just the foundations. Now, these boxes come finished, floor to ceiling. Fixtures wired and insulated. This means that you've got an extra sound barrier between the first and second floors. The stairs to the second floor will also come installed with just a piece of plywood covering the opening at the top. So once the second floor, with all the bedrooms and the bathrooms, is in place, that will be removed and you'll be able to check out both floors by the end of the day."

"That's going to need a lot of tarps to keep it dry if it rains overnight," Tom said.

"Well, you'd think so--but no it won't. You see, the roof is already hitched with hinges to the second floor. It's folded so it can fit under the overpasses on the highway. When Bert finishes putting the second story in place and it's all bolted; he'll use the crane to lift the roof. It will unfold on its hinges, and will just settle into place. All the knee wall struts for the attic are hinged to the roof, so the men just have to pull them forward into the precut slots, fasten them. When the final roof sections unfold into place, you'll have your attic. It's supposed to rain or snow Saturday night, but by then, all the shingle joins will be finished, the master, the bumpout, and the porch roof will be in place and everything will be watertight."

"Amazing," Gwyn, Ann and Tom said in unison.

"And we get to watch this all happens tomorrow and Saturday," Ann whispered.

Kate watched Sean chat with Mr. Edwards about the timing between the arrival of each truck. Mr. Edwards pointed out that once emptied, one of the long-beds would be lifted onto the bed of another truck so that by the end of the day, there will only be two long trucks to maneuver out and the rest would just be the short cabs. This eased the exit traffic problem and sped up the ride back to the factory.

Mr. Edwards and Bert left, so they could check into their hotel. They announced they would be back here by five-thirty in the morning and the trucks would be arriving about six. "With these short winter days, we will be moving fast to finish everything. Ann stepped forward to explain that a hot meal would be served at lunchtime in the house opposite and beverages and drinks, both hot and cold will be available all day for the crew. That news brought a smile to Mr. Edward's face and had Bert rubbing his hands with glee as they got into Mr. Edwards's car.

Sean told them he'd be back later but had work to finish up before he could focus on what was happening here. Kate tried to get him to wait and eat lunch, but he wanted to get work out of the way. Harry pulled a couple of containers of soup and some homemade bread which needed slicing from the refrigerator, then Kate handed him a platter to hold sandwich fixings. Soon everyone was sitting around the table chatting about other things in their lives. Gwyn and Dani were discussing their favorite movies and video games. Tom and Harry were deep in conversation with Maeve about new security equipment while Kate told Ann, Sybil, and Padraig about the new exercise yard and how they had put it in earlier that morning.

"It may come in handy today since, at four o'clock, I am holding a rehearsal of the search dog team-dog dancing group. This year, they'll be doing their usual routines at the Christmas Pageant, but they will march in the parade with the addition of the kids who are in the junior handling classes Kate explained that the kids had decided to come up with a theme. They've chosen the Magi. The audience is going to have to overlook the small problem that Balthazar, Melchior, and Caspar will have the company of several extra kings plus two queens. But I figure it's the thought that counts and I'm sure Fr. Joe will get a laugh out of it. We should warn him though when we see him at Mass on Sunday."

Everyone chuckled. The rest of us go traditional with Santa, Mrs. Claus, and a bunch of elves with their dogs. Ann explained that she and Tom started doing it years ago to show the people in town what a well-trained dog could do. It brought attention to the boarding kennel and the training business, plus it was lots of fun. Kate was an elf first with Rory, then with Liam, and most recently with Dillon. "We're going to have to get you and Quinn trained for next year Harry, to keep the family tradition going," she said with a hitch in her voice. "Good times. Agnes is the elf who passes out all the fliers."

"And she'll be back in time to do it again this year," Sybil said with a sniff but a determined force to her voice.

CHAPTER 6

Thursday afternoon late

J ust before four o'clock, the cars belonging to members of the search team and the kids in the junior handling class began to arrive at the training barn. Kate got Dillon from the exercise yard. With Dani, she headed over to meet everyone in front of the barn only to find people gathered around Carisa Amaya. Kate noticed that the girl didn't have her Borzoi bitch, Kira, with her, and she was crying. Kate headed over to find out what was wrong. When she asked, Carisa said, "It's Kira. She's... She came in season, so I can't have her in the pageant."

Kate looked at the girl and came to the conclusion that she was crying more because she couldn't be in the pageant. "I may have a solution. Now you're used to showing a big, calm hound and I assume you have made a costume to fit her. How about working a greyhound bitch? She's not quiet as tall as Kira, but she very well-trained."

"Really?" The tears turning to sunshine.

"Really. Agnes had to be away this weekend, so I have Twisp and Thorin staying with me. Thorin is the most experienced, so I think she'd be perfect with you. She's used to crowds and noise. I'm sure Agnes wouldn't mind. Let's go get her."

Kate unlocked the barn so that everyone could go in and then told Dillon to wait. She and Dani walked Carisa over to the kennel. When she reached the door to the Samoyed exercise yard, she called Thorin before opening the door. Using her body to block Quinn, she eased Thorin through. Once inside, she had Carisa run her hands over the bitch and let the bitch get used to the girl's scent. Soon Thorin was bouncing around with her tail wagging. Kate grabbed a lead from the rack on the wall as she headed back to the barn. Once through the far door, she told Carisa to move Thorin out in a circle. They moved together very smoothly. The teenager's lanky legs were a definite asset in moving the gaze hound.

"Excellent. Let's go inside and get ready for the

rehearsal. Did you make a costume for Kira?"

"Yes. It's in the car. My brother brought me over. He's visiting your brother Tim talking about basketball." She ran to the car and grabbed a bag from the back. When Kate opened the barn door, Dillon immediately trotted across the floor and began heeling at her side sitting perfectly as she stopped. She reached down and snuggled his head. "Let's get to work, Big Guy."

Richard had spotted the new exercise yard and thought it was a great addition to the training barn. She explained that she needed a place for her dogs while house sections were flying overhead tomorrow. He told her he'd try to stop by to get a peek at the show.

The next hour was a perfect example of controlled chaos. The members of the search team who were also part of the drill team became one-on-one coaches for those who were new to the routines. Once they were grouped, with an experienced marcher, guiding each beginner, Kate turned on the music. To get them into the idea of marching, she had them just march forward and back in line, encouraging those who shuffled, to pick up their feet and those who anticipated, to count with the music. Soon the line began moving, first in a circle, and then in a spiral, finally having the spiral unwind, so they could experience moving with their dog in heel position going face-to-face with another dog. The power of the music seemed to keep each dog's attention on the handler rather than other dogs.

Basics covered, the juniors moved forward with their dogs in costumes appropriate to accompany the three kings--in this case four kings and two queens in their trick to visit the holy child. The kids had gone all out on their costumes. Tawanda Johnson even came up with an idea of a pillow with small handles sewn onto the sides so that for part of the time marching during the parade, she could carry her Pomeranian like an offering. All in all, it was spectacular and the dogs seem to enjoy it as much as the Juniors.

When all the basics were down pat with the new marchers, Kate did a quick run-through of the finale with experienced the drill team. These members and dogs had been doing that exercise for several years, including when they were televised last February at the Westerland Show in New York City. Once the music began, the handlers and dogs worked in sync through a dozen different maneuvers down to the final flag trick that allowed Dillon to show off. When done, everyone applauded including the audience which had gathered unnoticed behind them. Ann, Tom, Gwyn, and Harry as well as their house guests, had quietly filed in and got to watch their last run-through.

"Okay, we are ready to go. Carisa, you and Thorin looked as though you'd been working together for years. Tawanda, great idea for Ace. He might get a bit tired with the length of the parade before the demonstration. I'll see you all next week for the real thing." Carisa gave Thorin a big hug before handing her back to Kate. The big greyhound bitch did a play bow with Dillon, and they both romped around Kate.

Her friends seemed impressed. Kate explained that the Search and Rescue team part of the group included the Berner, Golden, Shepherd, Newf, and Chihuahua as well as Dillon. The others were part of a dog dancing group that worked their dogs for fun. It also kept their dogs focused and improve their obedience trial scores. She explained that this was the first time the new Junior Handling class got to try anything different from the breed ring, and they seemed to enjoy it.

Dani said, "Okay Kate, I want to see you get the troopers to do that spiral thing the next time we have search training."

"That's a great idea, but first I'd have to get Sgt. Gurka to go hide in the woods because there is no way he'd ever approve." Everyone laughed.

While Kate put away the music and props, Harry caught Richard and pulled him aside for a chat. When he came back into the barn, everyone decided they were hungry and headed back inside. Maeve and Padraig were going to spend some time talking with them so the rest of the family, plus Dani headed up to Ann's. Dani volunteered to cook supper telling Ann she enjoyed working in the kitchen. Kate saw that her grandmother not only agreed but look relieved. All the stress of the day was taking its toll on her. Having Dani in her kitchen might be just the change of pace she needed.

Maeve sat at Kate's kitchen table and looked at the others. "I've been thinking about this whole thing. I have a passing idea of what Bill did in his business. His was a small but lucrative think tank which created technology that he sold to various departments of the government. My first question would be how did anyone know that he was talking with Agnes? Is our killer someone from his company--which I think has only a half-dozen employees--or was it, someone connected with the bank? I'd need to know if there were a board meeting that day? What would mark the visit to bring it to the notice of someone? Did the person who had him killed know that he planned to give the information to Agnes? There are too many unanswered questions. Someone needs to find the answers." Maeve pulled out her phone and dialed. "Sadie, we need some information."

Kate had taken her laptop and pulled up the pages of photos in her research of Bill Salverson. She knew she had missed something earlier. There had been something in the array of photos that had seemed off, but she'd been distracted before her brain had identified what it was. This time she checked the pages again, looking carefully at each photo. The first page contained shots dealing with Bill's business. Formal headshots and group shots of him working with a number of people. She studied the people surrounding him in the group shots. When they were identified, Kate made a note of each person identified either by name or by position. She slowly worked her way down the page which she'd bookmarked to a new file. Glancing at her list, she noticed a certain repetition with several people. It could mean nothing or everything. It was too early to tell.

She glanced up to see the others grouped

around a stack of papers that Harry had taken from the printer. Maeve still had Sadie on the phone. Both women had worked in security since the time of the Cold War and knew about as much as you could about espionage and covert operations as possible. They had both run operations within their bureaus, though on opposite sides of the Atlantic. When Maeve married Donovan and settled in New York City, she appeared to be just an upper-class housewife to a husband who was an affluent manu-facturer, but in reality, she had still been working the occasional undercover operation for her former bosses. This continued up until a few years ago. At least Kate didn't think they were still giving her assignments. Because of this, she and Sadie knew everything about everybody.

Kate was just about to ask what they'd found about why Bill was murdered when her phone rang. It was her grandmother telling them to get them-selves up to the house because dinner was about to be served. Kate passed on the message. Dillon rose from where he was sleeping at her side, and she turned to let him out with the others when Maeve said, "No. From now on, until this mess is over, Dil-lon should never leave your side."

"Maeve is right. When we come home, he can

play with the others and I'll help you with the boarders. Let's go. I don't want to make Ann wait. Oh, and here are the new camera codes. I had him put two cameras on the back of the barn, one for the pen and one to watch the woods. I also had him put a camera high on the front of the kennel under the bedroom windows. It's got a wide-angle and will show the parking lot plus give you a different view of the exercise yard, the back of this place plus the new house.

Kate keyed in the various numbers as they strolled up the hill. The angles were great. She pocketed the paper, having memorized the codes when her phone dinged. The code for the driveway automatically came up showing her brother Will's car pull in and circling her mother's house to park by the garage. He saw them walking and waved. Once parked, he trotted up the hill to join them.

Hugging his sister he asked, "Did I make it in time for dinner at Gram's?"

"Your timing is perfect. Gram is planning on feeding lunch to all the men working to install the house tomorrow, so maybe you can take that over. The last few days have been rough around here which you will find out about soon enough."

They mounted the steps to their grandmother's

porch and went inside only to have Will stop in his tracks and sniff. "That's chicken piccata."

Harry sniffed the air. "Smells good. I know I'm ready for it."

Ann was sitting quietly at the head of the table as Tom and Gwyn poured wine in glasses around the table. As the new arrivals joined those at the table, Will stood behind his chair and asked, "Who's cooking?"

"Dani," Sybil said, "and it smells wonderful. Will, dear, will you go carry in the salad for her?"

"Chicken piccata?" He asked the woman standing at the stove.

"Italian comfort food. I assume you're one of Kate's brothers. If you would carry in the salad, I'll bring the platter with the piccata, and we can all relax and eat."

Will who had been staring at the woman, snapped out of it. "The salad. Right, the salad." He picked up the bowl, pulled the serving spoon and fork from the drawer by his side, and turned to follow the enchanting woman from the kitchen looking as if his mind was spinning. "Beautiful, and she cooks," Kate heard him whisper to himself as he passed her.

Kate watched her brother follow Dani in with a

dazed look on his face. She stood when he got near and took the salad to put it on the table. "I think there are a couple of introductions still to be made here. This is my brother Will who is completing his Ph.D. at MIT in June and will be joining K and K. Will, the girl with the purple hair is my longtime friend Dr. Gwyn Braxton who is a forensic pathologist. The woman with the Bouvier des Flandres sitting politely at the table beside her and our chef for the evening is my friend Trooper Danielle DeFelice who will be guarding me and Sybil against a murderer this weekend. So now that everybody knows everybody, let's eat."

CHAPTER 7

Thursday night and Friday morning very early

Following the delicious dinner, they all sat at the table enjoying coffee and tea, discussing the next day's schedule. Kate spotted Will stealing looks at Dani and wasn't surprised to hear him say when he finally, he leaned over to Dani and in a low voice that didn't interrupt the main conversation asked, "Where did you get the capers. There is no way they came out of my grandmother's pantry?"

Dani grinned. "I brought them with me. When I go on a job like this. It is best to be prepared for any eventuality. I pack my emergency box of spices and herbs and in this case, a jar of capers."

"You cook like this and you're a cop? You could have your own restaurant."

"That's the pot calling the kettle... I ate what you prepared for Kate and Harry's wedding reception, and you're a mathematician?" She lifted her chin. "I love what I do. I cook because it makes me happy."

Kate watched Will stare at her and then watched a grin slowly spread over his face. After a minute, Dani wore the same smile. Kate turned back to the main conversation and nodded at Harry's raised eyebrow. Kate listened to her family to discuss various plans to keep all of them safe.

The room was warm, and she was full of wonderful food. So, when her head started to nod and her eyes close, when her phone dinged, she was too tired to care, when a pair of hands gripped her arms.

Harry whispered in her ear, "Hey sleepyhead, it's time for bed. Tomorrow is another early day." He pulled back her chair and helped her to stand. Padraig held her parka and helped her to slip it on. Harry wished everyone goodnight, and they headed out and down the driveway.

They had almost reached their front steps when a voice came out of the dark. "This makes three times in less than a month with someone trying to kill you, Kate. Don't you think that's a little excessive, even for you?"

"Sal!" She ran up and hugged the man who was sitting on the front porch. Harry moved forward and gripped his hand.

"I take it Gurka called you. I don't think we can blame Kate for this one. Like February, it's Agnes who they are after. They're just willing to take out Kate, Sybil, and Agnes' bitches to convince her they are serious. Come on inside. I'm going to put sleepy-head to bed and I'll give you the rundown. Dani is staying at Ann's tonight but will be glued to Kate this weekend along with Dillon and Jake. Maeve and Padraig came today. Roger had been too busy to cover the kennel, but he will be here tomorrow. Sean will be doing traffic, but he'll have his Golden Patrick with him. The problem is that we don't have a clue who this killer is. He could be anyone, and he could be part of the crowd who will be here to-morrow or Saturday. It's going to be an interesting weekend."

Once inside, Harry steered Kate into the bed-room, took her coat, her shoes, her jeans, and then tucked her under the covers.

Kate tried to fight her exhaustion and say some-thing but instead just gave in.

Harry headed for the kitchen where Sal had al-ready made himself a cup of coffee. The dogs had been let in and were snuggling their friend. Liam sat with his head in Sal's lap, the former cop's massive hand resting on the head. Sal told him that he'd bunk down in one of the kennel bedrooms since his family wouldn't be back for a week. They both went out to let the boarding dogs in and bed them down. While there, Harry played the threat that he'd copied to his phone. Sal slammed his hand against the chain-link gate beside him.

"Why do they go after Katie? She is the sweetest, kindest person I've ever known and these bastards always come after her with hatred."

"I think it's more that they're frightened. Kate notices things and figures things out. If you are trying to hide something, she will probably find it. I don't think it's hate, I think it's fear. They are frightened she'll keep hunting until she finds what they are hiding. We think that Tuesday will be the day when whatever they are afraid might happen--will. Maeve and Sadie are trying to find what it is. But our job, for the next forty-eight hours, is to keep Kate, Sybil, and the bitches all alive while we try to find out who is behind this and stop him. Did you ever meet Salverson?"

"Yea. It wasn't well-known in the family, but Sybil and Bill have been seeing each other for several years. They weren't married but were a couple. Ann and I would often go to dinner with them. He was a genius as well as a really nice guy and since Sybil was a Killoy by birth and mathematical by nature, they had a lot in common and could speak the same language. Sybil must be devastated."

"She is. But she's also out for blood. She's determined that Kate finds out who did this. It frightens me that people assume that my wife will be at the front of the line in every battle against crime. I know she's taken chances in the past, but now..."

"I agree. Sean let your secret out. With a baby on the way, Kate can't take the chances she has in the past. We've got to make sure she is protected whether she wants that or not." He stretched and yawned. "Four hours on the interstate wore me out after skiing all morning with my son. I will see you two very early tomorrow and help move the dogs. I'm looking forward to seeing the new yard."

"You'll like it. I also have some new security codes for you to put into your phone app. We added three new cameras: one for the new dog yard, one to show all the entrances to the woods, and one on the front of the kennel with the view from upstairs here looking out at the parking lot, the back of both the small house with the dog yard and the new house.

You can get them in the morning. Agnes managed to slip in and out of here undetected, so Kate wanted more coverage."

Sal went to get his suitcase and settle into one of the bedrooms on the second floor of the kennel and Harry returned to the house. He allowed the dogs one more trip outside to pee and then bedded them all down, chatting to each. He noticed that Shelagh had bonded with the two greyhound bitches and shared her usual spot. The last stop was the kitchen for a packet of crackers then he then headed for bed.

***

The alarm buzzed and Harry muttered, "Crackers on the nightstand."

Without lifting her head, Kate reached out and slid a couple of crackers from the package and then closed it. She nibbled carefully, normally preferring her crackers with peanut butter or jam. However, just the thought of those toppings led to queasiness. Plain crackers were fine. After she finished both crackers, she lay still listening to Harry talk to the dogs as he let them out. He laughed at Quinn's "turtle on it's back" routine as the pup pretended that he had yet to figure how to right himself before being able to stand.

She faced a similar problem. How to stand without making a complete mess of things. Working in slow motion, she pushed the covers back, and inch-by-inch raised herself to a sitting position. She stopped. A faint disquieting spasm came over her but then faded. She reached for another cracker and slowly nibbled. Again she waited, staring inward, gauging how far she could move before nausea descended on her, forcing her to race to the bathroom rather than she throwing-up all over her rug. Steam rose toward her face. She opened her eyes and focused on the mug of tea being held out to her.

"Sip this slowly. Don't rush it and don't move until you have at least half the contents of the cup inside you." Harry's voice commanded. He eased himself onto the bed making sure not to jostle her, and waited. After several sips, he noticed that she sat up straighter. Without moving too quickly, he wrapped his arm around her shoulders and urged her to lean into him. They sat like that until she finished the entire cup. Standing, he took the cup from her, set it aside, and then took both her hands. With his hands supplying balance, he urged her to stand and walk to the door of the bathroom. The smile on Kate's face when she achieved that goal warmed him through, and he leaned in to kiss her gently.

"Take your shower while I get breakfast ready. I'll shower when you're done. And I need you to wear your wedding present from Sadie. No arguments. I will worry less."

Kate looked at him, following his gaze to her belly, she nodded. "I'll wear it."

"Thanks. We've got to feed these guys and get them moved before the hoards of helpers descend on us."

Sal arrived and took the pile of dog bowls and began preparing the food. Kate had switched to giving the dogs half a meal twice a day. Spreading the calorie intake over the day seemed to keep their weight under better control and seemed to calm them. They didn't need to wait as long between meals and were happier about the whole process. Sal and Kate had laid out the bowls and the dogs were eating by the time Harry got back. He went to the biscuit bin on the counter and began pulling out fistfuls as Kate and Sal picked up the dishes. Handing Kate one stack of biscuits while he grabbed the rest, he opened the door and each dog stacked and got a biscuit then took off running to their favorite spots.

"I have a stack of pancakes ready to be heated that I took from the freezer last night. Do you want bacon or sausage?"

"Bacon. My daughter-in-law has decided that I am old and should have my diet restricted to pablum and dry toast."

"Going to be eating more meals here for a while, I take it. Well, feel free. Will came home last night, and we found out that Dani is a fantastic cook after eating the wonderful supper she made us," Harry told him.

Kate said she'd have bacon with her pancakes and went to prepare her tea while the men opted for coffee. They ate quickly and then bundled up warmly, collecting leads for the dogs who were not as reliable on their own. The sharp bite of bitterly cold air greeted them as they stepped outside.

The dogs were surprised to be going somewhere in the pitch dark but were eager for adventure. Having three people sped up the process as they headed out across the parking lot toward the barn. They stopped when their phones dinged. Looking up the driveway, they saw a green sedan that had stopped there. Harry took the leads Kate held and stepped between her and the car while she pulled out her phone and keyed in a code. Two seconds later, the car backed out onto the highway which luckily had no traffic at that hour, and drove off to the north.

"Got it," Kate said.

CHAPTER 8

Friday morning before dawn

Kate had started after Sal when Harry grabbed her from behind and held her tight to his chest.

"No. They aren't trying to kill Sal. They are trying to kill you."

She pulled out her phone which she'd shoved into her pocket and keyed in the camera on the front of the kennel. It showed a light green sedan stopped at the end of the driveway. It also showed Sal jogging up the driveway casually, looking as though he were going for a run. He had almost reached the end of the driveway when the car began moving, Sal pulled a gun and sprinted toward the car door, but the car swerved onto the highway and took off at high speed. He'd turned back toward the barn when a state police patrol car pulled up beside him, stopped, and then hopped into the passenger seat letting it bring him back down the driveway.

Sean and his dog Patrick got out of the car as Sal exited the other side. "Kate. Sal says you may have the license number for the stalker."

She hit a few buttons on her phone and then said, "You've got it."

Sal went into the barn and returned with Liam and Dillon. "Harry, you're on your own. Kate, I don't want to see you without Dillon at your side. Sean, keep Patrick nearby while doing traffic. Liam and I are headed up to Ann's. I'll send Dani down to join you. Sean, call in that number in now. We need a possible name to deal with as soon as possible."

The three of them stood watching Sal's retreating back, then turned to each other grinning. "Now there is one happy man," Harry said.

"He looks ten years younger. They never should have made him retire." Sean added.

Kate looked at them as Sal moved out of sight. "For my sake, I'm really glad he's here. I must say, I love seeing him in full cop mode."

They reached the kitchen and just had time for a hot drink and a piece of one of Will's coffee cakes warmed up when the sound of a ding on each phone followed by the noise of a massive engine had them moving toward the front door. Harry and Kate stood on the front porch while Sean, with Patrick at his side, jogged over to meet Mr. Edwards. They directed the first truck to drive straight down the driveway and park in front of the kennel. The second truck arrived just as the driver and crew were exiting the first truck's cab. Using lights similar to those used at airports to guide planes during night-time parking at the terminal, Edwards guided the movement of the second truck into a space right next to the first.

Bert, who had gotten out of Edward's car, trotted over to his crane and scrambled up into the cab. The floodlights on the front of the barn and the kennel lit up the operation as the crew, armed with box cutters, began clambering up onto the first section. The sheeting covering from that section of the house began to come off.

"This is so cool." Dani, Will, Tim, Seamus, Sal, Ann, and the rest had gathered behind them on Kate's porch. "Does everyone have a phone?" Kate asked. "We're going to need lots of pictures of everything happening." Her phone camera was already at work getting shots of the men crawling over what would be the back of the first floor.

"I need to go get a look at the kitchen," Will said and took off running over to the far side of the first truck.

Ann turned to her twin grandsons Seamus and Tim and pulled rank. "What we really need are all those chairs I had you find last weekend, lined up across the porch of your house. That will be the best place to watch everything."

Harry ducked back into the house but returned a moment later. He handed Kate two more phones and a portable charger. "I figure you could use another phone or two when you need to charge the first. That way you don't have to stop."

"Wonderful." She told him, smiling--her eyes shining. They followed her younger brothers across the driveway and soon Sal, Tom and Padraig had joined the project and a dozen chairs, mostly Adirondack chairs, but some were old wicker chairs that probably dated back thirty years and had been repainted many times were arranged across the porch. Ann opened the front door and started passing out stacks of quilts and afghans. "Exciting as this is, if we sit still in this weather for long, we're going to freeze. These will help keep the chill at bay for part of the time."

When Mr. Edwards joined them five minutes

later, he admired the view. "You people have the best seats in the house. You'll be able to watch every detail. A couple of ground rules. First I see a bunch of dogs. They can't be allowed to run around."

"That won't be a problem. Kate has trained them all to stay at our sides."

He raised his eyebrows but said, "Good, good. The other thing is your little house must stay empty. It's for safety's sake, though Bert probably won't even rattle your china, the insurance insists on it."

"Understood," Harry told him. "I'll go lock it up now so that nobody wanders in looking for a bathroom."

"Once the men have both boxes cleared of wrappings, we'll begin backing the first truck into position. These trucks move slowly, but I'd rather people didn't walk behind them. The backup cameras make it a lot easier than it used to be when it comes to aligning the box with the crane, but it would help if everybody stayed clear when the trucks were moving." He looked back over his shoulder at the men working on the house sections. "It seems they're ready to go."

Kate spotted Will jumping down from the box he'd been exploring. From the grin on his face, she'd bet that he more than approved of the kitchen. He trotted over and squatted down in front of Dani who was sitting next to Kate.

"Wait till you see this kitchen. It is heaven. The stove cries out to be used to create masterpieces. That island with automatic waste disposal is mind-boggling."

"So you won't mind if Harry and I ask you to cook Christmas dinner for the family in that kitchen. Mr. Edwards says it will be ready in time for us to spend the holidays there."

"That soon. Fantastic. I've got to start planning the menu. With all the kitchen has, feeding fifty will be a walk-in-the-park."

Kate laughed and reached out to muss his hair. She chuckled when he immediately reached up to put it back in order and blushed. Will was the closest to her in thinking as well as age, being what they call an Irish twin because he was born eleven months after she was. "I ordered everything on the list you gave me," she told him. "I figured if you picked it, I would love it. I certainly love the kitchen you designed for us up at Camp in Lake George," Kate told him.

"The kitchen at Camp is enough to have a girl who had spent the previous year cooking over a hot plate in my rooms above the morgue, a heart attack. I had oven-envy," Gwyn told them. Everyone laughed.

The sound of a monster engine starting focused everyone's attention as the first truck began backing up. Harry looked around. "Everyone. Twice this morning, a light green sedan showed up at the end of our driveway and acted suspiciously. We got the license number, and Sean is checking on it, but keep an eye out. I don't know if it's our threat or not but better safe than sorry."

When the first section reached the right spot for lifting, the workmen began threading cables through marked slots on the base. These spots were marked to make sure that the multi-ton section was lifted, it would be perfectly balanced. The women each grabbed a quilt to wrap around their legs. Kate whipped out her phone and began taking a video, sweeping the camera in an arc encompassing everything from the beginning of the driveway to the far side of the crane. Using the zoom on her camera, she got a close-up of Harry and Will pointing to the area of the kitchen which would overlook the dog yard. Kate loved the placement of that window which would be by the breakfast nook. She could picture herself sipping tea and watching her dogs play.

Kate had been so busy watching the construction going together, that she hadn't noticed a crowd had arrived. Her knitter's cars were in the section saved for them. Tim and Seamus were parking visitors out of the way. The idea was to allow people to witness this unusual event but to make sure that nobody got hurt. Several people from her classes waved to her as they watched. Sean was spending as much time directing visitor traffic as he was the big trucks.

Both Will and Harry stopped talking to watch the first section be lifted up into the air and slowly moved across the foundation. It was guided by only three men holding cables and then was gradually lowered into place. Kate's telephoto lens on her camera followed the entire thing. She moved the shot in as close as she could when the section descended and was impressed by the gentle and perfectly accurate settling of the section onto a waterproof membrane installed between the foundation and the house itself. That padding meant that when the box settled in place, it was a relatively quiet joining. The membrane would keep out the wet and the drafts. Everyone had stopped talking to hold their breath, but as the first section landed, they cheered.

Harry jogged up the steps, kissed the top of her head, asked if she was having fun then jogged back down the steps to go talk with Edwards as the second section was backed into the prime position for the crane to lift it. Kate chuckled at Harry's kid-like enthusiasm. He'd hadn't really had a childhood, so she felt he should have some fun as an adult. It was easier to record now since the sun had managed to put in an appearance. Like the first section, the second moved smoothly into place. The placement seemed almost delicate, inching its way down to sit perfectly onto the foundation. A man began ratcheting the two sections tightly together matching up marks that had been put on the base of each section for that purpose. Another man began pulling the cables from under the second section of the house. Groves had been placed and marked in the bottom plate to achieve a perfect balance with the cables run through them, Edwards had explained.

Men then disappeared into the basement. Kate remembered Edwards telling them that temporary columns would be put into place to support the long sections that would later be replaced with permanent columns. While they were working down there, two men had climbed onto the top of the sections and were bolting the two sections together.

Her zoom was getting a workout. She switched cameras to get shots of them attaching the side walls together and hitching it to her tiny house. Finally, one worker opened the front door. Kate could see straight through the living room to the French doors leading to the back deck. The room was filled with light. Glancing to where she'd last seen Harry, she spotted him with Edwards, Tom, and Will, all heading in her direction.

She picked up her phone/camera and went back to work. Earlier this month, when she and Harry took their honeymoon, she found her great-great-grandfather's photo album with black and white photographs showing every step in the construction of the family's vacation home almost two hundred years ago. It was this vacation home which she and Harry bought on the banks of Lake George in New York last month. They'd spent their honeymoon there and the history of the place thrilled her. She was glad that Harry wanted to keep the place in the family.

Kate decided to keep a similar photographic record of this house. She photographed the construction of their foundation and the company had sent her photos of the house as it was put together. Now, with the arrival and assembly of the house sections, she'd see her dream home brought to reality. This time she would be recording it for her great- (however many great) grandchildren to have as a record. She lifted her phone camera and began taking more photos. When they paused to adjust something, she sent out a series of texts asking all the family and friend who photographed the day from different angles to post copies to the link she listed, so she could work them into the story. This would be the perfect project for her to work on once her pregnancy kept her from doing all the running around that was part of her normal schedule.

Kate finished adding a bunch of her shots to the file in Dropbox which Harry had created online when a mug appeared in her hand. Harry settled himself on the arm of her Adirondack chair. "Getting it all recorded? This is the perfect spot to see everything that's happening."

"I am. I just texted people to upload their photos to the file you created in Dropbox. It will be a great place for people not only to send their shots but for our friends who couldn't make it to the real thing, to see the process by visiting the site. This way we'll be able to make a wonderful study of the building of our home to preserve for generations.

Harry hugged her, "My wife, the anthropologist".

CHAPTER 9

Friday noon

It was a good half hour before Harry waved to her to say that it was time for their tour. Will was serving a buffet inside for the workmen and as Kate stood, she called to him that it was time for the tour. She headed down the porch steps, but had to force herself to concentrate on where she was going. As she moved around to an area near the trucks, it was too tempting to stop every few steps to take photos from different angles. She took a few of her grandmother sitting on the front porch of her mother's house wrapped in her quilt, with Sal standing behind her and Liam at her side. Her mind imagined what it might be like to sit on their new porch, looking across to this one. In the summers to come, their children might be running around playing on the lawns stretching out on either side of the driveway. Or in winter, they'd be watching as their kids took turns riding on the dog sled pulled by her dogs down the length of the drive.

Seamus approached. He and Tim had gotten permission to miss school today so long as their work was done. Because Seamus was competing with his girlfriend to be valedictorian that wasn't a problem. Tim had pushed the assignments out so it wouldn't hurt his status on the basketball team. Seamus was now accompanied by his girlfriend, Satu. Both were extremely bright students and re-searchers and both were already on Harry's payroll part-time.

Kate pulled Seamus aside and asked him for a favor. It occurred to her that what would show the total view of the project in action would be a bird's eye view. She asked if Seamus could get Rex, his search and rescue drone, to take some stills and video of what was going on. His face broke into a grin. "I've got this. Mr. Edwards said they are about to take a break. Satu, could you interview the crane operator and one or two of the guys who work the guide ropes for our paper. I'm going to slip into the whelping room and get Rex. I'll fly him out of the kennel copula again. Satu, I'll text you when we're

ready to fly and you can record it and link it to Kate."
The girl grinned and gave him a thumbs-up as she
raced to intercept the crane driver.

"I'm amazed at how quickly the sections are
going together." Tom said as he took her arm to
stroll toward the now completed first floor. "This
house is going to be even bigger than Mom's. Once
the parts are assembled, I'm told they only have to
back fill around the foundation, connect the plumbing and electrical heating, finish building the front
porch, deck off the back, and finish the fireplaces
and siding and it will be good to go."

"We hope to celebrate Christmas there. Will is
already planning a fancy dinner since I let him design the kitchen, pick all the appliances, and design
the fancy island."

Harry came hurrying toward her. "Edwards says
that while his men take a lunch break, we can do a
walk through of the first floor. Come on!" He reached
out and grabbed her hand, and they headed for the
front door followed by the others.

The beams which would comprise the base
for the front porch were already in place and Mr.
Edward's crew had placed several two-by-twelve
boards to make steps and a safe walkway to the
door. As they crossed what would be the porch and

Harry stepped ahead of her to open the door. Then, startling her, he reached out to lift her into his arms, kissed her, and carried her over the threshold to the hoots and cat-calls from crew, friends and family. Kate felt her cheeks burn, but she loved the gesture. She looked over Harry's shoulder and saw Will and Dani head for the kitchen.

As Kate's feet hit the floor, she turned in a circle taking in the space. Having lived in a tiny house for couple of years, the amount of space was overwhelming. The living room extended from the front of the house all the way to the back, with two large casement windows on the front and a set of French doors banked by smaller casement windows on the back. Light flooded the room, and would highlight the warmth of the wide oak floorboards which were now covered to protect them. Kate looked up at the beautiful crown molding along the edge of the ceiling. It was mirrored by a modified version in the baseboards. Edwards pointed out that each box came complete with floor and ceiling. When put together, it gave an extra layer which kept the noise between floors to a minimum. She was happy to see the number of electrical outlets including several in the floor.

Mentally she placed a sofa in the middle of

the room facing the fireplace with two wing chairs flanking it. A long table would go along the back of the sofa which could hold lamps, and vases plus would be a great place to set down the book you were reading when you had to get up to answer the door. Kate looked at the area where the fireplace would go which now contained only the fire-box and the flue. A door to the left of the fireplace would lead to the master-bedroom suite which was due to arrive tomorrow. Dillon quietly explored the room with his father, Liam. The dogs were busy taking in all the new smells. Kate smiled at the thought that her dozen Samoyeds would sack out happily in this room and there would be plenty of room to walk around them.

Harry took her hand and pulled her into the library. They both were avid readers so this room was a given. All four walls were covered with beautifully carved oak bookcases, though the wall along the front wall of the house, had the bottom shelves replaced with cupboards that extended eight inches beyond the book shelves into the room. This allowed for the large casement window to accommodate a window-seat. Edwards pointed out that the section below the window seat opened to reveal a storage cupboard for pillows and blankets. Harry described where he would put his massive oak desk which was made from the same oak as the book-cases. Plus he had ordered a matching wood and lea-ther swivel desk chair. Maeve asked if her library had inspired them, and both Kate and Harry said yes.

Everyone walked back out into the living room past the staircase which rose part way up to a small landing then split to go toward different ends of the second floor hallway. This allowed room beneath it for both a double coat closets in the living room and a built-in china cabinet in the dining room. Ann mentioned that with the bump-out section of the dining room, the large table could run the length of the room with overflow directly into the living room and the children's table could be in the bump out where they could look down into the dog yard.

Edwards began hurrying them along saying his men would be finishing lunch and getting ready to install the second floor. Ann reminded him to be sure to eat as well. They walked into the kitchen to find Dani and Will talking about the fact that there was an oven in the stove plus two build into the wall next to it--one strictly a warming oven.

Ann and Gwyn began raving over the disposal system on the island. Its purpose was to allow the disposal of vegetable waste into a recycling bin simply by stepping on a pedal near the floor. After you finished cutting up your vegetables, what you weren't using could be pushed over to an area near the stainless steel disk. That disk covered a hole in the counter, whoever was cooking would step on a pedal causing the disk to move aside giving access to the recycling bin below. The vegetable scraps would be easily slid in and when the foot was removed the lid would close. "When full, it can be brought outside to the garden for the mulch pile." Dani explained.

"A garden," Kate whispered longingly. She had never had the time or a good space to grow a garden. But now, with a family on the way, she loved the idea.

"Now that there are two of us, we'll be able to do many of the things we enjoy but didn't have time to do." Harry told her as if reading her mind. After admiring the breakfast nook overlooking the dog yard, they turned to the other end of the kitchen. The island didn't take up as much space as Kate had thought. It was a nice size, big enough for food prep but not so long that it was a hike to go around. What this meant was there was plenty of space under the windows that faced out onto the front porch for a large table. Kate remembered one that she'd seen one evening this fall when Harry had been away. She had bookmarked it in her computer and now thought it would be perfect for the space.

"Time's up folks. We've got to get back to work. We'll be loosing light in four-and-a-half hours," Mr. Edwards said as he herded them out the door. When they left the unfinished porch, Kate's phone beeped. She glanced at it not concerned since with all the visitors kept it beeping all morning. But it wasn't the driveway that came up. Someone was coming out of the woods and heading for the dog pen. Kate began to run and yelled, "The dogs." Harry passed her his long legs covering more space quickly with Will right beside him. Sal had his phone to his ear as he followed them. Dani stayed running at her side but Dillon, Jake and Liam all raced ahead of the men, seeming to know what was happening. As they rounded the end of the kennel, they headed for someone who was moving toward the dog pen carrying what looked like a stick. As she ran, Kate keyed in the code for the new camera and hit record. She checked the display on the phone's screen as she ran, and noticed the man pause and kneel, lifting what she realized was a rifle and point it at the dogs who were lined up along the chain link enclosure, barking at the stranger.

Then, two things happened at once. The inside door of the run opened and someone made a noise. The dogs all turned and ran through the door, just as the massive Bouvier shot across the grass and jumped, knocking the man to the ground as a shot rang out. Two Sams were on him almost at the same time, with Dillon grabbing the rifle and pulling it away and Liam grabbing the man's coat. He pulled it up over the guy's head which managed to keep him from using his arms. As the men rounded the corner of the kennel, Patrick flew by to provide backup to the dogs holding the shooter. Sean met the men as they came in sight of the shooter. He pulled out his handcuffs and called off Patrick. Dani shouted to Jake to hold as Kate did the same to Dillon and Liam. The dogs surrounded the man just daring him to move. Sean had just cuffed the man when a patrol car pulled up and Sgt. Gurka jumped out.

Kate's phone buzzed with a text. Satu had the whole thing on video from the man moving through the woods and approaching the kennel to his preparing to shoot. Rex's overhead camera had even gotten perfect coverage of the takedown by the dogs. Once the man was cuffed, the dogs were given their release to return to their handlers. Jake came racing up to Dani and jumped straight up while she reached out to hug him, swinging the big dog around. Both Dillon and Liam crowded Kate, getting hugs and their ears rubbed as they were told how wonderful they were. Patrick bounced around carrying his tennis ball in his mouth. Gurka confiscated the rifle. The shooter wasn't talking except to say he was going to sue Kate for damage done by the dogs.

Kate stepped up to the man. "Just remember one thing if your get out on bail," she said as everyone looked her way. "These dog, plus all the dogs in that yard now have your scent. If you come anywhere near this property, they will know, and they will remember today." With that she spun around and walked with Dillon at her side back toward the construction unit which had continued working in spite of the excitement. Dani and Jake fell in beside her. When she reached the barn's side door, Kate opened it to find Roger with a pail full of tennis balls, throwing for all he's worth and the dogs having a marvelous time. Kate grabbed a box of dog treats from the shelf and yelled, "Clean-up." As the dogs ran to retrieve the balls and get their treats, Kate laughed. "I wondered how you were able to get them inside so fast."

"I knew it was their favorite game and I didn't even have to call, I only rattled the pail, and they were in here ready to go. Then it was just a matter of throwing balls until they caught the guy. Sal texted me that there was a threat on the dogs. I was putting some equipment into the closet here since I'd finished cleaning the kennel, so I just got the bucket and the rest was easy."

They all laughed and Dani walked up and high-fived the retiring trooper. Will walked back next to Jake and Dani, and Harry moved into position on Kate's right side, so he and Dillon created a Kate sandwich. She told him that Seamus and Satu had captured everything using Rex. As they approached the corner of her house, they watched the back of their home's second floor fly up in the air. Kate and Dani and Will had begun filming when Kate and Harry's phones beeped. They looked at the end of the driveway just in time to watch as green sedan, pulled in, stopped, turned and quickly pull back onto the highway. It looked as though his boss was checking up on the shooter. If the idiot made a call, she wondered who would be on the other end.

CHAPTER 10

Friday afternoon

"Somehow I didn't think that doofus with the rifle was the brains behind this operation." Kate said, nodding at the retreating green sedan.

Harry broke away and ran across the driveway as Sgt. Gurka drove up with the prisoner. "Did you get anything from the license number Sean gave you?"

"Stolen."

"He was just here. Probably checking on this idiot."

"I don't know what he'll pull next, but we'll be ready. If he dares come after any of our girls, he's a corpse."

Harry turned back toward Kate and noticed that she was focusing on the sight of the first part of the second floor being put in place. Instead of hiding, she was photographing the workers who were bolting the first and second floors together.

As they mounted the steps to the lineup of chairs again, Ann and Sybil came out with trays of sandwiches for them. Will ducked inside and returned with a stack of plates and a bowl of pasta salad. Tim followed him with a carrier loaded with utensils and an urn of coffee, followed by Padraig with one of tea. Lunch was now served on two folding tables which had been set up while they'd been with the dogs.

They ate as they watched the back of the top floor get attached to the bottom floor. The men worked smoothly and fast, like a ballet. Bert was moving the crane into position to accept the final section for the day, when a car pulled into the driveway and Lt. Leon Holmwood stepped out, reaching into the back of the car for a box. He approached the porch and asked, "Mrs. Forester?"

Sybil stood and went forward. "Can I help you?"

"We spoke on the phone, about Mr. Salverson. My name is Lt. Holmwood."

"Yes lieutenant, how can I help you?"

"I know this may be hard, mam, but it might help in our investigation if you could look over the thing that he had with him in the car and see if anything stands out as being unusual?"

She looked from him to the box in horror. "I... Bill's things? I can't..." Kate was beside her instantly holding her arm and walking her back to her chair. Ann reached in to hug her and Maeve stepped forward to talk to Holmwood.

"Lieutenant, I'm Maeve Donovan, Mrs. Forester's sister." She said as Kate joined her.

"She is also former MI-5, lieutenant. If those are Mr. Salverson's things, I suggest you leave them with us. Maeve and I can sit with Sybil this evening and go through the contents of the box. Believe me, I am just as anxious as you are to find who is behind this murder. Whoever this person is has begun his attempts at frightening Agnes. A shooter tried to kill her greyhounds about an hour ago. Luckily, our security system caught him coming out of the woods behind the kennel carrying a rifle. Three certified police dogs and one other went after him, while an off-duty trooper got the dogs to safety. Sgt. Gurka took the man into custody, however, the car driven by the man who we think might be the brains behind the outfit, was seen turning around in the driveway right after the arrest was made. You might want to check and see if Gurka got anything out of the man--though I doubt it. "

Maeve spoke up. "Leave the box with us. We'll let you know if we come up with any possible leads. And thank you lieutenant for your help in this matter."

He looked at Kate and added, "I'll go by the barracks now and see what Gurka has gotten. Give me a call if you find anything out of the ordinary."

"Will do."

Kate and Maeve watched him return to his car. "I think you, I, and Harry should go through the box first. Then if we find anything, we can talk to Sybil. Going through this is going to be upsetting."

Harry came forward and picked up the box. Then avoiding the final truck which was backing into position, he trotted across the drive, unlocked the door of the small house and went inside. He was back out in under a minute and locking up. Kate watched him stop in front of the kennel and shout something up to Seamus who was in the tower above the kennel. Then he disappeared inside.

Kate walked over to where Sybil was sitting and squatted in front of her. Taking her hands, she explained what she, Harry and Maeve would do with the things that Lt. Holmwood had brought.

"If we find anything that you might help explain, we'll ask you about it. I know it is like opening a wound over and over when you are forced to deal with these details about someone you cared so much about, but if there is something there which might save Agnes' life, or ours, you'll need to tell us."

"Oh, Katie, I'm not brave like you or my sister, but I'll try. Bill had more faith in me than I had in myself. He often told me that I could do anything I want." She took Kate's head between her hands and whispered, "Bill and I were planning on marrying quietly, after Agnes and Sean's wedding was over. We didn't want to distract from the kids."

"Sybil, I can see you loved him very much. We will not stop until his killer is brought to justice."

"Thank you, Katie."

Kate nodded to her grandmother who handed Sybil a cup of tea and put an arm around her." She sighed and returned to her seat next to Dani. The front section of the top floor settled into place perfectly and Kate noticed a long cable extending from the crane to which the men were attaching to plywood triangles that had been lying on top of the section. These were the gable end sections of the roof. The men nailed them in place quickly and Kate looked up to see the first hinged section of the roof along the back of the house being drawn up.

Raising her camera she began taking close up shots as men seemed to be everywhere on the top of the second floor. They began by pulling the hinged knee-wall into place. Each two-by-four was wedged by two men into slots in support beams which ran along the second floor ceiling. Then they bolted these in place. Other men quickly went along and bolted the first and second floor sections together.

Next Bert went back to work and swung the crane back over the second floor and the ground crew attached cables lifting the next section of the hinged roof. As soon as each of the lower roof panel was in place, he went back to lift each of the final two sections comprising the peek of the roof, and the attic was complete. All that needed finishing was the papering and shingling of the hinged joining sections and the roof would be water tight.

Kate had been filming this whole process when a hand took her camera and pulled her to her feet. "Excuse us everyone, but Kate and I want to explore our new home."

"Go ahead. We'll look when you are done," Maeve spoke for all of them.

They didn't talk as they walked down the hill hand-in-hand toward their front door. Bert was busy stacking the flatbed sections, on top of another semi so that there were fewer long trucks dealing with that traffic challenge on the trip back to the factory. Harry gave him a smiling thumb's up as they walked across the boards and went inside. Closing the door muffled the sound of the crane somewhat, but they could still hear the workmen finishing work above their heads. Strolling around the living room, they'd stop to comment on where to put what. Kate's imagination visualized the finished room far better than Harry's.

"When they complete the fireplace, I want to put shelves on either side where I could display some of the dog's nicer trophies. They've been sitting in a carton in the closet of my office for years."

They stepped into the library and Harry closed the door. "I wanted to talk to you without everyone listening."

"What is it?"

"Tom just called me. I gave him Agnes' phone to examine. There was a new message."

They walked to the window seat and sat. Taking a deep breath she asked, "What did it say."

Harry paced for a minute then joined her at the window and sat. Reaching into his pocket, he pulled out his phone and pressed play on the recorder as he wrapped his other arm around her.

The same voice as before spoke. "You are a stupid bitch. You think you can hide with no consequences. Well, your wrong. Your ugly mutts are dead, so I hope you are happy. You never cared about them anyway. But they were only the first. It's going to be that pretty cousin of yours who owns all those white dogs next. Such a pity she won't get to live in that fancy house they're building. She'll be gone in 24 hours if you don't give me what I want. Believe me. She will die and it won't be painless."

CHAPTER 11

Friday afternoon, late

Neither said a word. Kate pulled up her knees so that she could sit sideways on the window seat and stare out the window, as Harry slid to the floor. Then he reached up, over his shoulder, to grasp her hand. The both let the silence hold them for a while. Finally, Harry leaned his head back, resting it on her leg.

"Remember when we were at the National. The situation wasn't much different from this. Someone was determined to kill you."

"That's not something I'm likely to forget," she whispered. "I was so scared."

"I know you were. But the interesting thing is nobody else did. They thought you were fearless. You looked a killer right in the eye."

"Right. Then he shot me."

"Details." Harry said with a wry grin.

Kate laughed.

"You toughed it out. When you recovered from being shot, even though you hurt, you went to talk to hundreds of frightened people. Your words reassured everyone. Anybody else would have taken to their bed and hidden under the covers."

"So, you think I should be brave and just brush this off?"

"No. You won't brush this off. You will be conscious of every iota of threat every minute. No, what I mean is I think you should be Kate. Weigh each fact and use your brain to figure the best course. Ask anyone in your family what Kate does in a crisis. They'll tell you the same thing they always tell me, 'Kate will find the answer.'"

Silence settled on them again. After a few minutes, Kate said, "I really like this room. I'm looking forward to sitting here when it's filled with furniture that's been mussed up by having kids and dogs crawl all over it."

Harry stood and pulled her into his arms for a kiss, which was interrupted by the sound of someone clearing their throat. A voice asked from just outside the door. "You folks want to check out the rest of your house?" They followed the voice and found one of the workmen standing by the stairs pointing upward. "We opened up your staircase and have completed the staircase to the attic. We're ready to wrap it up for today. Your roof is tight, though the bad weather looks like it's holding off until tomorrow night or Sunday. We'll be here to-morrow to get the last sections in place." He looked around. "This is a nice house you people designed. I really love that library and kitchen. Most of the time, these are the standard blueprint houses, but you've really put some thought into the place. Con-gratulations." Two of the other workers came down the stairs and all three left.

"Do you feel up to checking it out?" Harry asked quietly.

Kate smiled a half-smile answered, "Sure, no worry. I'm tough. Just ask my husband and my brothers." Chuckling softly, they headed up the stairs. The climb began with five steps from the liv-ing room to a landing, then turned left and went up eight steps to a second landing. This had sets of three steps going in opposite directions to what Kate laughingly dubbed the north and south wings of the second floor.

They took the south wing steps which led to

two bedrooms, one facing front and one to the rear. These two bedrooms shared a Jack-and-Jill bath at the end of the hall. They entered the bedroom on the front of the house, which had a view of the two Killoy homes as well as, Bert's crane. At the far end of the room they walked into the bathroom which had separate toilet and sink areas, but a shared tub and shower. The back bedroom had a beautiful view out into the woods. In autumn, it would be spectacular in full color.

Leaving that room, they went back along the hall, past the door to the attic and reached an area with French doors. These would open onto a balcony created by the flat roof of the dining room bump-out which they would install tomorrow.

Kate mused, "I think this would be a wonderful playroom for the kids. By splitting the staircase, we created an open room full of light with cupboards fitted into the area above the stairs, to hold toys and puzzles. We gained enough floor space for a pair of overstuffed chairs. We could even put a table near the French doors where the light would be perfect for working jigsaw puzzles."

Harry laughed. "This will be the place for them to do homework. We can add a row of cubbies to keep their books and backpacks as well as bookshelves and a stack of cushion for flopping on the floor. This way they'll have their own space away from grown-ups."

Walking on, they explored north hall which held three bedrooms. One bedroom was on either side of the hall, and a larger one sat at the end of the hall. Kate had originally planned for it to be the master-suite but when they decided to move the master-suite downstairs, it became an elaborate guest-room with its own bath. Another bath off the hall would be shared by the two bedrooms.

"I know when we fill this with kids racing around with hockey sticks or baseball and soccer equipment it won't seem so big, but after living in my tiny house for a couple of years, the amount of space is overwhelming."

They finished exploring and went back through the children's playroom to the door that faced the staircase. Opening it, they climbed up to the attic which had been put together as if by magic. There was tons of open space which had Kate sighing. "Storage, at last. This is culture shock," she said. "I can get my Christmas ornaments out from under my old bed and take my summer clothes out of the spare bedroom above the kennel." Harry laughed.

"It's getting late. Do you want to see if they put

in the stairs to the basement?"

"Lets. If this is boggling my mind, what will the basement do? I'm so used to just a hole in the ground. Now it will be a massive part of the house."

As they descended to the second floor, Kate smiled again at the sight of the future playroom which had her looking forward even more to the birth of their child. Going down the stairs they heard voices. They followed the sound to the kitchen and found a crowd discussing Christmas dinner.

"Hi, everyone. We've been to the attic, so now we were going to explore the basement if the stairs are in." Harry opened a door off the end of the dining room opposite the powder room, and saw a staircase running down into what was a massive basement.

Seamus gasped, "Cool, you could have a media room, and a workout room..."

"And a basketball court." Tim said, dribbling an imaginary ball down the court for the layup. "And Killoy scores again!" Everyone laughed.

They headed back upstairs, since it was getting late and people had to be fed. Kate and Harry wanted to go through the box that Lt. Holmwood had brought. Kate would be the first to admit that she was ready for sleep.

Will leaned over and quietly told them that he had just put their dinner into the refrigerator. All they had to do was heat it up. Kate hugged her brother then stepped back to take Harry's hand. Harry locked up the house with the set of keys he'd gotten from Edwards. Then Sal, Dani, Sean, Kate and Harry walked to the barn, to bring the dogs into the house, while everyone else headed for Ann's.

"Sit," Harry told Kate gently pushing her into her chair. He and Sal grabbed the dog's bowls and filled them. Soon the dogs were outside, full of food and biscuits and happy to be home in their own yard.

Sean and Dani had been going through the box on the table, laying everything out to be examined. Kate spotted a day-planner and opening it to the first day of the year, she began going through it slowly, noting each entry, hoping to find a pattern to Bill's days. By the time she reached the end of the March entries, she knew that Sybil was the most important thing in his life. What might prove interesting for them was that he had meetings with Jannah Mastalski. When Kate was doing a demonstration of police dog work at the academy, she'd also met her. The congresswoman was giving an award for meritorious service to a now retired trooper, whose name Kate couldn't remember but his dog was named Curtis, for breaking up a drug ring. It appeared the congresswoman had been working with Bill, but their meetings were always held at various office buildings not connected to either of their jobs. She represented the first congressional district and was from New Britain. Kate made a note to herself to check and see what committees Jannah was on.

Sean reached the bottom of the box. Dani had checked off, on the evidence list, each item as it came out. The last thing he found was a key fob which was square with a Celtic design on it holding two house keys. As he handed it to Dani to record, she saw the edge of a tiny memory card inside the fob which she managed to ease out with her fingernail. "We need a computer," she called out. "Hopefully there is something on this card."

"Card?" He grabbed the list to check. "There's no card listed."

"It was in the key fob."

"The one with two keys, one of which is listed for his house." Sean told her.

"The other might be for Sybil's place," Kate mentioned. "He spent a lot of time there."

Harry laid his laptop on the table and turned it on. Dani handed him the memory card. When loaded, he found it contained forty folders as well as dozens of graphic files, both png and jpg. Harry clicked on the first photo and saw a group of men sitting around a table in a restaurant. The angle of the photo managed to capture their faces but Harry suspected that they didn't know there was a camera pointed their way. Of the six men at the table, most were strangers but two looked vaguely familiar, as if he'd seen them somewhere before. He couldn't remember where. He pulled up a blank Word document and began opening the various photos and pasting them, four to a page. When he finished, he printed them out making two copies of each page.

Looking up, he saw that Kate had taken a casserole from the refrigerator and was placing it in the microwave. Next she put a covered glass bowl filled with broccoli on the counter and put a loaf of what smelled like garlic bread in the oven to warm. His stomach told him he was more than ready for food.

By the time dinner was ready, Harry had managed to print out all the documents in two of the file folders. At this rate, he would be in for quite a long evening. Stretching, he stood and took the casserole from Kate as she put the broccoli in to warm up. Sal laid out plates and silverware for everyone and Sean reached into the cupboard to get glasses but stopped. "Ah," he said opening the refrigerator. "There's a bottle of wine to go with the meal. I'll get wine glasses."

"I'll have water, please." Kate told him. He poured wine for everyone else and they all settled in to eat.

Kate looked around the table and began, "We need to find out if there is a session of Congress going on next Tuesday that involves an investigation of some sort. It might be Appropriations, Armed Services or Judiciary. See which one might include Representative Jannah Mastalski of Connecticut's First District."

Dani asked, "You got all that from his daily planner?"

"Well, when a person begins having multiple meetings with governmental officials in out of the way places, I for one suspect an undercover investigation. And, I think Bill was gathering information which he was passing on to congress. I think what Agnes might have is a copy of this disk. Our stalker wants what Bill gave her returned. Now it might be what we have here, a card with the same thing on it, or it might be something else entirely."

Dani pointed to the printouts which held the photos. "I glanced at these photos and all it tells me is there are groups of middle-aged men who like to eat out at fancy restaurants. The second photo and eighth were both taken at Cristoforo's which is a membership only club in Hartford."

"I've never heard of the place." Harry said.

"My uncle was chef there for many years. It is very exclusive and expensive."

Kate looked at her. "Did your uncle teach you to cook?"

"Yeah. My mom hates to cook and believes in TV dinners, so he figured if she wouldn't feed us right, he'd teach me. He would really love your new kitchen."

Kate grinned.

Harry called Sadie to do some research on Rep. Mastalski and what committees she was now serving on. Also, he wanted to know if any of those committees might have meetings next Tuesday.

Kate suddenly yawned and felt that she could fall asleep right where she sat but she still had more to do. "I'm going to go bed down the kennel dogs. I'll be back in a few minutes." She stood and pulled on her parka as she headed out.

"I'll come with you." Sal grabbed his parka and

followed her.

They'd almost reached the door of the kennel when the phone app sounded in both Kate and Sal's pockets, and a car raced down the driveway toward them. Sal spotted the muzzle of a rifle sticking out of the window on the passenger side. He lifted Kate and dove behind the concrete knee-wall which divided the walkway from the parking lot. He landed hard with her on top of him and then pushed her down as he rolled to free his gun hand. A spray of bullets rained against the other side of the wall sending concrete shards flying everywhere. Without even looking for a target, Sal fired back over the wall toward the sound of screeching tires. He pulled back when he heard the car's fire being returned from the front of the house. They heard a loud 'bang' followed by a grinding noise and a flapping sound as the car raced away. Sal peeked over the edge of the wall as the back door opened and Harry raced out screaming, "KATE!"

CHAPTER 12

Friday night

"I'm okay," she said as she extricated herself from her position half under Sal. Harry swept her into his arms and hugged her so tight she could barely breathe. Kate didn't care. To be alive and safe in his arms was what she needed.

She turned to where Sal was using the wall to help him stand. "Sal, are you hit?"

"No, just bruised. I haven't done that in years, and I think I'm out of practice."

Dani ran through the door out of breath. "Sean and I got off some decent shots and Sean blew out the guy's tire. I called it in. He's not going to get very far riding on the wheel rim in that sedan. He's also leaking fluid, probably gas, so here's hoping he's not in traffic if he blows up." Her phone rang. After listening for a few seconds, she disconnected and swore explaining, "A patrol car found the sedan abandoned by the state park entrance. There was no sign of the driver or shooter though the motor was still hot. They are going to tow it and see if they can find any prints. There were fresh tire tracks from a second vehicle crossing over the track made by the blown tire. So, they had an accomplice."

Kate bent to look around Harry's shoulder. "Where are the dogs?"

"I threw open door to the yard when I heard the screech of tires and yelled. They all came running. Luckily I kicked the door shut the instant they were all inside because Dillon and Liam suddenly realized that you and Sal were outside. I thought they were going to break through the wall to get to you."

They stopped talking at the sound of running feet. Seamus, Will, Satu, and Tim raced around the house to where they were gathered. Gwyn and Tom came right behind. Tom shouted, "I told the others to stay inside. Maeve's armed and I gave Padraig my spare Glock."

Sirens filled the air. Patrol cars raced into the parking lot. Gurka jumped out of his car and ran toward them shouting, "Anybody hurt?"

"Bruised, but unbloodied." Sal told him. "We're going to need some patrols by here for the next few days. As near as I could tell, he was watching us from the spot in the bushes right outside the entrance the driveway. When he saw Kate and me leave the house to walk to the kennel, he gunned it. His partner leaned out and emptied his AR or whatever assault rifle he was firing. Luckily, I was able to pull Kate down behind the wall, so except for being stiff from being out of practice on football tackles and bruises from flying concrete chunks, we're fine."

"The dogs?"

"Inside."

"Thank goodness. This is getting out of hand."

"Agreed."

"Kate, we'll go put the boarders away. You go lie down. Tomorrow is another early morning." Satu said while pushing Seamus and Tim toward the kennel door.

Harry looked at Kate and then turned to the others. "I'm going to take my wife inside and get her to lie down. This has been a ton of strain on top of being exhausted. We'll continue our research on Salverson's murder later."

They'd almost reached their bedroom, working their way through the milling bodies of clinging, upset dogs when Kate, who'd been half asleep stopped. She reached into her pocket and pulled out her phone, relieved that it was still intact after her fall.

"The camera," she said. "The new camera." She pulled up the app and keyed in the code. She requested everything for the last four hours and downloaded it. Then she opened the camera located on the front of the kennel. She pushed the play button and they watched the replay twice. Then Harry took the phone, and they continued into the bedroom.

Harry grabbed her pajamas and after taking off her parka and boots, he helped her undress and get ready for bed. Tucking her in, he said he'd be back with tea and saltines, and went into the kitchen. When he returned, she was asleep. However, he noticed she slept with her phone back in her hand, and the video of the shooting playing over and over in a loop. He eased the phone from her hand and put it back on the nightstand and plugged it in. Kissing her forehead, he slipped out of the room.

Sal sat at the kitchen table, a cup of coffee in front of him. Everyone else had left except the patrol cars in the driveway. Harry showed Sal the video and suggested he download it and forward it to Gurka. Then he packed the contents of the box and placed it in the back of the closet in Kate's old room under a pair of cross-country ski-boots. Next, he loaded the printer with a ream of paper and instructed the printer to print all the files in each folder they'd found on the disk.

He sat and waited. Sal looked at him but Harry didn't move.

"When did Kate start wearing a bullet proof vest?"

Harry smiled. "Sadie gave it to her for a wedding present. The one she sent her when we were at the national specialty was damaged when Kate was shot." Sal just stared at him.

Not saying more, Harry sat and let his mind go over all the times he'd come close to losing her. The number of times she'd been shot at. It was unreal. He knew it would destroy him if he lost her. The mere idea of someone trying to rip her from him tightened the fist that gripped his heart. He also knew what was coming. Her fear—that terror which didn't show at all on the outside when things were going wrong. It was when things were going insane, that this amazing woman he married would hold it all together. No, his Kate clinched her terrors in a tight grip which she hid neatly inside—held tight so nobody would be upset. But they would escape when she wasn't watching. And that's why he waited. He knew what would come. Raw pain that she tamped down would burst forth, tearing at her. When the anguish that ate at her slipped from her grasp, it would free itself and tear her apart. It was his job to sit and wait and be there when it arrived.

"I'll tell you, Sal," he said as he stared straight ahead, out the kitchen window, "the high iron gate I have at the entrance to my driveway at Camp is not looking like a luxury any more. The fact that he could spy on us and then just swoop in and attack you and Kate terrifies me. The fact that he's doing it just to blackmail Agnes is beyond belief."

He picked up the day-planner Kate had been working on as well as the pad with her notes. He noted the important names, dates and facts she was listing in one column and the questions she was developing in a second column.

It seemed Bill was working undercover compiling information on a case. How it involved a congressional committee remained a question. Harry realized that the contents of the files were probably evidence of criminal activity. But the question was, what activity? Who was involved? These needed answers and that meant research tomorrow—in their non-existent spare time. They needed to talk to the congresswoman. She might not even know that Bill was dead. If she did, she might feel she'd lost the battle she and Bill were waging. Knowing his wife, her great-aunt, and her cousin, the battle may have been lost, but they would win the war. Walking to the door of their bedroom, he looked in and made sure that Kate still slept.

Back in the kitchen, he checked the printer and added another ream of paper. Taking what was printed, he closed the paper tray and watched it continue to print. Then he resumed his vigil and sat to wait.

Sal still sat at the table speaking softly on his phone. From his tone of voice, Harry suspected he was talking with Ann. He seemed to be discouraging her from coming down to check on Kate. After a few minutes, he switched his argument to having Dani escort her. Harry was listening with half an ear when he heard the sound he'd been expecting. It started as a low howl which bounced off the walls, then rose into a heart-breaking cry that filled the house and brought the dogs flooding into the bedroom. Harry found Kate sitting up swaying back and forth, her eyes wide open but not awake.

Harry kicked off his shoes and climbed onto

the bed, pulled Kate into his lap, wrapped his arms around tightly her, matching his swaying to hers—not fighting what she had to do—just sharing the journey. His voice, was calm and soothing as he said, "Sing your song, Kate. Sing it to the end. The dogs will sing with you." The dogs had begun to howl along with her. They climbed onto the bed and lay around her and beside her.

"What's happening?" Sal asked, standing frozen in the doorway of the bedroom, horrified.

The front door opened and slammed shut. Ann and Dani rushed in. "Oh, my sweet Katie. I knew this would happen when the shooting started. She'll need tea and something to eat."

"Ann," Sal asked, "What's happening to her?"

"PTSD," she whispered. "This is how she handles being shot at." She watched Kate sway as she screamed with the dogs joining her song. But as she watched her, her eyes were caught by the movement of Kate's hands, which were splayed across her stomach one above the other. Was the stress giving her a stomach ache or...? She watched as Harry laid his large hand over hers, without breaking the motion of her swaying. Then it dawned. Pregnant. She grabbed Sal's arm and whispered, "Katie's pregnant!"

As they both stood looking at her, they saw

Quinn suddenly stop howling and push his head forward past the others to stare into Kate's face. Then, he shifted and grabbed her hand pulling it from under Harry's, tearing it away from her stomach.

"Ouch!" Kate blinked. After slowly looking around, she rubbed her sore hand and then placed it on Quinn's head. "That hurt, Quinn, but thanks. I needed you to bring me back."

"Good boy, Quinn," Ann said approaching the bed and patting the puppy on his head. "What would you like with your tea, Kate?"

"I don't know, maybe toast? I'm fine, everybody. It was just an allergy attack. It turns out I'm allergic to people shooting at me."

Harry hugged her and helped her get out of bed, then put on her slippers and a warm sweatshirt. Once in the kitchen with everyone gathered around the table, Kate apologized to Sal and Dani for scaring them.

"How long has this been going on?" Sal asked.

"It started in New York in February. I didn't sing my screams in that one, but the shut-down was longer and more severe. The screams began when we went to Texas to get Quinn. I'll tell you; those needle-like teeth of an eight-week-old puppy can hurt. It happened again at the National when I was shot at. Surprisingly though, when I was actually hit, I didn't do my sing—probably because it would have hurt with all the bruising I got even with the bullet-proof vest. I don't remember if it happened with all that confusion surrounding the wedding, but it happened during the honeymoon. Quinn seems to have a talent for bringing me back to reality at just the right time. You are a good boy, Quinn," she said, scratching his head and then reaching for her tea. "I honestly don't do anything to invite people to shoot at me—they just do."

"It's not the first time Agnes set you up to be shot," Harry grumbled.

"She didn't know they'd try to kill me. She ran to keep us safe. Remember, we have her phone. She doesn't know any of this is happening. If she knew, she'd be here in a flash and we don't want that. What we've got to figure out is who the person is behind this and how to stop him. And in keeping with that thought, what did you get off that memory card you found?"

"I don't know yet. I've been printing out the files figuring we could go through them this weekend."

"I don't think we have that much time. I think we should look at them now."

Agreement resonated. Kate picked up the day planner and turned back to the beginning to go through it again. The group sat around the table going through the piles of papers. Murmurs of 'Oh, my God,' and 'I can't believe it,' burst forth as papers were passed back and forth.

Kate double checked each page in the day planner. When she was half way through, she turned a page only to realize that it was really two pages stuck together. She reached over to get a butter knife from the drawer when the front door opened and Sybil, Maeve and Padraig came in. Harry rose to greet them as she gently pried apart the pages.

"What has you frowning so hard?" Sal asked.

"It's just that I found two pages stuck together with what looks like..."

"Jelly." Sybil said. "Probably from a Dunkin' Donuts jelly donut. They were his favorite. Katie dear, are you all right? I couldn't believe what happened. The world has gone crazy. Why is someone doing this?"

"I find it's usually the case of a greedy person wanting to get what they don't deserve and willing to do anything to get it. It's not the first time I've been their target."

In spite of being surrounded by people, Kate

couldn't fight yawning. Harry was beside her in two seconds. "I think we all need a good night sleep. Why don't we pick this up tomorrow after they finish putting more stuff on our house."

After everyone left, Harry tucked Kate back into bed and went to let out the dogs for a minute. He put the day planner with the piles of paper. Then he let the dogs back in. He checked that the patrol car was parked in the driveway and finally shed his clothes and crawled into bed. Reaching out, he pulled Kate tightly against him. Only when he heard her soft relaxed breathing did he allow the sleep he craved to take him.

CHAPTER 13

Saturday very early morning

T he alarm went off before any of them were ready for the new day. Even the dogs were tired. Kate lay still waiting for the first signs of nausea to hit. She carefully reached for a few saltine crackers and began to nibble while Harry dealt with the dogs. Once she got a couple of crackers into her stomach, she was able to roll to her side and sit up. She felt a vague disquieting feeling with her stomach, so she sat still and nibbled another cracker. A cup of tea was pressed into her hand, and she breathed in the steam, then sipped.

"You are a saint," she muttered.

"No, I'm just someone who loves you and realizes how lucky he is that you are carrying this baby because he'd be a whimpering mess for nine months if the job fell to him."

Kate laughed and after a last swig of tea, stood and headed for the shower. Harry had breakfast ready when she emerged from the bedroom. They quickly fed the dogs and then Harry dashed into the shower while Kate cleaned up and put the dogs out.

Sal knocked at the back door and then walked in. "Ah, coffee. Harry's a saint."

"That's the second time he's been told that today. He's racking up points in heaven left and right."

"So, what's the schedule.

"The truck with the final pieces should be pulling in about thirty minutes. First we move the dogs to the new run. They've been fed. I'll do a quick clean up of their run before the truck arrives. The workers wouldn't enjoy stepping in anything. Then we'll go watch them deliver the final parts of the house. The finish crew will begin as soon as the sections are in place. They'll back fill around the basement first, then complete the porch. Tomorrow the crew comes to do the siding and then paint everything to match. Due to the slope of the land, the big house is higher than this one, so this porch will be connected to the other one with two steps. It will differentiate the house from the business and

I think it will look good. They've already matched the shingles.

"Electricians and plumbers can do their work at the same time. Next week they'll finish the fireplaces and chimney. We decided that since the fireplace backed up to the master suite, we'd put one in there as well sharing the chimney. So there is still a lot of work left to do, but we want to be in by Christmas."

"This is amazing. I'm glad I came back to see it."

"The eggs and bacon are in the warming oven so get yourself a plate. Harry will be out in a minute, and then we'll move the dogs."

"Um, Ann told everyone last night you were pregnant."

Kate smiled. "I guess I couldn't fool her. How did she know?"

"Apparently when you were screaming, your hands went protectively to your stomach and so did Harry's."

"Well, she's right. So I'm glad that Roger is close to retirement, because I've been told that I will be getting tired more easily as the baby grows."

"Or babies," Harry said as he walked into the kitchen, grabbing another muffin off the counter.

"Twins?" Sal asked.

"It's nothing. I just had a dream and Harry's convinced that was a premonition."

"Well, I have every faith that whatever happens, you'll handle it. Let's go move dogs," Sal said giving her a hug.

As they started across the parking lot, Sean and Roger both pulled into the driveway, stopping to talk to the troopers in the patrol car. Kate's dogs and the greyhounds settled themselves quickly so, Sal joined Roger to begin letting out the boarding dogs. They walked back through the kennel and Harry went to a drawer in her office and pulled out one of the new phones and loaded the app for the security. He handed it to Roger and told him Sal would fill him in on all the security and how to spot any intrusions. Then he and Kate headed back toward the house when they heard a beep and saw Mr. Edwards and Bert arrive.

Meeting them at the front door, and they offered coffee and a quick breakfast. It was well-received. Kate put the plate of muffins on the table and began dishing up scrambled eggs and bacon.

Dani and Kate's brothers were next to arrive with Satu in tow. She was explaining about the head start she'd gotten on the paper she was writing for extra credit on the house instillation for her math class. She immediately sat down next to Mr. Edwards and Bert and peppered them with questions. Seamus whipped out his pocket recorder rather than taking notes. Kate chuckled over the fact that these two were locked in a battle for valedictorian and at the same time were going steady.

The beeping of their phones had her and Harry heading for the door as the last flatbed eighteen-wheeler pulled into the driveway with the final sections of the house. Kate pulled the extra phones off their chargers and headed out. Bert climbed into his crane and cranked the engine up as Edwards, Harry and Sean went to meet the driver and the car with the crew. Dillon and Jake moved into heel position as she and Dani with Will staying close headed across the driveway to the porch. They would stay out of the way until everything was ready to go, but move to the rear when Bert swung the bump-out into position. They settled into a group of Adirondack chairs and watched what appeared to be a ballet as the truck slid into position and the crane arm swung down to meet it. Harry mounted the porch to tell them that the first thing that would be moved would be the bump-out.

Kate looked up toward the entrance of the driveway and saw two troopers putting sawhorses across it. Harry saw her.

"It was Roger's idea. He said your boarders are not coming or going today and the gawkers got their looks yesterday."

"Thank goodness for that. We need as much protection as we can get." Sybil said as she, Ann, Maeve and Padraig arrived. I got a call from our friend Lt. Holmwood early this morning. It seems that Bill's younger brother Charlie just found out about his death. He contacted Holmwood about getting Bill's things that he had with him when he was killed. Charlie told him that he didn't have much to remember Bill by, so he'd like to have the few possessions he had with him on his last day."

"That sounds very sentimental. I didn't know that Bill had family."

"He didn't. One of the greatest sorrows that remained with him all his life was the death of his brother Charlie at age two. It seems the family had been invited to a party at a friend's home. It was a hot weekend and the friends had a pool. Bill was eight years old and had taken swimming lessons. He was eager to compete with his friends in swim races. Charlie was sleeping in his stroller. While their mother was talking, apparently Charlie woke up and managed to crawl out of the stroller. Before anyone had a clue, he managed to toddle over to the edge of the pool, probably drawn by all the noise. Bill said that they had just lined up at one end for a race when he spotted his brother standing on the edge of the pool, take a step and fall in. Bill screamed and then dove to get his brother. He pulled him out, but his lungs had taken in too much water, and he died. Bill never swam again not even when we went to the Cape last summer. So, I don't know about you, but I'm eager to meet this ghost of Charlie who wants to get his hands on Bill's stuff."

"Well, I'd better go pack up the box so that it is ready when the ghost arrives," Harry said.

"Copy the pages of the day planner, and remove the pages with the jelly on them," Kate told him. "They're the only ones I haven't examined thoroughly yet. I don't want him to get his hands on something vital. Also, when our ghost shows up with Lt. Holmwood, he can ask to be let in. It will also tell this bastard that we're ready for him if he's the shooter. Oh, and Sybil, is one of these keys yours?" she asked handing her the key fob.

"Yes, this one." She pulled the key from the ring. 'I'm glad you thought of that, so I didn't have to have my locks changed."

"Good. Let's go concentrate on our new house

and try for some joy stolen from us yesterday."

They all walked down to the driveway, watching the bump-out be delicately lifted high over the house and then slowly lowered it toward that section of the foundation. The men grabbed the ropes to guide it as they came into reach. One man was standing in the opening of the dining room using hand signals as the house section settled onto the foundation. Through the windows, they could see the man inside give a thumbs-up indicating that the fit was perfect. The outside operators pulled the cables from under the house section and began moving toward the end of the house to do the same thing for the master bedroom suite.

Dani looked up. "I wondered why you had French doors on the second floor. You're going to have a balcony overlooking the dog yard and the woods."

"Yes. That's where the children's playroom is located. There will be a white Baluster balcony railing with a Plexiglas lining. This way if small puppies get smuggled up there, they won't accidentally fall off the balcony."

"I'll tell you Kate, I can't wait to see this house with kids running all over it being chased by dogs and laughing. I think it's perfect."

"I can't wait either."

"By the way, the cat's out of the bag. I overheard Ann tell Sybil last night that you are pregnant."

"Harry and I just wanted to keep it to ourselves for a while before people begin to fuss. However, I could do without the feeling I'm going to barf when I wake every morning. Harry has me eating crackers before I get up and it seems to help."

"You got a good one when you married Foyle."

"I agree. Plus, he's going to make a wonderful father."

The subject of their talk walked up at that moment accompanied by Sal and Liam. He leaned in to Kate. "Holmwood just arrived with the ghost. They are just coming through the barricades. How do you want to play it?"

"I'm rather interested in what our ghost looks like. I don't think that we should expose him yet. Let him take the box. It might be good to let him pass off the information. It's possible it could lead us to more players in this game. The card isn't in the key fob anymore, right."

"Right. But I don't think we should act suspicious. I think he should just take it and go. In fact, his taking it might help identify him. Seamus had a new toy that I made use of and added to the collection. It was a bug like the ones used on us at the National only more sophisticated and with a longer range. I had Tim bring the box up to Ann's. Let's walk over and watch the show, plus that's the best place to see them install our master bedroom--my favorite room," he grinned.

They reached the porch at Ann's house just as Holmwood and a stranger were exiting their cars. Ann, Sybil and Maeve all walked out of the house together and stood looking at the men. Dillon stepped forward and stood with his hackles up between Kate and the man posing as 'Charlie', a low hum-like sound coming from him. The subject of the scrutiny looked disconcerted and stepped back from Dillon.

Liam was by Sal. As the man watched Dillon, Liam;s prey drive kicked in, and he began creeping up behind his target. He was almost close enough to grab him when Sal said, "Hold." The man swiveled and saw the big white dog crouched, ready to strike, and his handler calmly watching. He looked from Liam to Dillon and moved further up the porch.

Holmwood turned to the women and said to 'Charlie'. "Of course you've met your brother's fiancée being as close as you were."

"Ah, actually, I didn't know he was engaged. We never discussed it," the man posing as Charlie Salverson said.

"But you said you were close. Wasn't that why you wanted his things?" Holmwood pushed the point.

"Yea. However, we've both been busy and haven't been able to get together recently."

Holmwood looked at him doubtfully. "Could I check your ID again?"

Reluctantly, he pulled out a California driver's license and a birth certificate.

Sybil stepped forward. "So you are Charlie. You don't look anything like Bill."

"No. I look more like our mother."

"I see." Sybil looked at him hard which made him turn his head away. That allowed Kate to get a string of good head shots.

As he looked up, she went back to taking shots of the bedroom wing. Clearly uncomfortable, he spotted the box, grabbed it and after checking the dogs, said goodbye and left.

As they watched the car drive away Kate said, "He drives fast for a ghost."

"Ghost? What ghost?" Holmwood asked.

"Talk to Sybil. She'll tell you all about the late Charlie Salverson. I'm going to go check on the bedroom and bump-out." Kate told him.

Kate, Harry, Will and Dani walked back down to where they were attaching the walls of the bedroom to the main house. Tim, Seamus and Satu met them.

"Did you test it?" Harry asked Seamus.

"Working perfectly. He called a DC number and told them he had the box. It came through loud and clear. The recording will remain on the dark web until we need it, and I sent Tom the number to check."

Kate smiled as her husband and brother slapped hands. They met up with Mr. Edwards, "You can have a look at the final additions while the men finish framing out the porch. Then Bert will finish of the roof on the framing and all the big pieces will be in place. Later this morning, the crew will bring in the equipment to back-fill around your basement and the basement doors will be installed. I guarantee that this place will be water tight by sunset which will be good because now they are talking about snow tonight.

"The subs for the plumbing and electrical will be here on Monday along with those doing any finish work that doesn't get done inside. You can take a look inside now and check out the finished dining room and bedroom. How are you planning to use that space at the top of your divided stairs?"

"That will be the children's playroom."

"With all the light and the deck outside, it will be great. I like the way you've planned this place for generations to come. You will always love it." Mr. Edwards smiled and then went to talk to his crew.

Kate was overwhelmed by the bedroom. It was big and fancy, with closets on either side of the entrance to the master bath. It had both a tub that was big enough for two, a separate shower, dual sinks with separate vanities, plus a linen closet. The firebox was set for the fireplace. The French doors were in place leading to what would be the deck that was shared with the living room. It would have three steps leading down to the main dog yard which she would enlarge. Dani turned slowly in the middle of the room. "You could have all twelve of your dogs in here at once and not feel crowded. Kate, it's heaven."

Harry wrapped his arms around her, kissed her and whispered, "It may not be heaven now, but it will be soon--I promise."

CHAPTER 14

Saturday, late morning

They quickly toured the rest of the house. Dani flopped down on the floor of the playroom at the head of the stairs that made use of the divided stairs. "This is such a great place to chill. Grownups downstairs. Nobody to bug you. It's perfect. Grab a book or a computer game and a dog to lean on and you have nirvana." Will chuckled." "When they get older, you can add a pool table."

"Too heavy," Harry said. "The pool table should go in the basement."

Dani sighed. "You need a comfortable rocker here Kate so you can sit and read them bedtime stories. I can just see it with kids and dogs and puppies all gathered around listening to you read or telling tales of Dillon and Quinn's adventures."

Harry interrupted. "Or listening to their dad tell them stories of their mother's bravery."

"Absolutely!" the others all agreed.

Kate blushed and decided to bring the focus back to the problem hanging over their heads. "Now that we've seen the whole house, we should go back to my tiny house and figure out how to stop this killer."

They waved at Bert and the workers who were back to completing some finishes on the house after consuming Ann's mid-morning snack. Deciding that was a good idea, Kate thawed one of Will's coffee cakes and got the tea pot heating while Harry took care of the coffee. Roger came by to tell them that all was well with the dogs. Sal had decided that since there weren't any classes until after the holidays, it would be a great time to check all the equipment and see what needed replacing or repairing. He said he had already checked the plows and the snowblower to be sure they were ready to handle any snow cleanup this weekend. "Tonight's forecast was supposed to be rain, but now there is snow predicted for Sunday night into Monday." Roger took a slice of coffee cake and headed back to work. Sal took Kate aside. "The parade is Friday night. Hopefully all the snow will be cleaned up by then and just remain on lawns and the green to add to the holiday ambiance."

"Don't worry. There are enough covers that make our boots look like elf shoes stored in the costume drawer from the last time this happened. It won't be a problem." Kate wondered if her life would ever get to the point where the most important thing in a day was worrying about parade costumes rather than about dying.

They had only just settled in to work when Maeve and Sybil walked in accompanied by Tom. Sybil came over to where Kate stood and took her arms. "I explained to the policeman about Charlie Salverson dying many years ago and pointed out the fact that the man posing as him was only trying to get his hands on the box. I told him he was lying. I also let him know about the shooting yesterday. He's beginning to see this as something larger than a car crash now. He told me he intended to make the FBI aware of what was happening."

"Oh goody, just what I need for Christmas. The FBI," Kate snorted.

"They may be necessary to guarantee our safety on Tuesday." Harry said.

Sybil sighed and said. "Do we know if the congresswoman is still planning on holding the meeting? This has gone on too long to let them use Bill's death to halt the investigation."

"Sybil, how much of this did Bill discuss with you?"

"All of it. We worked on the project together. I was the better researcher and could handle the math involved better than he. Being a Killoy has its benefits."

"Could you explain to us why Bill was testifying to this committee?"

"To explain I would need to tell you some of Bill's background. He founded his company when he was quite young, only in his early thirties. Personal computers weren't available and companies used mainframes. A single disk could be two-feet in diameter and would only handle a couple of hours of memory. They were heavy and had to be unscrewed and changed out carefully. Unscrewing them needed two hands, and they had to be lifted straight up and carefully stored in an airtight plastic case. The process was then reversed to install the new disk. I worked with a system like that at the bank. It was arduous, but the amount of man-hours saved was incredible.

Bill's company instead of working to develop a personal computer like Apple or Microsoft, worked instead to develop smaller and faster business computers, similar to IBM, but more specialized. As his business grew, he saw the need for this type of technology as part of our national defense. He began producing computers to control rockets and more recently ballistic missiles. He sold the company about twenty years ago and concentrated on the software development aspect of the field. In recent years, he's specialized in developing defensive software aimed at protecting troops in the field. He's been fine-tuning it and has recently been involved in trials with the army.

"Last year, during one such trial, the troops, working with the prototype in the field during the trial, were attacked. Three men were shot. One survived. The fourth member of the team disappeared along with the vehicle. The vehicle turned up later stripped of all the equipment including the computer with the software. They got less than they anticipated, though. Bill had had several break-ins at his business along with his home. So when he set up the test, he did not tell anyone the fact that the program couldn't be run without a release code. He planned to give the code to the troops in the field just before the missile was fired. Since the attack and theft happened first, what they got was a program that didn't work. This software was a system that could be used in the field to divert incoming missiles. It would not only send an incoming missile in another direction, but had built in a calculation which could choose the new target making sure it contained no live inhabitants. "Needless to say, many people, as well as other nations, would like to get their hands on this technology.

"The army investigated the attack but found neither the driver nor the men who attacked them. Bill did not tell the brass that the program wouldn't work. He had his suspicions about who was behind it, but he had no proof. This year he spent time and money trying to find that proof which included using a private investigator friend of his. His investigation is what I assume you have before you." She pointed to the stacks of paper on the table.

"This is what we got from the memory card which was hidden in the key fob."

Sybil gazed away for a minute. "I gave him that for Christmas last year. He was delighted at the secret compartment."

"Well, we gave him a little extra that tells us that his first call after he left was to his bosses informing them he got the box," Seamus grinned.

Kate looked at Harry. "Do you have the information from the day planner? There was something on the pages that had been stuck together that I needed to see."

"Yup. But Satu had a better idea. She had a similar day planner since they were both undated. She was able to create a similar planner with information made vague and telephone numbers, and dates missing. It still kept his social calendar which would be available to be checked, but technical stuff she re-coded with slight adjustments to the information. It should keep them busy for a while since they don't have the key to the code."

"What did she choose for the key?"

"Their trigonometry textbook."

Kate laughed. It was the first real laugh of the day and it felt good.

Harry handed Kate the pages she wanted from the day planner.

She decided that there wasn't enough time to investigate everything all over again. They would use what Bill had and hope for the best. Pulling out her phone she dialed the number that was listed in Bill's day planner and put it on speaker.

When a voice answered, she said, "Hi Joel, it's Kate Killoy."

"How did you get this number?" came the gruff

reply.

"Well technologically I got it from Bill Salverson."

"Salverson. Do you know where he is. The congresswoman has been trying to get in touch with him?"

"Yes, I do know where he is. Joel. Bill was murdered on Wednesday."

"Oh my God, we didn't know."

"I suspected she hadn't heard. The reason I'm calling is that before he was killed, he entrusted some intelligence to trusted allies. He suspected that he was in danger and wanted the truth to come out even if he might not be there to complete it himself. He hoped that the committee would still meet."

"How do you know about the session?"

"Technically I didn't. I just reasoned that if Bill did all this work and developed a presentation he was probably going to present it to someone who could do something about it, and since his day planner was filled with covert meetings with your boss, I assume it would be Tuesday's session to which he'd be presenting and would be in the House of Representatives. If I am wrong on anything so far, just tell me."

She could hear muted talking at the other end. Voices were upset. Then a voice came on.

"Miss Killoy. Joel tells me that Bill has been killed but that you and some other people have the evidence that he planned to present to my committee."

"That is correct."

"I would like to meet with you personally. Joel says he has met you, but..."

"Believe me, I understand. I have already had an attempt on my life over this. Probably the safest thing to do would be for you to come here, preferably in disguise. The people who killed Bill, have been trying to get his research and are still attempting to kill those associated with him. My cousin, Agnes Forester was threatened. She has gone into hiding. However, she guaranteed the safety of the information."

"I could be there at five. We need to stop this threat. Your life should not be threatened by these horrible people."

Good, then, Congresswoman, we'll see you at five pm."

Sal looked at her and asked, "What was that all about? You call up a member of congress, and they come running to visit you. How did you contact her.

You have to go through the congressional switch-board"

Kate looked at him. "Sal, remember Joel from the beginner's class this fall?"

"Nope. Don't remember any Joel from any class."

"Do you remember a two-year-old Siberian Husky bitch?"

"Yea, Tania. She was so smart. Her heeling was absolutely perfect, and she learned to respond to hand signals when the rest of the class was still working on 'sit'."

"Well, the person at the other end of Tania's lead, was Joel. He is the representative's administrative assistant. I recognized his phone number in Bill's day planner, so I thought that it would be good for us to get together with Representative Mastalski. She'll be here at five."

"Just like that?" Dani asked.

Sybil smiled at her. "Never underestimate the power of a Killoy if faced with the impossible. That's when they get going. Now one of the things I didn't have time to do was to come up with a synopsis for each section with the accompanying graphics. I think if we hand her all of this, and the session is on Tuesday, it will never be ready on time. I'm just not sure I can get it done in time."

Seamus spoke up. "You have the power of a Killoy many times over here. Tim, Satu and I can all help. Satu is an honorary Killoy. Tom and Will said they'd pitch in. And Kate said that she'd see what more she, Harry and Maeve could find about who is behind Bill's murder and the crime spree here."

Ten minutes later Kate, Maeve, and Harry were working to follow up on names of those who could want the software at all costs. She contacted Sadie who went into files she wouldn't say how she got, and a few minutes later Kate was reading the report of the Army's investigation of the murder/kidnapping and theft. After reading through the report twice and checking the testimony of everyone involved, she was convinced it was a cover-up. They had never located the body of the missing soldier and no country claimed credit for the theft, even though many would have considered it a coup and worthy of bragging rights.

"Harry, are you a nosing about on the dark web to see if there is any scuttlebutt about the crime or Bill's murder? If stolen for money rather than to benefit another country, there might be some gossip floating around."

"Good idea. If the session on Tuesday reveals things they want secret, I could see why they would try to stop us."

Maeve sat back from her computer and sighed. "A friend of mine at MI 5, said there was some underground chatter about the US Army not being able to keep their technology from driving off right in the middle of a demonstration. He didn't have much, but the guy who pulled off the heist apparently went into hiding when the big cheese behind it found that the program didn't work."

Tom spoke up. "I've got someone who says that the Army purposely gave short shrift to the investigation of the theft on word from one of the high ups. The word is that someone in power, and the guess is that it's not somebody military, is keeping a lid on this. They say anybody who can make sure that program comes into the right hands, would be a wealthy man. He said he pitied anyone who has that piece of software, because the guys signing up to try to get that golden apple are not nice people."

"No wonder they are so determined to use whatever means possible to get Agnes to give them the information." Padraig said.

"There is one thing I need to know, Sybil. Is the program anywhere among this mess of intelligence covering the table?" Kate asked.

Sybil stopped what she was working on and

asked Harry to show her the files he had on the two micro cards. He pushed the computer toward her, and she began checking the higher numbered files.

"He might have put it somewhere else, but I don't see it here. I remember the coding that started the program," she said and recited two lines of code, "but I don't see it in any of these files. All we have is information on the crime and other related crimes Bill found once he got investigating." Kate looked at Sybil. "Do you think Bill would have gone to so much trouble if he didn't have the program he could place in safe hands or at least proof of a successful test."

Sybil looked at her and then screamed. "Why didn't I think of that. The graphics. We've got to check all the graphics. The proof could be right here in front of us. How many files are there?"

"Lots, but none of them are video files."

CHAPTER 15

Saturday afternoon

"**N**o video files?" Sybil slumped back in her chair. She stared straight ahead for a few minutes and then said, "Well there may not be videos but those files are here for a reason. I'm going to find out what that reason is."

A knock at the door interrupted their work. Harry went to answer and saw a smiling Mr. Edwards. "We're getting ready to leave for the day, so if Trooper Connelly is able to help get these trucks on the road, we'll be heading out. You and the missus might like to come and check what we've done. The siding crew and the plumbers and electricians will be here on Monday but it is all tight and safe against the weather. They're saying snow tonight so our timing worked out well."

Kate shook her head to get her mind out of the work she was doing and made a dash for the door. She and Harry grabbed their coats and headed out. They'd only reached the edge of the porch when Kate said, "It's graded. While we've been working, a backhoe has come in and pushed all the soil back against the foundation and smoothed it all out. The porch roof which had been propped up with temporary two-by-sixes, now had the permanent posts installed. The finish crew had given the porch a floor and steps. And, as they walked around the outside, they saw that the basement door was installed and Mr. Edwards guaranteed it was watertight. "With all the drainage that your people put in when they built this basement, it will be dry as a bone."

They had reached the back of the house and saw temporary steps leading up to where the deck would be. "That's scheduled for Wednesday, after the finish work on the siding is complete. The temporary stairs will allow you to get in and out that way until it's finished."

He suggested going inside. They walked into the living room and Kate stopped. Coming in from this direction, she was able to look to the left and see all the way into the kitchen. Harry took her hand as they walked into the dining room to see the new view from the bumped out section. As you passed from the living room you could look out the windows and see the kennel, the barn and the woods in the background. Looking from the kitchen end of the room, was the view of the edge of what would be their deck, and the glorious expanse of the woods beyond. Kate looked at the ground just beyond the fence of the dog yard and thought it would be the perfect spot for a garden. Though there were many farm stores in the area, it would be nice to eat food she'd actually grown herself. There would be plenty of winter left for her to learn how to do it so that when spring arrived, she'd be all set.

The kitchen was bathed in the late afternoon sun which gave it a golden glow. Kate sat for a minute imagining her years ahead sitting right there at the end of a day of work, relaxing before starting to cook supper or for Harry to cook and thanking God what a wonderful life she led.

Minutes later, she was walking out through the French doors onto the top of the bump-out which was now the second floor balcony. Mr Edwards checked the papers in his clipboard and told her that the railing would go in on Thursday. She realized that from this height, she could look over the roof of the kennel and see the dogs playing in the new yard on the back of the barn. Mr. Edwards was pointing out to Harry all the finishing of the joining so that it was impossible to see where the sections were attached. The final plastering of the joins and the removal of the floor covering would happen once the interior work, especially the brick work is done. They headed back downstairs and walked into their bedroom. With windows on the front and back sides and the smaller clerestory windows above the bed, the room would be bathed in light all the time.

Mr. Edwards headed out, saying that he'd be back next week to check on any of the finishing which needed completion. Harry locked up the French doors, and then they followed Edwards out onto the front porch. After waving him off and calling thanks to Bert for all his good work, they stood watching the last of the big trucks maneuver out of the driveway and onto the highway. Kate took a few more photos to put a coda to the adventures of the flying house. While taking in the view from the front porch, she heard a click and saw Harry taking her picture. She pulled out her phone and pointed it at him, with the porch and house in the background. Harry laughed and pulled her into his arms for a kiss.

A car pulled into the driveway and stopped before the house. Richard stepped out and stood looking at the place. "I had to come by Kate and see just what could be accomplished in just two days. I can tell you that people who come to my bank now asking for a loan so that they can build a home, will be told all about this. It is fabulous.

"The other reason is that I've been trying to get in touch with Agnes, but with no success. She's not answering her phone and it's important I talk to her."

Turning back toward the house, Harry unlocked the door and invited Richard in. "Oh, goodness, this is huge." Richard said. "The reason I need her is that I have to be in Ohio for a last minute meeting on Monday. That was when Agnes and I had a meeting scheduled, and she was to pick up some things she left with me. She stressed that she didn't want certain people looking at what was in the box before Monday. I have no idea what it involves, but since I'll be out of state when she needs it, I got the idea to ask you to get it to her."

Kate kept her voice normal as she could as she smiled at Richard and said, "I can do that. I've been so tied up in the house, I really have no idea where she is at the moment, but her girls are staying with me, so I'm sure I'll see her when she gets back from wherever she is."

"Great. The box is out in the car. I hope she'll be back in time to do her thing for the parade. Thanks for taking care of this for me. I'll see you two next Friday. I really love the house and congratulations on your home together."

Harry took the box and said, "Thanks." They watched him drive away and then looked at each other and the box. "Do you think...?" Kate asked.

"I'll lock up, and we can go find out."

They found everyone hard at work, except Ann who was getting ready to go make dinner for everyone. Dani and Will had volunteered to help her, and they passed them on their way out, bundled up against the cold, even with the short walk between houses.

Sal asked, "Well is the house all set and the equipment all gone? If so, Roger and I will go now to bring the dogs back."

"Good idea. They are gone. The finish work will be done by Wednesday. I only hope that if it snows, it's not so much that it holds things up." Harry told him. "Richard stopped by. It seemed that he had a meeting with Agnes scheduled for Monday to give her back some stuff she'd asked him to hold for her.

He has to go to Ohio on Monday, and since he hasn't been able to get in touch with her, he left it with Kate to make sure she gets it."

"Do you think it is something about the investigation we could use? The fact that she wanted it on Monday...," Sybil asked.

"Well there is only one way to find out. If it has nothing to do with Bill, then we'll seal it back up and put it aside for her." Kate went to the kitchen drawer to get scissors to open the package. Disappointment filled her when she saw the gaily wrapped packages in the box. One by one, she removed the packages and read the tags. "It looks like Christmas presents from Bill."

Sybil gasped. Fighting tears, she got up and went into the bedroom. Kate took one more package from the bottom and stopped. The label said, 'Open before Christmas'. Kate put all the rest of the boxes back in the box and stared at the final present. She hadn't known Bill well, but having observed him around her family, she felt that this might be the most important package of all. The 'To' part of the card wasn't filled in. Looking at those sitting around the table she shrugged and said, "Merry Christmas."

Removing the wrapping, she opened the box and took out three thumb drives and a stack of notebooks. On the bottom, a small box turned out to contain contained receipts from restaurants and hotels, airports and gas stations. Kate handed Harry the first drive and watched him insert it into his computer. It contained three files that were video files. He clicked the first and it showed a missile being launched towards a target and then at the last minute turning to the right to touch down, exploding harmlessly in the desert. The video kept playing as everyone cheered. Then a voice came in from someone standing out of view. "Well Bill, you said it would work and it does. We'll run two more trials to get the data and then you can present it. But what are you going to do about Roosevelt Heller? He's not going to let this go. He wants you destroyed." The video ended and everyone sat in silence.

Kate walked to the other end of the table and typed the name Roosevelt Heller into the search engine. "There seem to be a lot of articles and photos coming up. But the one that was most interesting was the one of him being sworn into Congress eight years ago representing the state of Missouri. It seemed that Congressman Heller is a member of the Subcommittee on Intelligence, Emerging Threats and Capabilities. Isn't that the same committee that Representative Mastalski is on? The one for which we are getting data. Was Bill murdered because he was presenting to this committee which has a member who wanted to destroy him or am I being melodramatic and out of line?"

"If he's a member of Congress, maybe we shouldn't be too quick to accuse him of..." Sal said.

Kate held up a hand and interrupted. "Who has the file with the graphics that Bill took of the men meeting together?"

Satu jumped up and carried her laptop over to Kate. "There here and I've arranged them chronologically."

Kate pulled up the first and then using the forward arrow, began skimming through them. On the eleventh photo she stopped. "I thought there was someone familiar in this shot. Remember the general who was booted out of the service for selling equipment to Eastern European countries about five years ago?"

"Vaguely Tom said."

"You mean Anderson Barkley?" Maeve filled in.

"Well here is former general Barkley, and he is sitting next to none other than Congressman Heller." She rotated the screen so that everyone could see it. "Explain to me why Bill would have photos of a former general who was on the take and a present day member of congress. Plus now I wonder who all the other men were, and why were they at what is obviously a dinner meeting? I'm afraid that we've stepped into a nest of rattlesnakes. The man who's hunting Agnes and thinks nothing of shooting me does not seem to be working alone. Mastalski is due in an hour. We've got to decide what to share with her and what to hold back until we get a better understanding of what's going on and who all the players are."

Her phone rang. Looking at the screen she said, "It's Sadie." Kate answered. "Hi Sadie, you're on speaker. What's up?"

"Maeve told me that the wedding present I gave to you is getting a workout. At the rate you're attracting killers, maybe I should be buying them in volume for you. Well, you keep wearing it, Kiddo, because you've fallen into a nest of vipers this time. I'm sending you some help, and I need you to be very careful who you trust. Bill may have trusted the wrong person. I met him a couple of times when I was working in Washington. He was a good man and a gentleman."

"A couple of names have come up so far that you might want to look at, Anderson Barkley and Roosevelt Heller."

"Barkley is scum out to line his pockets. He bought his way up the ladder by doing favors for people with power. Heller, hum, I heard something about him but I can't think of it now. It will come to me."

"I'm going to send you a bunch of photos that Bill took or had someone take of people who seem to be involved. Send me anything you can on them. Also, it seems that Bill was working with Congresswoman Mastalski. Her district is east of here in the Hartford/New Britain area. She and Heller are on the Subcommittee on Intelligence, Emerging Threats and Capabilities. That is the committee Bill was supposed to present to on Tuesday. Also, there's a video of a successful test of Bill's software. Before the video ends there is someone talking to Bill and warning that Heller is out to destroy him."

"You people never do anything by halves. I'll get to work on this."

"The congresswoman is due to come visit in about twenty minutes to find out what we know."

"Take my advice. Give her the bare bones, no pictures, no video. Give her an outline of what Bill found with a bit of his presentation. Just enough for her to show which side she's on. My present to you should arrive in about an hour. You take care and keep your head down."

Maeve stood. "Okay, clear the table. The box with the new stuff goes into Kate's closet along with the original print outs. Satu, did you finish the rough outline?"

"It's done," she said. "It gives a brief outline of what Bill wanted and quotes from his presentation. I'm printing it out and I'm adding the photo that Dani said was taken at her uncle's restaurant. We can see if the congresswoman can identify any of the players. Laptops should go out of sight in Kate's room which I like to think of as my future office thank you," she chuckled.

"Okay, tea, coffee and get the stack of furniture catalogs from the top of the refrigerator under the sleeping. Macbeth will have to move." Kate muttered to herself as she dumped the stack of catalogs on the table. "You guys are helping me come up with ideas on how to furnish that massive house." She no sooner sat than her phone went ding.

CHAPTER 16

Saturday - Late afternoon and evening

Harry went to answer the door and Sybil once more joined them. Joel entered followed by Congresswoman Mastalski and a large man who remained at the door. Kate came forward indicating that they should join those at the table. Then she introduced everyone.

When they all were seated, she said, "Thank you for coming Congresswoman. I'm afraid that the situation with Bill Salverson supplying your committee with information has gotten out of hand. Bill asked Agnes Forester to be his backup and keep a copy of the information safe just in case. He was murdered on the way home from that meeting. Agnes, who is my cousin, then received a death threat. She decided to hide the information and go into hiding, leaving her phone behind so that nobody could trace her. We located her phone, and additional threats were also delivered. They were against her dogs, the greyhounds you see lying by the door, also against me and against Agnes' grandmother, Sybil Forester," she reached over to take Sybil's hand. Sybil was engaged to Bill prior to his death. They were to be married in the summer.

"So far there has been an attempt to shoot her bitches, which was stopped due to the fast response of three police dogs, and an off-duty trooper. Last evening, there was an attempt on my life and that of my kennel manager, Salvatore Mondigliani," she grabbed Sal's hand. "As we went out to take care of the boarding dogs, a car sped into the driveway and a man sitting in the passenger seat began shooting at us with an assault rifle. Thanks to Sal's experience and speed plus a concrete half wall, we survived. Unfortunately the shooter escaped."

The congresswoman stared back at Kate in horror. "This is unbelievable. I know they are desperate to stop this information from coming out which is why we've gone to such extremes to keep it secret, but murder, and attempted murder. No, this has got to be stopped."

"We're working on it. We weren't able to identify the shooter tonight, but we did get video from the security camera above the kennel door." Kate angled her laptop and pulled up the file. As it played out, she watched the faces of those around the table. The only reaction was a flicker of recognition by the man standing at the door.

Joel swore. "Kate. Words don't describe this. You could have died."

"Yes, I know. The man who murdered Bill and tried to murder me is still out there. However, I have another photo to show you in case you might recognize this person." Kate pulled up the grainy headshot she'd gotten of the stalker and turned the laptop toward those at the table.

"I've seen that man. I don't know who he is but I've seen him. I can't think where, but it may come to me?" Joel muttered.

"Howard." The voice from the doorway replied. "He's Heller's fixer, though he's more of a hit man. When people need convincing, Heller sends Howard." The man stepped back into the living room.

"Heller? I know he opposes this but to send someone..." The congresswoman said. "To send someone to murder..."

Joel patted her shoulder as Harry realized that it was getting late. "Congresswoman, earlier today, the detective in charge of Bill's murder dropped off a box that held the things that were on him and in his car when it was pushed off the highway, and he died. Mrs. Forester was listed as his contact since they were engaged. We began checking out what was in it. About an hour ago, Mrs. Forester got a call from the detective asking for the box back. It seems that Bill's younger brother Charlie wanted his things."

"I didn't know Bill had a brother."

Sybil spoke. "His brother Charlie died at the age of two when Bill was eight-years-old."

"So this is someone who is posing as his brother using his birth certificate and other information which is real and on file." The congresswoman mused. "I've heard of criminals doing that."

"This morning while they were moving in the final parts of our house, this person came and collected the box."

"You must have found something about this investigation in the box to know to call me."

"Yes, we did. However, the box no longer contains that information," Kate told her. "The box now contains what looks like tons of research all written in techno-babble and a phony code which is not for a missile shield. I know because I wrote it several years ago. It's for a crochet designing program."

The congresswoman stared at her and laughed. "They'll sell the program."

"I imagine they will. Their buyers won't be happy when they try to test it."

"So the real program is safe." Joel asked.

"I assume so. I suspect that Agnes has it, but we haven't heard from her."

"But Bill was doing research."

"The research is also safe for now."

"Who are you people? Why do I feel I've been dropped in the middle of a superhero movie?"

Kate grinned and as she gazed around at who was sitting at the table, she said, "I like that, but no. The only ones with superpowers here are in the dogs who are very talented. They caught the criminal who tried to shoot Agnes' bitches. However, we do have experience. My husband is former FBI and now has his own cybersecurity company. My brother Tom is head of Killoy and Killoy Forensic Accountants. Sybil and Agnes own Forester's Bank in New York and are well-trained in fighting corporate crime. My great aunt, Maeve Donovan here is former MI-5. Sal is the former head of the police chief's association. Gwyn is a Forensic Pathologist for the state. We are also working with two Connecticut State Troopers. Seamus and Satu are very talented researchers who work for my husband. And this is my brother Tim. I'm just a fashion designer who shows dogs. However, in the past, I have come up against criminal elements and met with some success investigating them. However, our super-power, as you put it, is mathematics and the skill to weed out and organize facts."

"I actually know of your brother Tim since he was high scorer in the game against my son's New Britain team. I got very used to hearing 'and Killoy scores' throughout the game." She looked around the table and then back at Kate. "So if I were to call the FBI and mention your name, they'd know it?"

"Not everyone in the bureau, but the AIC for DC and New York, definitely."

"Okay, I'm going to trust you and pray I don't regret it. Bill came to me last year as his con-gresswoman. He was seeing things happening in the tests that the army was running on the new mis-sile system he'd come up with. When the final test came, the vehicle which was carrying the deflector, was stolen and two soldiers were killed and one wounded. A fourth soldier is missing and assumed dead. Bill came to the conclusion that what hap-pened was not carried out by a foreign power but by someone inside the service or the government. He'd wrote the software for that deflector system and the missile, but he told me he left out a vital piece which he would have had the soldiers enter during the test at the last minute. He suspected something like this was going to happen prior to the test.

"I told him if he could get the evidence I would see that all those involved would be called before my committee to answer for what was going on. He told me he had the evidence and I went ahead and scheduled the session for next Tuesday. With Christmas coming, everybody wants to leave Washington, so it was a push to get this session. With Bill not here to present the evidence, I don't know what we can do. I understand the broad concepts he talked about, but even with a written report, I'm not sure if we'll be able to speak strongly enough to stop these men from what they're doing. If there had been someone at his firm that he discussed it with who understood it, that would be different. But he told me he didn't discuss it with any of his employees. For Bill's sake, I'll go ahead and leave the committee meeting on the schedule, but I don't know if just the written report, without explanation, would be enough for us to succeed."

Sybil's quiet voice came from the end of the table asking, "If you agree to still have the session, then I shall present Bill's information, so he didn't die in vain? I worked with him on all the research and helped him write the presentation. I know it and the information behind it."

"Put like that, how can I not agree. I am so sorry for your loss. Bill was a fine, patriotic man. The meeting will begin at 10 o'clock Tuesday morning. I will have Joel contact Kate with all the details. Let me know which of you will need security passes and I will see you get them." She rose and left, leaving behind a quiet group. Finally, Kate said, "I don't know about the rest of you, but this superhero needs to dinner and rest. Building a house is hard work." That broke the tension as laughter filled the room.

They were all gathering their coats to head up to Ann's when the phones dinged on several phones announcing someone's arrival. Harry opened the door as a car stopped in front of the house and a man stepped out. "Where in the world did that house come from? I was just here and I swear there was not this huge, though beautiful house attached to your place, Kate."

"So you are Sadie's surprise, Des. Your timing is impeccable. We were just heading up the hill to Ann's for supper."

"Looking at this group, I know everyone except

this lovely lady who looks like your cousin Agnes."

"Sybil, this is our friend Deshi Xiang of the FBI. Des, this is Agnes' grandmother, and Maeve's sister, Sybil Forester."

"It's wonderful to meet you. I know your granddaughter and, of course, this gang here."

"You mean this gang of superhero's Sybil said laughing. That's what a congresswoman called them a few minutes ago."

"I won't argue with that. Hey, there's my main man Dillon. Hi there, boy. How is it going?" Dillon bounded forward to get a scratch from one of his favorite people.

"Well in the last few days he helped send a criminal to jail who tried to shoot Agnes' bitches. So I'd say he's keeping up his end."

"I'll need to see Quinn later. Since I've dropped in with suitcase in hand, I'll be begging a bunk at the main house if Seamus and Tim don't mind"

"We don't mind. Will is home for the holidays so the food will be good."

"If your brother is cooking, it will be great."

Kate opened Ann's front door and called, "We've brought company for supper."

Ann looked around the corner and then raced over to give Des a hug. "Des, I knew someone was missing from our merry band, and here you are."

Sybil laughed. "Now we are a merry band, when minutes ago we were superheros. I don't know if that's a promotion or not."

Des had only gotten to know them in September when the Bureau and the NSA worked with Kate, Harry and Maeve to stop a group trying to disrupt the economy of the country. Kate had been shot, but luckily had been wearing a bullet-proof vest. When he'd just hugged her, he noticed that the vest was back in place.

"Oh, Des, I have a question. Have you ever heard anything about Congressman Heller's assistant named Howard?"

"That sc... excuse me ladies, that person is not someone you want to run into on a dark night."

"Apparently the night was dark enough, because Sal and I ran into him last night when he was driven into the kennel parking lot as we went to bed down the kennel dogs, and unloaded an assault rifle at us. Luckily Sal hasn't lost is ability as at football tackle. We hid behind the concrete knee-wall until his driver left. Sean managed to take out his tire, but he had an accomplice with another car which allowed him to get away. Congresswoman Mastalski's bodyguard identified him from a shot from the camera at the driveway entrance I'd taken earlier when he was stalking us."

"I'm glad I'm here. You can fill me in on everything you're involved in this time. But if Howard is hunting you, you'll need all the cover you can get. Now, to talk of pleasanter things, how in the world did you get a house built here in such a short time. I just saw you at Lake George on your honeymoon."

Dani turned to him and asked, "You went on their honeymoon?"

Des and several others laughed as he told her, "Everybody and his brother went on their honeymoon."

CHAPTER 17

Saturday night

The meal, with talk about the house and what everyone was doing, allowed Kate to relax. Harry took some teasing about getting Kate pregnant so soon after they got married. Ann pointed out that it was a Killoy tradition. All the Killoy women did it. Even Kate's mother got pregnant with Tom on her honeymoon she told them. Des grinned and contributed to the teasing, but was horrified underneath knowing the threats that Kate was facing. Des muttered to Harry, "The congressman's hit man has come by his reputation honestly, but the bureau hasn't been able to get enough evidence to put him away. I don't want Kate to be hurt or die just so that we can catch the piece of shit."

Harry stared at him. "It's our job to see that never happens."

"So what is the plan?"

"We've got two main jobs. Organize all the evidence for the presentation on Tuesday while keeping Kate and Sybil unharmed, oh and find Agnes."

"Any ideas on where she's hiding?"

"I don't. Kate might. She knows Agnes best. But she keeps her own counsel until she's ready. If Agnes has the software for the missile deflector, The best plan would be to place it in the hands of the government at that session in public with lots of witnesses."

"She knows the deadline. The ball is in her court. But we're running out of time."

The meal continued until dessert was served and then people began breaking up into groups. Gwyn came up to Kate and pulled her aside. "Kate, I got a strange call from my cousin George this afternoon. He said to let you know that he's been checking up on Camp and your property is fine. However, he wanted to talk to you and he suggested that I call and let you use my phone."

"Hmm, he might think mine is tapped. Go ahead and call."

Gwyn dialed and when it went through, she

told him that she was with Kate. Then she handed her the phone.

George was very concise about the princess he saw in the tower when he was leaving Camp. He said that since Helen hadn't mentioned her being in residence that the public was to continue to think that only the caretakers were in residence.

Kate breathed a sigh of relief. "The princess needs to be guarded at all cost. There are people out to harm her. Tomorrow I will send her prince to you. His Golden is named Patrick so you'll know who he is. It may take both of you to smuggle her back here safely Monday. He will fill you in on the details when he arrives. And thanks, George. Harry sends his best. We've decided to spend the holidays here but start thinking about getting a date for a Valentine ball at Camp."

His laugh, reassured Kate, and she disconnected thanking Gwyn.

Soon the gathering broke up. Kate and Harry headed back home and Seamus drove Satu to her house. Des, Will and Tim headed for the main house. "I still can't believe you built that house so fast." Des said in awe.

Tim laughed. "Wait until you see the videos of the flying sections of house sailing over Kate's tiny house and into place. Putting the whole thing together was amazing. Kate and Harry are planning to host Christmas dinner there."

Will chuckled. "They will host but I shall cook. Wait 'til you see the kitchen. They got everything I suggested so it's going to be a joy to cook anything there. I'm already planning the menu."

Sean pulled into the driveway as Kate and Harry approached the house. "I got your text Kate. You said that you needed to talk to me."

Harry looked at her, but Kate just motioned them inside. Once coats were put away and the dogs let in, Harry put on the kettle while Kate and Sean sat at the table. "I sent you the text so that you could arrange with Gurka to be free for tomorrow and maybe Monday and Tuesday, depending on what happens. Tomorrow I need you to drive up to Camp, our place on Lake George. I need you to meet with Sgt. George Braxton of the Bolton Landing Police. He's Gwyn's cousin."

"And I need to drive to Upstate New York, because...?"

"Because George spotted a princess in one of the towers at Camp today. You have to know that George shows Alaskan Malamutes and grew up showing dogs with us when we went on the Adirondack Circuit." She let the information sink in and suddenly a grin covered his face.

"You found her."

"Technically, George found her. He called Gwyn today and asked her to have me call him using her phone. He was afraid that if Agnes was hiding there to the point where Helen and Otto, our caretakers didn't mention it when they had him to dinner, it was probably serious. George didn't want to take a chance on my phone being bugged. I told him to expect you tomorrow. He knows your Golden's name is Patrick. Also, if they are watching me, they are definitely watching you. You need to go completely undercover. Think of a way of getting there without anybody knowing that you are not still here."

"I'll visit my cousins and disappear into a crowd of guys who look enough like me to be my twin. Then we'll play the old shell game. Hopefully they won't guess which shell has the pea." Gurka can have one of the troopers leave a car at the hockey rink. We usually work out on Sundays and all of us wear our old league team jerseys. I'll manage."

Harry had been listening quietly. He went into Kate's old room and returned with his go-bag. Reaching inside, he pulled out one of the burner phones he carried and handed it to Sean. "You can't be traced with this phone. Use it as your only communication with us."

Sean stood and gave Kate a hug and shook Harry's hand. "I'll bring her home, no matter what." Going to the door, he waved and left.

"Did you know she was there before George called?"

"I didn't know for sure, but it was at the top of my list of possibilities. That's why I specifically didn't call Helen. I knew she wouldn't lie to me, but it would make her uncomfortable to have to choose between me and Agnes. You see, Agnes was always Helen's favorite."

They got the dishes out and began feeding the dogs. Quinn stopped and sniffed her. Then looked around. Kate chuckled. "You'll see him tomorrow, Quinn. Des is here, but he won't be able to visit until morning. Speaking of morning. We're going to have to check the people who follow us into Mass in the morning. Both Sybil and I will be exposed. We can't count on it being the same shooter each time."

Harry held her as the dogs ate. He didn't want to let her go. The fear of losing her had him on edge, but he was careful not to smother Kate. That had been a bone of contention between them while they were courting. He'd promised her, he'd respect her ability to make her own decisions. She often scared him by taking chances. However, he noticed that she seemed slightly more cautious this time. It could be that though he wanted to protect her, now more importantly she wanted to protect their baby.

When the dogs finished, they picked up the dishes and Kate pulled out the biscuits, giving each one his biscuit, and sent them racing into the yard.

"Tomorrow, we've got to get all the evidence organized for the presentation. I am hoping that Agnes either has or knows where the Bill's software is. I'll leave that to her, but we've got to see how many of the players we can identify from the photos. Knowing the players and who your enemy is makes things safer."

The front door opened and Sal came in. He had a box with him that smelled a lot like dinner. "Your grandmother sent Roger a meal since he volunteered to stay down watching over the kennel and your dogs while we all went to supper. I'll get this out to him and then bed down the boarders. What's the schedule for tomorrow?"

"Mass in the morning followed by breakfast, and then we need to go through all the new information that was in the package that Bill left for us and go through all the photo files to see who we can identify."

"Sounds good. I'll see you two in the morning. Katie, get some sleep. You need your rest." He headed out the kitchen door to bring Roger his dinner.

"And so it begins." Kate said with a huff.

"What begins?"

"The comments from everybody. 'Oh, don't strain yourself, Kate.' 'Did you remember to take your vitamins?' 'Did you get enough sleep?' 'Oh, don't carry that it's too heavy.' Etcetera, etcetera, etcetera. I'm about to spend eight and a half months being babied as though I didn't have any common sense just because I'm pregnant. I'm carrying a baby, not missing and arm or leg., for heaven's sake."

"They just love you, Sweetheart."

"I know, and I feel guilty about getting mad--but that doesn't stop me from wanting to bite."

Harry chuckled. "But you're a good dog, well-trained, so instead of biting, you're going to sit quietly and lull them into believing you are safely in your cocoon and when their backs are turned, you're going to sneak out and conquer the world."

She turned in his arms and kissed him. "You know me so well."

They let in the dogs and locked up. Then they

both went to bed. The last few days had been four weeks long and Kate freely admitted she was exhausted. But at the same time, she was wired and knew it would take a while to settle down. As she crawled into bed, Harry placed a stack of saltines on her night stand and a stack of furniture catalogs in her lap. "Find us a kitchen table. I'm going to go take a shower."

Kate sorted through the pile to find the catalog she'd been going through before their world went insane. It had been one of handmade oak furniture ones. Since she hadn't remembered to mark the page which had the table she liked, she had to go through the whole catalog again. She felt herself relax as she paged through the collection of unusual and beautiful pieces. Finally, she found the table she remembered. It looked like a traditional round pedestal table that would seat six. However, the series of photos that followed showed a child being told that they were having company. The kid pulled a lever under the edge of the table and pulled. The six pointed diamond design in the center of the table then slipped apart and a similar design in a slightly different shade of oak rose in the center. When the boy finished pulling, the table that had seated six, now seated twelve. Kate grabbed her phone and went to their website. She found that they had the table in stock and it could be shipped with a dozen matching chairs immediately. This would be even better than her kitchen table which was long. Here everyone could see everyone else. She filled in the order form and clicked to place the order. Relaxed, she set the catalogs on Harry's side of the bed, leaving the catalog open she had marked the table as ORDERED. Then turning out her light, she slipped deeper under the covers and went to sleep.

When Harry emerged from the bathroom, he found the catalogs and spotted Kate's block capital lettering. He stared at the table. It was perfect. He shook his head. There was no doubt about it, he was the luckiest guy on the face of the earth. Once again, he thanked the Lord for finding Kate for him, and then crawled in next to her, and slept.

CHAPTER 18

Sunday morning

F r. Joe stood on the top step of the church entrance and grinned. "Welcome back from your honeymoon. You both look wonderful and I see you've brought my friend Dillon to visit and the family is visiting to see the new house go in. I just stopped by for a few minutes to watch from my car as they lifted a section up and lowered it into place on Friday. I shall have to come by and bless the house. It boggles the mind that a house could come together so quickly. How soon will you be moving in?"

"We'll be celebrating Christmas in our new home. We'll begin furnishing it next week, so we're looking forward to eating breakfast in our own kitchen any day now. The Christmas tree goes up next weekend."

"I'll let you know when I have a free night and come by."

"Oh, and Fr. Joe, when you see the kids marching in the parade with our group, you might want to overlook the number of Magi that brought gifts to Jesus." Kate told him as they filed in to find their pew. The priest's laughter followed them.

Harry noticed that he wasn't the only one checking out the congregation as they filed in. Sal, Tom and Will were all casting eyes over the faces surrounding them. Any stranger was noted and kept under surveillance. When the doors closed and the choir began singing, he let out the breath he hadn't realized he was holding.

When Mass ended, Kate noticed that Fr. Joe went to sit by Sybil in a pew listening to her talk. She wondered if she and Bill had already spoken to the priest about their wedding plans. She suspected so. And now Sybil must plan a funeral. Ann, Maeve and Padraig were waiting several pews away and Ann signaled for them to go ahead.

Harry checked the area before they went to step out of church and head down the steps. He pulled her back behind the heavy wooden doors when he spotted a green sedan going down the street more slowly than the rest of traffic. It finally passed the church and turned the corner to disappear behind a building which held medical offices. Quickly gripping Kate's arm, he hurried her down the steps and into the car. Then he headed up the street in the opposite direction from home. They drove for about five minutes, making turns, and doubling back whenever possible on side streets. When they passed the church on the return visit, the parking lot was empty and there was no sign of the green sedan. It was a relief when they arrived back home.

Des was in the yard playing with Quinn and all the other dogs. He was surrounded by happy Sammies and the two dignified Greyhounds. Sal had the coffee started and Will was standing at their stove creating wonderful smells. Kate hugged her brother. "Its good to have you home."

"It's good to be home. You know I love cooking for a crowd. I talked to Edwards, and he says that your kitchen wiring should be finished by Tuesday at the latest. So expect me to be underfoot, stocking your pantry and playing with your new toys."

"I'm looking forward to it." She laughed and then reached to take her laptop off the counter to get to work.

"Leave it! Will commanded. When I cook a

meal, I expect it to be eaten by people who give it their full attention. Your choice. Research or food?"

"Your tough. But I choose food."

"Smart. Always good to stay on the right side of the person putting the food on the table."

The egg, cheese, spinach and mushroom casserole had spices that Kate couldn't identify, but the flavor was wonderful. There was little talking around the table as the food was consumed. When they finished eating and cleaned up, Will gave them permission to go back to work. Kate grabbed her laptop and took one of the thumb drives from the box Harry placed on the table, inserted it and opened the first folder. A collection of twenty JPEG files opened showing photos of men in various settings. The first ten displayed a background that told Kate that this wasn't in the United States.

"Harry. Can you give me any idea of where these photos might have been taken. It doesn't look at all familiar."

Harry stepped behind her and looked over her shoulder as she enlarged each photo. "If I were to guess, I'd say one of the countries in the former USSR. But I couldn't say which."

Des walked up. "That's the Belarusian State Museum of the History of the Great Patriotic War in

Minsk. And, damn it, the person standing in front of the museum is a reputed ghost. He was thought to be murdered like his companions when the vehicle carrying Bill's missile deflector was stolen. The man in front of the museum is Corporal Pavlo Turchin, the missing soldier. Does the photo have a date? I have a friend in the CIA who would kiss your feet to get a lead on him. It's been driving her nuts that the man disappeared without a trace. People were even thinking that he was buried in the desert."

Kate hit a few buttons and Des' phone dinged. "There is your photo with the metadata included. I hope your friend gets him." She went back to work sorting the photos by trying to choose one person and link him to all the photos in which he appears. Then she went back to pick a second person and went on another search. Sean and Satu arrived and settled in to work. When she got up to get a cup of tea, Satu stopped to look at what Kate was doing.

"There is an easier way to do that."

Kate blinked pulling her attention from the screen. "Matching individuals to groups of photos?"

"It's something I just got. Give me a second to download it to your laptop from the server. Okay, I'm going to tag this guy. Now you type in this code and hit enter." Kate watched when some photos from the batch were copied into the man's file. But what blew her away, was when photos appeared from other folders on her computer.

Kate stared at her. "Wow. That's incredible. Remind me to tell Harry to give you a raise."

Satu laughed and went to get her tea. Kate opened the collection of photos which had been connected. The first three photos were of a group of men at a restaurant which included Des' ghost, somewhere. The next two showed a meeting between the man and someone else in a park. She opened the final group which seemed to be at a test site in the desert. A group of high ranking officers were either standing or bent over a table covered with papers. In the background, in uniform, stood the man in the other photos. This wasn't Corporal Turchin. This was someone else entirely.

"Des," she called.

"What's up?" He looked over her shoulder at the screen.

"Don't say anything. Just watch this series of photos."

"Working backwards from the desert shot, she clicked one by one until she finished with the final shot in the restaurant."

"Send me that file. Now." Des hurried back to his

laptop.

"Sent. I'll send you all suspicious files."

Kate went to the photo of Turchin and ran it through Satu's program. Then she sat back. One file after another was being gathered by the program. When it finished, Kate flipped through the collection. Beginning in Belarus, she checked each shot. Turchin got around. He bounced around Europe, and then the shots came to the US. Looking at the buildings behind him, she could approximate that he'd been meeting people in New York, St. Louis, Seattle, and then the shots cover him wearing fatigues standing with a bunch of officers and enlisted men in the desert. In the final desert shot, there was a civilian with the group--Heller. She sent the bunch of photos to Des and waited.

It took a full minute for the yelp to come from the other end of the table. "Damn it Kate, you're dangerous. No wonder bad actors try to shoot you. Your a bleeping miracle worker. He pulled out his phone and dialed. "Risa, you're going to owe me dinner with champagne. Check out your in box and tell your husband to stand back because you're going to explode. I'm sending you some files." He waited for a minute and then heard a scream coming from the phone. "We're working on Bill Salverson's murder and the theft of the deflector and its software," he told her. "Bill had someone apparently tracking all the players taking photos. And Turchin, our man in Minsk, is straight-line connect. Yea, I'll send you anything else we find but, this is on the QT because there is a House session on Tuesday where much of this is going to come out." He listened for a few minutes. "If you can pull it off, that would be the cherry on top. Go for it."

Des walked to the other end of the table to look at Kate's laptop again. She had the software building files of linked photos for each of the folders on the drives. "This is becoming much bigger that we first thought. It's more than Bill's project. I think that there is something going on that involves both our defense systems and threats against us from foreign actors. I think we're under attack and don't know it yet."

The room was silent. Harry stood up and walked to Kate, wrapping his arms around her. "If we have to figure this whole thing out by Tuesday, we're going to need help. Do you think Malcolm can help us without word getting out?"

"Des looked at Harry. He owes you guys, big time, but he'll be at home this morning." He looked at his phone and frowned. Harry told him to wait and went into Kate's room and got out his bag of tricks. He pulled out what Kate recognized as the scrambler and a phone that was safe. He clicked on the switch and handed it to Des. Before I call, I need everyone to agree that nothing that is said leaves this room. Everyone agreed and Des nodded and dialed.

"It's Xiang, sir. The phone is one of Foyle's toys that is secure. I'm afraid that my original assignment has escalated beyond what we originally estimated. I sent Risa some information and graphics but what we originally thought was a politician on the take, might involve some of our friends from Minsk. There is a congressional hearing on Tuesday morning of the Subcommittee on Intelligence, Emerging Threats and Capabilities. The crew here will be testifying. From what we're starting to uncover, they'll be walking into the meeting carrying a bomb which could go off in their faces. Heller's involved and his man Howard has already tried to shoot Kate and Mondigliani. They survived, but he won't give up. However, neither will my guys here. Kate's great-aunt Sybil was engaged to Bill Salverson. Agnes Forester is in hiding from threats and there's very little time left."

Des listened and then dropped his shoulders in

relief. "Oxford Airport, one o'clock. You'll be met." Des stared at the quiet phone for a minute and then handed it back to Harry. Harry switched off the scrambler and packed everything away. Then walked to the counter, picked up Kate's kettle to fill and get heating for tea, and refilled his coffee maker.

Satu leaned over and whispered something to Seamus. He nodded and looked toward Harry. "Satu thinks if we all take a graphic string of photos about one person from Kate's collection, and research that person, we could speed up the research. She also thinks that we should get Maeve down here with her laptop, and even send a batch to Sadie."

"Good idea. I'll call Maeve. You send a folder to Sadie." Looking around, he asked where's Tim?"

"He and Padraig had a chess game scheduled for after church. He's probably at Ann's." Seamus told him.

Harry dialed Tim's cell phone and after several rings, was finally picked up. "Tim, I need you to pick up Malcolm Bullock at Oxford Airport at one o'clock. Good. Who's winning?" Harry laughed and ended the call. "We're all set. He's got Padraig in a corner and says the game will be over in three moves, so he'll be there on time."

Tom laughed. "I didn't realize that Padraig had

never played him when I heard him talking last night. I was tempted to say something, but then decided that everyone should get the opportunity to be thoroughly trounced by the family jock. Wait until he gets to college on a basketball scholarship. His victims will be lining up ten deep. I think when he plays chess it's the only time he's ever really still."

CHAPTER 19

Sunday midday

Maeve arrived armed with her laptop and after being given a folder and a quick outline of the task at hand, got busy. She said that Sybil was napping and Ann is taking cooking lessons from Dani. Tim has gone somewhere and Padraig is reading one of her brother Tom's old books on chess. "He suspects my brother created a hustler when he taught Tim to play." The quiet laughter in the room told her that they were all aware of her great-nephews talents.

"Tell Padraig he's not alone. We've all been skunked by Tim at chess." Tom told her. "Grandpa was the only one who could beat him, which he did--regularly."

The room fell into a library-like atmosphere

only broken by whispered questions about a person or place. The stillness of the next hour was disturbed only by occasional fists shooting into the air.

Kate had found a good deal about Turchin's life in the last two years, but prior to that, the man was a ghost. He joined the army twenty-five months ago and rose quickly in rank to corporal. He'd worked hard at becoming invisible once that rank was achieved--a man always in the background or slightly off screen--but always there. As she checked the photos, he appeared in all but two, not as someone to notice, but invisibly present. He must have become aware of the photographer after a while, because he managed to hide most of his body behind equipment or other soldiers. The photographer was good though, because most of the shots were taken from waist height. He'd pretend to take his shot and then lower his camera with it still pointed in the right direction. In four shots, Turchin is in the act of stepping out from behind someone.

Kate was bothered that she couldn't find any record of him prior to the army. She reached for her phone and texted Sadie. How do you find information on someone who doesn't exist prior to joining the army?

It didn't take long to hear back.

He probably joined under an assumed ID. If he signed up at one of the smaller offices, they may have checked it for priors, but that was a far as they went. If he was charming, he could have gotten by easily. His physical might have shown something, but not enough for red flags. Get Des to do a facial recognition on him if he will.

She looked around the table and noticed that Harry and Des were conferring quietly at the other end of the table. Picking up her laptop, she walked down to them and asked the same question.

"Turchin?" Des asked.

"Yes. Prior to twenty-five months ago, the man didn't exist. I went searching for him through records the Army has. His application is very lean with no fingerprints and this physical is gone."

Des opened a program on his laptop which she noticed had many more apps than hers. He pulled up the folder she'd built of Turchin's photos. Clicking through them, he found one that had a clear shot of his head. He enlarged and cropped it, then moved it to another program. "This will take about an hour--if we're lucky. The program is good but slow. What have you found about him so far?"

Kate told him about the man's army career to date. He rose to the rank of corporal and then did everything he could to stay there. He is there but not there. I did notice that he appears to know these three men. One is another corporal, but one's a staff sergeant and one a second lieutenant according to their insignia. While you are running the facial recognition, I think I'll see what I can find out about his buddies. Oh, and don't disappear too far into your research. Ann will be calling soon about Sunday dinner and with Will and Dani helping, I expect a fantastic meal."

"I can't wait."

She reached for her laptop but stopped. The front door had opened and her brother Tim, Seamus' twin, came in followed by a huge man with the build of a linebacker who was very familiar to her. "Bullock, your timing is perfect. We were just about to go up to my grandmother's for Sunday dinner. I guarantee you the food will be fantastic."

The giant man stepped forward to sweep Kate up in a hug. Her fair coloring and blond curls a contrast to his dark skin and short regulation FBI haircut. "So this is where the brain trust works on its cases. I heard that Salverson had a connection to your family."

"He was engaged to my great-aunt Sybil who is Agnes Forester's grandmother and my late grandfather's sister. You'll meet her because it was easier to protect her by keeping her with us. Both she and I are on the hit list of the people who want Bill's information."

"Well I'm glad to see you're wearing your vest under that pretty sweater. Better safe than sorry."

Kate laughed. "Sadie gave me a replacement one for a wedding present since the one I wore out in Kentucky is too badly dented to wear. Before we head up, let me introduce you to the crew. Maeve you know. This is my brother Tom."

"I know Tom. I've worked with Killoy and Killoy in the past."

"This is my brother Seamus As you can see he's Tim's twin, and this is Satu Mituzani. They work part-time for Harry. They'll be working on their degrees at MIT in the fall. The man standing by the door is Sal Mondigliani, former head of the Police Chief's Association and now my kennel manager. Sal and I run a training program here which includes the police dog work. And finally, the lady sitting next to Tom is Gwyn Braxton. Gwyn is a Forensic Pathologist for the state, and a friend of mine since childhood. She is the newest member of this group."

"Well it's good to know that Numbers and Kate have such a good team. I'm Malcolm Bullock. AIC for

DC. Des works for me."

Kate's phone buzzed with a text. She smiled and looked up. "Sunday dinner is served. Let's go."

Harry held her coat and then told his old boss, "Des will fill you in as we head up the hill." He wrapped his arm around Kate but as they headed for the driveway checked to be sure there was no green sedan nearby.

Over dinner of roast beef, Dani's spinach-Parmesan casserole and Will's garlic mashed potatoes and homemade dinner rolls, conversation tended to be about the house rather than the investigation. Kate told them about the table for the kitchen, and they explained that Jimmy would be over next week to extend the dog's exercise yard to align better with the rear of the new house.

Will surprised them with his plan to put in a greenhouse between this house and Kate and Harry's. This way, there would be fresh vegetables all year long and if Kate wants a garden, she can start her plants there and then move them outside. Dani told him that her uncle has a bunch of Italian herbs growing on his windowsill. Once the greenhouse is built, she'd bring him cuttings.

Padraig asked how he was planning to heat it since he wasn't attaching it to a house.

"I've been looking into solar. That space is open with no trees to block the sun. I have plans to build a series of solar generation units that can be wired into storage batteries. The batteries will provide power for the heating units as needed. Plus, the greenhouse will act as a solar collector itself." Padraig asked him about the thermal glass he was planning to use and other conversations broke out around the table.

Harry was checking on old friends who were still working for Malcolm when Kate's phone buzzed with a tweet. She collapsed into her chair, her face turned up and a slow smile spreading as she let out a breath. "Agnes is coming home. Sean and George are with her and will guard her here. George got the time off from his boss. They will be here by supper time." As a cheer went up in the room, she suddenly sat up straight. "Nobody must know she's here. Her being in hiding is the only thing that is keeping her safe. As far as we know, she's still in the wind, and we're worried about her."

"Agreed." Everyone at the table said thoughts of danger tempering their joy. The silence only broke when Will asked, "Anybody for desert?"

Full of good food the group walked back down the driveway to Kate's little house. Stopping in front of the new house, Satu said, "If there were grass on the dirt surrounding it, the house would look as though it had been here for years. The porch gives it that finished look."

"I will have to take a look inside before I leave," Bullock said, "but now we have an impossible task to complete in an absurd amount of time."

It was a subdued but determined troop of researchers that settled around the table to work. Ten minutes into their search, Des' laptop dinged. "Konstantine Lazar. Romanian mother and Russian father. Parents moved to Minsk when he was eleven. Was a bright young man who was later trained at 'The Conservatory' also known as the Defense Ministry's Military Academy which prepared him to move to work with the GRU. His assignments are not listed, but I can tell you where he has been recently. According to this, his father died four years ago and his mother still lives in Minsk. That, Kate is your Corporal Pavlo Turchin. We now know his background prior to joining the Army."

"So the Army took on a Russian spy, trained him, so he rose in the ranks, and created an opportunity to be part of sensitive missions involving the testing of cutting edge military equipment. Then they allow him to steal it. If it hadn't been for Bill's foresight, his deflector would be part of the Russian arsenal. I wonder if Turchin had help with this career advancement. Des, where did he live when he signed up to join the service?"

Des scanned the screen for a minute and then looked at Kate. "You knew?"

"No, but I suspected."

"You were right. Pavlo Turchin signed up at a registration office in Heller's district. Heller's wife was one of the people who recommended him."

"Send everything you've got to Satu, and Satu, I think the corporal needs his own section in Tuesday's show and tell. Make it complete with photos."

"You've got it. I think I'll research Congressman Heller's wife as well. It's interesting that she recommended him."

Malcolm was startled by the assumption of those around the table that Kate could pull these rabbits out of the hat. "You wouldn't want to work for me would you Kate?"

"I don't think so Malcolm. Plus I don't think there would be room for a dozen Samoyeds in your offices, and they'd shed all over everyone's black suits."

Everyone laughed. Sybil stretched and went to the kettle to fill it for more tea. As she waited, she wandered over to watch the greyhound bitches now asleep in the exercise yard resting sandwiched between Liam's daughter Shelagh and her mother Kelly. Kate came to stand next to her.

"Bill really loved those girls. This was his breed, and he felt they were fantastic representatives of the breed. He really loved the fact that they were so well-trained and congratulated me and Agnes on it. I had to admit that you had trained them both. Agnes had been away most of the time and I didn't have the energy to take on more puppies at my age. A few weeks ago, Bill came to supper. Agnes was out with Sean. He gave me my engagement ring telling me that I could keep our engagement from distracting from Agnes and Sean's wedding, but I was going to have a ring even if I don't wear it for everyone to see." She reached for a chain around her neck which was looped through a beautiful diamond and emerald engagement ring. "He told me the emeralds were to remind me of the Ireland of my birth. At the same time, he gave each of the bitches beautiful collars. He said that these princesses needed treasures of their own. I miss him so much."

Kate reached out and hugged her as they both watched the peaceful sight of sleeping dogs. The sound of a click behind them had them both heading to the counter to make more tea.

Kate's phone announced the arrival of another text. We're going to break the trip in Albany just to be sure we aren't being followed. I have cousins who live there. You'll see us early tomorrow morning.

Kate showed Sybil the text.

"That shows good sense. Travel in the wee small hours of the day will help them keep on eye on traffic and make sure nobody is after them."

Kate told the others about the change in schedule.

"Smart," Malcolm said. "We need to have this whole presentation ready to go by noon tomorrow."

Harry nodded at Kate. "The congresswoman just emailed me that passes would be waiting for Sybil, you, me, Agnes and Satu for Tuesday's session. She says if graphics will be involved, we should have someone other than the person testifying handling that. She suggests that we get to the building as early as possible in order to make it through security."

Malcolm said, "I think that you should fly down with me tomorrow evening. You can stay at my house and I'll arrange for cars to take you to the Capital. I will also make sure that Des and I, plus our link in the CIA will be present." He looked at Kate for a minute and then said, "Also, I'll make sure that Kate can have Dillon with her. It might be pushing the rules, but it can be done. If he has a police dog jacket, he should wear it."

Kate smiled. "He'll look very handsome wearing his police dog coat. Plus it will boggle a few minds that he's neither a German Shepherd or a Belgian Malinois.

CHAPTER 20

Sunday evening

Roger checked in to see how everyone was doing and to get Sal, so they could feed the boarding dogs. Kate looked up and realized that the afternoon had vanished and it was dark outside. Harry stood and went to begin filling the bowls for the dogs and Kate worked at adding any extra supplements specific dogs needed. Then, splitting the pile of bowls, Kate walked over to the door and opened it letting the dogs in. She allowed these very social canines to visit their favorite people but then said, "Dinner."

The dogs immediately moved to their positions in a semi-circle around them. Kate and Harry began at opposite ends and moved toward the center laying down bowls in front of sitting dogs.

When done, Kate stepped back and quietly said, "Eat."

The food quickly disappeared. She noticed that both Quinn and Shelagh were eyeing their parents bowls, but both ended up disappointed. As the last dog returned to a sitting position. Kate and Harry repeated their walks gathering bowls. That done. Harry took the large stack of dishes to the sink while Kate pulled a bin forward and began grabbing fistful's of biscuits handing some to Harry. She walked to the door and one at a time called each dog to halt before the door in a show stack, gently take its biscuit and then dash outside. This was repeated, oldest to youngest. As Quinn flew out the door hoping to find someone who'd dropped a piece of biscuit that he could eat. Kate realized that her puppy wasn't the only one hungry.

She was returning to the table when the front door opened and Padraig walked in. "Hail, ye merry band. I come bringing news that supper is being served. Just leave everything and head up the hill. Harry stood and gathered up the thumb drives. Kate made sure everything she'd been working on was saved, and shoved her notes into a folder. The others did the same thing so that within a couple of minutes the kitchen was restored to its domestic facade. They were just heading out the door when a car pulled into the driveway and stopped in front of her house. Joel, the congresswoman's aid stepped out and approached Kate.

"Hi Kate. My boss asked me to drop off your passes for the session on Tuesday and to remind you to be sure to be there early."

Kate was about to take them from him when Dillon stepped in front of her. She looked down, curious that he wasn't acting aggressive, but he was making sure to be between Kate and Joel. "Thanks Joel. We know how important getting this testimony right is to your boss."

Harry stepped forward and took the envelope from him and said, "I'll just put them inside. Thanks for bringing them by."

Joel hopped back into his car and drove out onto the highway. They continued up the hill toward her grandmother's, but Kate was distracted. Something was off. She couldn't tell what it was, but something was off.

Ann stood out on the front porch greeting them and explaining that dinner was a face-off between her two rival chefs. Everyone was laughing when they walked into the house only to stop and appreciate the wonderful smells emanating from the kitchen. Kate's stomach grumbled, but she wasn't alone. Dani entered carrying a tray loaded with small plates which initially looked like salad but in reality was individual antipasto. Will followed it with Creamy Parmesan Garlic Mushroom Chicken. Ann had done a simple vegetable of green beans with sliced almonds.

Everyone was full, but Padraig decided to get in on the challenge and had made two dozen cupcakes, with mint chocolate frosting. Since time was of the essence, these got boxed up to take back to eat later after they completed more research.

When they got back to Kate's house, she went to grab the envelope Joel had brought to put it away. When she reached for it, Dillon blocked her, knocking her back against Harry.

"Everyone freeze!" she screamed.

She stared at the envelope for about thirty-seconds and then pulled out her phone. Scrolling through her numbers she dialed the congress-woman. When she answered, Kate said, "Congress-woman. I wanted to thank you for sending us our passes for Tuesday." Then she pressed speaker.

"Passes. No, I didn't send you passes. I told them to hold them for you at the entrance. You'll need them when you go through security. Security is almost as bad as the airport, but they do let you keep your shoes on."

"Oh, my mistake. An envelope came and I assumed it was from you. We are almost ready and will see you at the meeting on Tuesday."

Malcolm went into the kitchen and got a pair of tongs from the drawer. Carrying it carefully, he took the envelope outside and set it on the lawn about ten feet from the house. Then Bullock pulled out his phone and began talking as everyone else filtered inside. Harry began pulling their research out of the closet as Satu and Maeve carried it to the table.

Kate slowly sank to the floor where she stood, wrapping her arms around Dillon and burying her face in his ruff. Harry went to the door to the kennel and opened it. Suddenly, Kate was surrounded by all her dogs who were thrilled that she was down on their level. It was a snuggle and cuddle free-for-all until Kate called "Uncle!"

Harry then reached into the pile of dogs and drew out his wife. Not caring if they were alone. He wrapped his arms around her and held her tight, whispering in her ear. He followed up with a kiss until the stiffness of her body gave way to a melting softness. As he broke the kiss, he asked, "Better."

"I think so. I don't know what is in that envelope, but Dillon didn't like it and I'll go with his judgment any day."

"So would I," came Malcolm's voice from the doorway. "The sniffer droid hasn't completely analyzed it, but it was able to identify it as an airborne pathogen. Anyone who opened the envelope would die as would anyone else in the room. New plan!" he shouted. "Kate, call Sean and have them be to the Albany airport at five o'clock tomorrow morning. They'll be met by a pair of agents who will escort them to DC and will make sure they are at the hearing Tuesday morning. Maeve, you and Sybil go pack. One of the agents outside will drive you two and Padraig to Bradley Airport as soon as you are ready. You will stay at a safe-house in DC and then be brought to the hearing on Tuesday morning. Satu, you will be escorted by an agent to your home to pack. You'll return here and you, Kate, Harry, Des, Seamus and I will leave for DC before dawn." He looked over his shoulder at an agent holding a small notebook standing just inside the living room door. "Got that?"

"Yes, sir," the agent answered.

"Good. Make it happen." The agent disappeared out the door leaving silence behind. Malcolm walked over to Sybil and took her small hands in his massive ones. "I promise you that we will finish what Bill Salverson began."

With tears streaming down her cheeks, Sybil said a quiet, "Thank you." She left with Maeve and Padraig to pack and head to the airport. Satu left with a female agent to get what she needed. Kate called Sean and after a brief explanation, handed her phone to Malcolm to give him the details. She looked around almost surprised to see William McKinley walk out of the living room to check his bowl of cat food on the corner cupboard. Macbeth, emerged from behind the kitchen door where she'd been hiding and joined him. The cats were used to dog excitement but the tension with the people in their house had them wary.

Kate texted Sal to bring Roger because something had happened. She realized she was sitting in her chair with no recollection of how she got there. Harry placed his go-bag by the front door and then walked into the kitchen as the kettle he'd filled, clicked. He made tea and set it in front of Kate and then sat beside her, holding her hand and waiting for her to tell him what she was thinking. She looked at him, not listening to the muted conversations at the other end of the table and asked, "Is it cowardly of me to want very badly to pretend that the last hour of our lives didn't happen? That it was all a dream?"

"It was a nightmare," Harry told her, "but one that can remain just that. Your friend Joel fooled a lot of people. He has been working for the congress-woman. He must have people who respect him to have reached this position. The fact that we didn't spot him for the murdering bastard his is, is not your fault."

"I remember wondering at the time he joined the class, why he brought a fully trained dog to attend the beginners class. He was just 'casing the joint' as they say. Checking us out because of our re-lationship to Bill. Even then, he was trying to stop Bill from succeeding. I wonder who his real boss is?"

She and Harry sat in silence for a while just holding hands. Finally, Harry stood up and took a box off the counter and put it on the table. Grabbing some paper napkins, he placed one in front of Kate and then put a cupcake on it. He did the same for himself and then told the men at the end of the table that brain food was available in the box. Des stood and slid the box down the table to the middle of their group.

When she heard cries of, "Ah, heaven. Padraig can bake." Kate smiled and began eating, but she still wore a frown.

"What has you thinking so hard? You've got your thinking face on to the point where I can see the wheels turning,." Harry asked running a finger across her forehead.

"There was something that someone said today that didn't seem important at the time, but now my brain is ringing bells and waving flags for me not to overlook it. The only problem being, I don't remember what it was."

"It will come to you. Finish your cupcake and go get your suitcase, Be sure to pack the royal blue suit that Agnes made you buy. You've only worn it once, but it looks beautiful on you--dignified and professional. You'll have all the congressmen eating out of your hands."

"I'll settle for them not falling asleep or trying to sneak out early." She got up and went to pack.

Sal and Roger came in and Roger said, "I smell chocolate."

Harry pulled the box of cupcakes back to their end of the table and explained what had happened when they returned to the house after supper. Both stopped eating. "Thank God for Dillon. Everyone was here. We would have walked in and..." Roger whispered.

"The bottom line is we are all decamping. Sybil, Maeve and Donovan are gone. Sean, Agnes and George will fly directly from where they are. Kate and I, Malcolm and Des, Satu and Seamus, plus Dillon will all fly out before dawn. Hopefully they won't know that we've decamped until it is a done deal. I called Gurka on a secure phone about ten minutes ago. This place will be guarded. You two, Ann, Tom, Gwyn, Dani, Will and Tim will still be here. As much as possible, just keep things quiet and low key but at the same time, be visible going between the houses and spending time at Kate's. You've met Williams, the guy who will be working on the house tomorrow. Just tell him there was a family emergency, and we had to go away overnight. We plan to be back Tuesday afternoon. I'd like you all to be nosy and in and out of the house all day. I trust the crew, but I don't want strangers sneaking onto the property."

"You've got it." Roger said.

"You'll take care of Katie, right."

"I'll take care of Kate--with Dillon's help."

"Okay." They headed out, talking quietly.

Harry went to look for Kate to see if she needed help. She was just emerging from the bedroom when he reached the door. "Here, let me get that for you,

Princess."

Kate froze. She stared straight ahead, not moving.

"Kate, what is it? What's wrong?"

"He gave it to the princesses. The treasurer. He gave it to the princesses!" she yelled, grabbing Harry's arm as she ran.

CHAPTER 21

Monday morning very early

Malcolm turned in Kate's direction as she raced through the kitchen and into the whelping room, then raced right behind.

"Earlier this evening, Sybil told me about the night that Bill gave her an engagement ring. He insisted that she have it even though she didn't want to wear it because she felt it would distract from the attention being paid to Agnes and Sean's wedding. While looking at Twisp and Thorin, she mentioned that Bill really loved those two bitches. You see, this was his breed. The one he'd always bred and on which he built his career as a dog show judge. He felt that these bitches that she and Agnes had bred were outstanding. But more importantly, he loved them. He called them his princesses.

"The night he gave Sybil her engagement ring, which was just recently, he gave his princesses new collars. They were beautiful but more than that, if I am right, they were also valuable. When the girls were in the dog yard, Quinn began chewing on their fancy collars when he played. So I took them off and replaced them with sturdy work collars that he couldn't damage. I took the collars that Bill gave the bitches, put them into a baggie and into the drawer where I keep all the fancy collars my dogs wear for Christmas."

Reaching out, she pulled open a drawer under the counter and took out a plastic bag. She opened it and removed the collars. Laying them flat on the counter, she took one and felt gently with her fingers, inching along. Malcolm did the same with the other. Kate stopped when she felt an irregularity. Reaching back into the drawer, she took out her sewing kit which included an embroidery scissors. Gently removing stitches without damaging the collar, she was able to separate the layers. Then taking a tweezer, she gently removed what was hidden. As with the key fob, a small memory card slid onto the counter. Malcolm slid the other collar toward her, his finger resting on a spot about a third of the way along. Kate repeated the action of removing the stitches then reached in to extract a second card.

Harry set his laptop on the counter and inserted the first card. It contained only one file which he opened. He heard Kate gasp. Kate's one outstanding math talent was the ability to understand computer code. She could read it like a novel. "Well?" he asked.

She smiled, "The princesses really did hold a treasurer just like he said. Sybil once recited the beginning of the code to the deflector when she was pointing out that the other memory cards weren't the right ones. She said that she'd been over it with him so many times, that at least the beginning lines, she could repeat verbatim. This is that code."

They checked the second card. This seems to be variations on the commands ordering the code to direct the missiles in different directions.

Malcolm said, "Excuse me Foyle but I've got to do this." With a grin, he reached out and hugged Kate, lifting her high off the floor.

Harry reached for her as soon as her feet touched down and kissed her. Then he went into Kate's old room and returned with two tiny plastic cases the right size for the cards and a larger holder to keep them from getting lost. He went to hand them to the AIC, but Malcolm held up his hand, refusing.

"I think that Kate should hold them. When the time comes--he stopped realizing the hour and checking his watch--tomorrow; I think she should give them to Sybil to present to the Army. If it is done publicly, the chance of possible theft is reduced to almost nothing" They nodded.

"Just to be on the safe side..." Harry said, and he reached out to press save as he closed each program. "Backup."

The next few hours settled into waiting. Harry wanted Kate to go to bed, but she preferred to sit with him on the sofa. Exhaustion defeated her resolve, and she ended up sleeping in Harry's lap. Satu returned and sat talking to Seamus and Des while Malcolm spent most of his time on the phone making plans. When the call came through at two o'clock, telling them the car was on its way to get them, Harry woke her, but made her eat a saltine before sitting up. She ate another when she was sitting and then was able to stand. The dogs woke and milled about so Harry let them out to pee. As the car arrived, luggage was moved out. Kate called Dillon and strapped on his police vest. Once bundled up, she grabbed her bag which held her laptop and everything which would normally go in a purse, including an easily folded purse to use if needed. Harry immediately took it from her and handed her Dillon's lead. Then he let in the dogs. Kate told them to be good for Sal. Finally, they left to get in the car.

The car picked them up and took them to Windsor Locks which is where Bradley International Airport was located, just north of Hartford. The drive on the empty highway, was quick. Here they transferred to a small jet which took them to DC. Dawn was still several hours off when they pulled up in front of a house in a quiet neighborhood of Arlington, Virginia. This was within commuting distance of The Capital so many of its residents held long time careers in the government.

When they got inside, Malcolm's wife was waiting for them, and after a light breakfast, she hustled them off to bed. Since Malcolm's children were either married or in college and not yet home for the holidays yet, there were plenty of bedrooms. Kate was surprised how calm she felt now that they were almost to the finish line. Her mind had been mentally organizing a to-do list on the drive from the airport, but instead, as soon as her head hit the pillow, she was asleep waking only for a minute when Harry climbed in next to her. It was almost one o'clock when Kate and Harry finally joined the others for lunch. Both were feeling better. Dillon had been fed by Seamus and was dozing in a spot of sunlight beneath the window in the kitchen.

Eleanor Bullock sat by her and said, "Call me Ellie, Kate. I've heard so much about you that I already feel I know you. Your Dillon is so handsome. Malcolm told me he is responsible for all of you being alive to be here now. I hope you don't mind, but he got steak with his food this morning for saving my husband's life."

"The number of times that Dillon has saved my life fills a long list. He is remarkable, but at the same time he's still--in my mind--just the beautiful puppy I bred and held in my hand the day he was born. Malcolm has probably told you that I spend most of my life surrounded by his relatives."

The conversation got more serious as lunch was finished and the dinning room table became home to laptops, thumb drives and the stack of Bill's notebooks. Seamus was assigned to go through the notebooks and enter any gems of information that might prove useful, into a word doc which Satu could access for the presentation. Des and Harry were going through the photos along with Karl and Anna, two agents Kate had met when she showed at the National Specialty. That had been her first experience wearing a bulletproof vest, but since it had saved her life, she no longer objected.

She had gone back to researching the connection between Heller and Turchin/Lazar. It seems his wife's family was very close to the Lazar. She grew up in Minsk quite near him and when she came to the U.S. to live with relatives, they stayed in touch. Lazar worked for her uncle's business when he first arrived. She had met and married Heller while in college, and he quickly got involved in politics winning a seat in Congress. Heller was the one who suggested that his wife's friend go into the army, according to the interview he'd had with the recruiter when he joined. Since Heller had suggested that he enter the service, Kate wondered if he'd also helped Lazar gain his new identity. As she found each detail, she entered it as a bullet point in a document which she then sent to the others.

As she started to research Howard, Karl called out, "Leave Howard to me. I've got several scores to settle with him. Just send me the details of your encounter with him."

Kate sent him a description of the attack on her and Sal.

It was getting late when she checked with Satu

on the presentation. They sat together and as Kate read through Sybil's speech which she would deliver describing Bill's work, she would have Satu key in a pause for either a photo, series of photos or a video. She also pulled up her laptop and quickly created a bullet pointed time-line. This was inserted at the end of the presentation with a reference to what had happened on that date and with references to photos coded for Satu to put on the screen.

Just as they broke for dinner, there come a knock at the door. An agent entered along with Sybil, Agnes, Sean and George. Kate jumped up to hug her cousin and to thank George for finding her. Luckily Ellie had been warned of their arrival, so she was prepared for a crowd when she served dinner. Kate, Harry, Seamus and George helped clear away their work and quickly get the food on the table. Malcolm suggested they hold business conversation until they were done eating. So talk turned to the new house flying into place and Agnes' raving over the changes Kate and Harry had made to Camp, Kate's family's long-time vacation home. Both she and Sean agreed that Camp was where they wanted to spend their honeymoon. George piped up, "Make sure you check the basement for dead bodies before you do." Everyone laughed which led

George to explain about Kate and Harry's honeymoon with the cast of thousands including thieves and murderers.

"To say nothing about FBI agents. Right Des?" Kate added.

"Sorry about that Kate."

Following dinner, they resumed their spots and Anna handed around sheets of possible questions the committee might ask tomorrow. Sybil was told she'd be sworn in and then given time to do her presentation. Malcolm introduced her and she began. Kate was impressed. When she'd said, she'd worked with Bill to build this presentation, she wasn't kidding. She knew it cold. Keeping one eye on her tablet with the speech, she was able to pause gracefully whenever a graphic needed to be shown, and to explain to the representatives what they were seeing. At the end of the presentation, she spoke about the deflector which Bill had created.

She'd go through the story of how the deflector had been stolen. Sybil would explain that Bill had not been satisfied with the army's investigation following the event. She also pointed out that what they had stolen had been useless since Bill had been warned by a friend of a possible problem with the test, he held back a coded-key step. The field team would only receive it to enter just prior to the actual test. With each question, Sybil would either go into how he'd launched a private investigation to supplement they government's, and he discovered the missing Corporal, instead of lying dead in the dessert, he was actually in Minsk. The graphics of people involved were listed.

Bullock stressed that they shouldn't lower the boom on Heller until the end. Everyone told Sybil it was an excellent presentation.

She smiled slightly and said, "This is worth every minute of work if it leads to the arrest of the men behind Bill's murder, but I had hoped..."

Kate moved to her side and knelt next to her chair. "Do you remember telling me the story about the night Bill gave you your engagement ring?"

Agnes gasped. "Bill gave you a ring? You were engaged to be married?"

Sybil looked at her. "I didn't want to wear it since all the focus should be on your wedding. We were going to be married quietly following yours."

Sybil unhooked the chain around her neck and placed the beautiful ring on her third finger. Kate smiled and asked, "Do you remember what else you told me happened that night, with Bill and his princesses?"

"Yes. He gave them gifts too. Beautiful collars."

"Well, last night it occurred to me that the safest place for him to hide the Salverson's Deflector's program would be to have it guarded by his princesses." Kate reached into her pocket and pulled out the box holding the two memory cards and placed it in her hands. "I think that Bill would be very proud if you presented this program to the Army in front of everyone as we play the video of the successful test."

Tears streamed down Sybil's face. She looked down at her hand that now not only wore Bill's ring, but held his software, and smiled through her tears. Then she reached out to hug Kate, holding her tight.

CHAPTER 22

Tuesday morning

The buzz on Harry's phone alarm had Kate opening her eyes and waiting. A saltine appeared in front of her face, and she grumbled, but began to nibble. Harry left the room along with Dillon and returned five minutes later when Kate had all but fallen asleep again, bearing a steaming cup of tea. He set it on the nightstand and helped her ease into a sitting position.

"How are you doing?"

"I'm fine, but I'll be better with that tea inside me and a hot shower."

"We leave in an hour. Malcolm wants to take a circular route to the Capital to make sure we aren't followed. An unmarked limo will arrive soon. Everyone else is up, so why don't you finish your tea while I jump in the shower? Then I can meet with the others as you dress. Hopefully you are not going to need to do anything but give Sybil moral support today. But, just in case, make sure that Dillon doesn't leave your side."

Ten minutes later, Kate and Dillon entered the kitchen filled with delicious smells of pancakes and sausages. Kate was glad that her stomach had decided to settle because she was hungry. Satu and Seamus had their heads together at the table, but she came over to Kate as soon as she walked in.

"I'm nervous this morning. I really hope that I don't ruin everything."

"Satu, it is not in your DNA to ruin anything. You will do a fantastic job. I will be sitting right next to you so if you have a doubt, just elbow me and point. I will have your back through the whole thing. Your biggest problem will be that Dillon is probably going end up lying on your foot to the point where it will go all pins and needles." Kate listened to the girl laugh and saw the tension leave her body. When they heard that breakfast was served, she watched her walk back to Seamus with her shoulders back. She stopped before she sat and patted Dillon's head.

"Rallying the troops?" Harry's voice came from

behind her.

She smiled, "Like the British, I think we should "Keep Calm and Carry On."

He laughed as he sat to eat.

All was organized when the limousine pulled into the driveway, so they quickly got inside with Dillon settling on her feet. The two agents from the day before, Karl and Anna were already seated. They chatted on the way to the Capital about the time when 'Numbers', Harry's nickname, worked with them at the bureau. It kept everyone distracted and relatively calm. The sun was up so Kate was able to enjoy looking out the windows at famous sights. Harry held her hand during the trip, and she could tell that though he was teased by his old friends and laughed, his mind was on their safety and how the day would go. When they pulled up at the special entrance to the Capital, he squeezed her hand and then helped her out of the car.

Kate noticed that their little band was suddenly surrounded by a group of armed agents. They hurried into the building leaving as little time possible for any ambush to happen. Des had gotten their passes, and they looped them over their necks and moved forward to pass through the metal detector. One of the Capital police stepped forward ready to object to Dillon in spite of his jacket, but Kate was ready and reached into the bag which had gone through the scanner and pulled out his badge and credentials, plus his pass, which Malcolm had secured. The guard was startled, but eventually nodded them through. Kate said that she'd like to use the restroom before the session began. Anna and another female agent went with her as well as Satu who thought that a good idea. Next they were escorted to a room where they could wait until it was time to go into the session room to testify.

Sybil and Agnes were there. Harry and Seamus, Maeve and Padraig came up and told them that they were going to find their seats and would see them inside. Agnes looked at her and grinned. "I told you that royal blue suit would look perfect on you. You finally look like a grownup."

"Thank you, I think. I like it but don't get time to dress up much these days. I figured I should get some wear out of it while it still fits."

"Are you planning on getting fat, Kate."

"Yes. That's what usually happens."

The look on Agnes' face as the penny dropped was priceless. "You're pregnant."

Kate just smiled as a man entered the room holding a sheaf of papers, ready to explain what would be happening. When he finished, they moved back out into the hall with Agnes and Sybil leading, followed by Kate and Satu with Dillon between them. Just short of the entrance to the chamber, Malcolm stepped forward escorted by a man wearing a very expensive suit. "This is Willard Chamberlain. He is an attorney and a friend of mine who specializes in this sort of thing. He's been briefed by me and Maeve. Sybil, give him a dollar."

"I wondered why Maeve stuck a dollar in my pocket this morning."

"You've now hired him to represent you and act as your legal counsel. Listen to him if he tells you not to speak. Though you are a witness, remember not everyone on this committee is happy that you will be here, and may try to unsettle you or trip you up."

Sybil shook hands with Mr Chamberlain, and they continued into the room. When they got inside, Kate's quick scan of the room showed that Representative Mastalski was not yet seated and so far there was no sign of Joel. Harry was seated directly behind her chair. Chamberlain held Sybil's chair for her and Harry reached out to hold hers. Satu stopped to talk to Sean who introduced her to the tech who had her graphics and a copy of the testimony marked. Satu said that they had added several graphics to the end of the testimony, but wasn't sure if they would be used as part of the presentation or the questioning. The tech assured her that all she had to do was have whoever was speaking say the number of the display and it would appear. Satu nodded, obviously relieved.

Kate watched, by seeming to talk to Harry, as chairs filled up in the gallery behind her. Then she changed position to observe the opposite direction by leaning over to talk to Seamus. As she did, something caught her notice. Two women, one of them old but quite tall, had entered the room, and they were seated in the third row about six seats from the end. Kate looked down at the floor for a moment and then quickly looked up. Turchin! Putting a hand on Sean's shoulder to whisper to him, she said, "Turchin is in the third row, sixth seat from the end. He's disguised as a very tall older woman and is wearing a red scarf around his neck. He is accompanied by the blond woman in the expensive black coat with the stand-up collar. Pass it on to Malcolm or one of his agents.

She was uneasy because she hadn't seen the man identified as Howard nor had she spotted Joel. There seemed to be an argument going on between the chairman, the minority chair and someone who was out of sight behind the high back chair of the chairman. Both the chairman and the ranking member kept glancing in Sybil's direction. Kate hoped that they weren't going to be told they couldn't address the committee. This was their safety net. If the testimony wasn't given, the threats and attempts would continue. After about five minutes, Congresswoman Mastalski emerged from behind the chairman's tall backed chair and moved to her designated spot. As she did so, her assistant, Joel, followed her in carrying a stack of papers. He was watching his step as he moved to the congresswoman's spot and placed the stack on her desk. Only then did he look up and lock eyes with Kate. His face lost all color and Kate was sure he was going to faint. He leaned over the congresswoman's shoulder and muttered something and turned to quickly walk toward the door through which he'd entered. As he reached the door, he spotted two agents standing there. He turned to head for another exit only to find a third agent behind him, directly in his path.

The agents spoke to him quietly, but not so quiet that the Chairman didn't hear what was said, and he twisted in his chair. As the two agents went to lead Joel out the door, the chairman reached over and grabbed the sleeve of the third agent. Covering his microphone with his hand, he held a quick conversation with the agent. Kate could tell when they got to the part about attempting to murder them. She was surprised the Chair didn't do himself an injury when his head whipped around. The agent also pointed to his boss, explaining that Malcolm was one the potential victims. Finally, the chairman sat back in his chair and stared at Mastalski. Then he picked up his gavel and after taking a deep breath, prepared to begin the session.

A voice from behind her whispered, "Joel's under arrest. He's not talking and is asking for a lawyer."

"Not surprising. With this many witnesses and the video from the cameras--wait did we save the video?"

"I downloaded it to my computer last night and sent Gurka a copy. Tom had added a camera to the front of Killoy and Killoy. It captured the whole episode."

The rapping of the gavel drew everyone's attention. The session began by the chairman asking them to stand, raise their right hand and take the oath. Once they were seated, he began his opening address. "Ladies and gentlemen, Ranking Member and members of the House of Representatives. We were scheduled to hear testimony this morning from William Salverson, who is well-known to members of this committee for developing technology that has been very helpful to the army over the years. Mr. Salverson's latest development, the creation of a deflector which deflects incoming missiles and sends them to uninhabited areas was stolen during a scheduled trial with the army. The theft led to the deaths of two service members and the wounding of a third. A fourth member of the team scheduled to use the new technology disappeared along with the truck holding the equipment and is assumed dead. Mr. Salverson apparently was not satisfied with the investigation which was carried out following the theft and proceeded with an instigating his own which he attested uncovered not only inconsistencies in the investigation but what he has claimed are crimes which involve not only members of the military, but of members of this house. These accusations are serious, and they are the reason I agreed to call this session. Such charges should not be allowed to stand without those being charged having the opportunity to refute them.

"As you may notice, Mr. Salverson is not in attendance here today. The reason for this is that he died last week. However, it seems that Mr. Salverson was not working alone. All of his research was saved and will be presented by his team today led by Sybil Forester who is its co-owner and retired CEO of Forester's Bank in New York City. She is accompanied today by her assistants, Agnes Forester, co-owner and present CEO of Forester's Bank and Kathleen Killoy Foyle owner of her fashion house and a dog training venue that includes training police dogs. I am told that Sybil Forester was also engaged to marry Mr. Salverson this summer. You have our sincere condolences, and we thank you for coming forth at such a time. According to the statement which was filed, of which the members have received copies, in the investigation of the disappearance of his software, Mr. Salverson uncovered what he contends is proof of other crimes. They are all included in the statement. I have been made aware of further crimes against his team since his death. This committee will wish to take testimony about the more recent crimes related to this investigation in closed session following this hearing.

CHAPTER 23

Tuesday morning, later

K ate scanned the chamber carefully as she listened to the opening addresses by the chairman and the ranking member. Heller was not in his seat but then there were several empty seats in the room. Either this was a small committee or they would rather be getting an early flight home for the holidays. As she looked around the room, her eye was caught by movement in the gallery off to her left. A man was standing at the far back wall, despite the fact there were a number of available seats. She looked back at Mr. Harrison, the ranking member, who had begun his welcome.

After a minute, she casually glanced to the left again taking in the representatives in attendance and looked slowly up into the gallery again. The man's head was turned toward the gallery door as he talked to another man who was wearing a charcoal suit with a blue shirt. She couldn't see that man's face, but she realized where she'd seen the one lurking in the gallery rear. It was Howard. Kate bet that the congressman was out of his seat for a reason. He was hatching a plan to deal with the fact that they were still alive.

She turned in the opposite direction, slowly scanning the seats of the members and the gallery above. A movement caught her peripheral vision, and she saw the woman sitting next to Turchin watching the two men in the gallery. From her expression, she knew what was going on, and she didn't like it. Kate noticed that one of the agents who'd escorted them in this morning was relaxing casually against the wall, watching the pair. Seamus must have been able to pass on the information.

The ranking member seemed to have a point to make, but Kate hadn't followed it. Writing a note, she passed it back to Harry, then she let her attention return to the hearing. After two more minutes, she concluded that the ranking member felt that today's session was a slap in the face of the army due to the fact that it questioned the investigation of the theft. Though he was sorry that Bill was dead, he didn't see the point in letting these women, who had no qualifications, appear and take up the committee's valuable time. Of course, it was phrased much more elegantly, but that was the gist.

Kate glanced over at Agnes who was sitting with perfect posture seemingly enthralled with the speakers comments. Kate looked at her hands and realized that she was nervous. She was fidgeting. Agnes never fidgeted. She was the walking personification of someone elegantly cool. But as she watched, it occurred to her that Agnes' life had never been threatened before, at least with her on her own. There was the time in February, but she was with Sean. Agnes was frightened.

Sybil, on the other hand had a serene calm about her that Kate could only covet. She faced the man who was trying to dismiss the importance of their appearance here today with the look of someone waiting for an untutored student to finish his excuses before she would tell him where he went wrong, why he'd failed to see the obvious and how he could redeem himself. There wasn't any fidgeting with her.

The ranking member concluded his opening remarks and the chairman called on Sybil for her opening statement.

"Chairman James, Ranking Member Harrison, Congressman Doggett, Congresswoman Schramek, Congressman Meier, Congressman Blanchard, Congresswoman Venti, Congressman Lovato, Congressman Nagel, Congressman DelGatto, Congressman Emmanuel, Congresswoman García, Congresswoman Mastalski," she paused as he slid into his seat, "and Congressman Heller. I thank you for this opportunity to speak with you this morning, both for myself and for William Salverson who was unable to present this to the committee do to his murder last week." The murmur of voices caused a rap of the gavel and quiet returned. "I am going to offer the opening statement that was prepared by my fiancé, Bill Salverson, and I ask that you submit our written testimony for the record."

Chairman James replied, "Without objection."

Sybil began, "The defense forces of the United States are of prime importance to keep its citizens safe and protect service personnel. Toward that end, the army and the other services strive to employ the latest tools to carry out that goal. One of those tools is the Salverson Defense Shield. The shield is a computer program which can be placed into any vehicle in which our troops travel, even something as small as a jeep. It is portable so that it can even be carried by a platoon when it goes into hiding to escape incoming missiles. The reason for its effectiveness, is that the Shield emits a signal which locks onto the incoming missile's signal which is directing it to its target, and then, can deflect that missile in another direction. One of the elements that make the Salverson program unique, is its ability to access the surrounding area for inhabitants, and adjust the missile's trajectory information to an uninhabited area, or if that is not possible, the one with the fewest signs of life. The purpose of the Shield is to protect our troops, reduce the numbers of casualties, and allow the troops into dangerous situations to have another tool to fight against a threat.

"Not to long ago, the army set up a test of the Salverson Defense Shield at their dessert testing grounds. Mr. Salverson met with the committee which would oversee the test. It was headed by General Cutter, and his team which included Congressman Heller representing this committee. It was during this test that the team moving the Defense Shield to the target site was attacked and the Shield was stolen. The attack not only took the lives of two soldiers, but serious wounding another, and led to the disappearance of a fourth. The army did an investigation of the attack and theft but though they located the vehicle, they were not able to find any trace of the Shield or the fourth soldier. It was assumed that the soldier had also been killed and his body buried in the dessert.

"Mr Salverson read the report of the investigation and spoke to the people involved, but came to the conclusion that the army had overlooked some possible explanations for the manner in which it disappeared and the individuals involved. Not wishing to put further burden on the service, in the search for something that they did not even know if it worked, he decided to carry out that investigation, bearing the cost himself." Sybil stopped to take a drink of water. Kate noticed that the room stayed silent. She had their attention.

"The first thing that concerned Bill was the well being of the missing soldier. He instituted a search for the man using several investigative companies. What he discovered was that Corporal Turchin had an exemplary career. His rise to Corporal had been swift, but he seemed determined to remain at that rank, not accepting opportunities for which he was recommended to advance. The other thing he discovered was that Corporal Turchin didn't exist prior to joining the army. In fact, various documents had been removed from his permanent file since he joined. In investigating his application process, it was discovered the Turchin came well recommended by the wife of a member of congress. One who is also a member of this very committee. Pursuing a deeper investigation, it was discovered that Corporal Pavlo Turchin was really "Konstantine Lazar. Born of a Romanian mother and Russian father. His parents moved to Minsk when he was eleven. He was a bright young man who was later trained at 'The Conservatory' also known as the Defense Ministry's Military Academy which prepared him to move to work with the GRU. His assignments were not found, but two years ago, he left Minsk and settled in the congressman's district. Soon after which Konstantine Lazar became Corporal Pavlo Turchin, a member of the United States Army."

A disturbance in the visitor seats to the right showed a tall older woman being restrained by two FBI agents. The woman who had arrived with him still sat, but instead of looking at the excitement next to her, she was staring toward the members of the committee, specifically Congressman Heller.

The gavel sounded bringing the room back to order. Chairman James asked Sybil to continue.

"The fact that the Defense Shield had been

stolen didn't concern Bill as much as finding those involved in the plot to do so. The reason he didn't worry was that he knew that if whoever stole it or whoever bought it from the thieves tried to use it, it wouldn't work. Prior to the test, Bill had heard that someone might try to acquire the Shield. So when he installed the software, he left out two vital pieces of code which he would have the soldier load into the program when getting it ready to block the missile's entry. However, neither the thieves nor the buyers took the time to test it, but instead removed it from the country. Where it is now, is unknown.

"In investigating Corporal Turchin, Bill found a number of his compatriots had met with Turchin both prior to and following the theft. Could I please have graphic one through four shown?" The large screen to the side of the room displayed photos of men meeting together at dinner, standing with drinks, and the shot of Turchin and Heller in the park.

"I would ask, Chairman James, that you will accept this submission as well as a detailed list of these meetings and the attendees names for the record."

Chairman James stated, "Without objection,"

while staring at Heller.

Sybil handed the papers to the clerk and continued. Kate listened to Sybil with one ear, since she knew what she would say and instead concentrated on Heller and his wife. She noticed that Howard had disappeared. The note she'd passed to Harry had told of his location. She could only hope it got passed to those in charge before he disappeared. She suspected that even if they nailed Heller and his wife, the danger would not be over. Howard struck her as someone who would carry out an order even if his superior was in jail.

Looking back over her shoulder, she saw that Malcolm was no longer there and neither was Des. They had probably gone to take care of Turchin. Taking a pen, she wrote a quick note that she passed to Seamus. He nodded and located one of the agents. By them both stretching, he was able to pass her note on. She didn't feel safe with Howard still on the loose.

She saw that Mrs. Heller still remained seated several rows behind her. The congressman hadn't moved from his seat; keeping his eyes on the desk in front of him.

Sybil was almost to the end of her presentation. She emphasized that, "Bill's first goal was to locate those behind this act which would remove a tool designed to keep our troops safe. But another was to complete what was begun with the trial of the Salverson Defense Shield. I have observed that General Cutter is in attendance today. Might I have your permission to address him?"

Chairman James looked at Cutter and receiving his nod said, "Without objections."

"General Cutter," Sybil said. "I can attest to Bill's disappointment in not being able to see your face as you watched a successful test of the Shield. If you could turn toward the screen, and if we could have video 1407, I would like to share with you the test that Bill and his technicians perform. It was also attended by members of the security firm which had helped in the investigation, and I was present." The video of the test played out on the screen including the final comment. When it ended, the general stepped over to Sybil and held out his hand to shake hers and thank her. She shook his hand and then holding his wrist, said, "This thumb drive has six video covering three tests from different angles. I'd like you to have it. And, I'm sure that Bill would approve if I also present the army with the complete software for the Salverson Defense Shield. His only price is that it be used to keep as many American soldiers safe as possible." Cutter stared at the box holding the two memory cards now in his hand and then back at Sybil.

"On behalf of the United States Army, I accept this program and thank you. Bill's work to save the lives of soldiers will not be forgotten by me or by the service." He gave Sybil as small salute and returned to his seat.

"With that, I'd like to thank you Chairman James and the committee, for this opportunity to testify before you on this important issue, and especially to thank Congresswoman Mastalski for her support of Bill's search for the truth and for her work in setting up this session. I do look forward to your questions and will be aided in supplying details by my team consisting of my granddaughter Agnes Forester, my great-niece Kate Killoy Foyle, and my assistant Satu Mituzani."

Chairman James looked at his watch and said, "Due to the time, and what will probably be extensive questioning, we shall take a forty-five-minute break for lunch and return at one-thirty." His gavel slammed down.

CHAPTER 24

Tuesday afternoon

Seamus and Satu led the way. Harry took Kate's bag, and she had Dillon move into heel position. Mr Chamberlain drew out Sybil's chair and offered his arm to escort her to lunch. She smiled at his courtly manners. Sean luckily quickly locked Agnes' arm to his as her fans began to swarm. Kate chuckled. "You can take the supermodel off the runway, but you can never take that style out of the supermodel."

"Sean will hate it."

"He'd better get used to it. One has only to look at Sybil to know Agnes will be swamped with fans into old age."

Des met them in the hall. "Will Dillon trust me? If so, I'll take him out to relieve himself while Anna guards you. Howard is still in the wind, so be careful. I don't think that he and his boss like you very much at this minute."

"Dillon. Go with Des. It's okay. Go out and pee." She watched them leave and then turned to Anna. "Now Kate has to go in and pee. Harry, could you get me a plate of food?"

"Will do." It looks like Seamus and Satu have already found us a table.

She used the stall and then came out to find Congresswoman Mastalski waiting for her. "Kate, I just found out all the details of what Joel did. I can't believe that I didn't suspect him. He was so nice and so efficient."

"I thought he was nice too. The only one who really didn't like him was Sal, because he brought a fully trained Siberian to a beginner class. At the time I thought it was strange. I suspected he was nosing around the place but couldn't figure out why. Dillon saw through him immediately and wouldn't let me near him. Dillon saved us all by not letting us open the package. We would have all died. If I were you, I'd avoid Congressman Heller. His wife, who was also involved, and was taken in for questioning by the FBI a few minutes ago." They had exited the restroom so Mastalski left and Kate and Anna headed for the table. She was almost there when Dillon slid into heel position, ready to get back to work.

Kate was starved. Harry had gotten all her favorites, and she noticed that he'd avoided salty food and other foods that the baby book she read last week suggested a pregnant woman not have. He pulled out her chair and sat next to her. "The tough part will come this afternoon. Bill wasn't that popular with the army traditionalists who think the answer to every war is more guns and more men. They are Luddites for whom the word technology is a red flag."

"Great. I'd love to take them on. I'll chop them up and Satu can sweep out the pieces.

Sybil leaned in. "You are welcome to them. I think I ran through my entire technology vocabulary this morning just reading Bill's presentation. I may know the math and some coding, but I can't pull rabbits out of the hat the way you do."

"Fine. We should first get Agnes to talk about her meeting with Bill. She can say that he gave her a box with evidence that backed up his theories. She can explain about the threats. You can send them to me to find out about the attack on the bitches, the adventures of Howard and his automatic rifle, and

Joel and the deadly pathogen in the envelope. Satu can give them dates, places, times and who was with whom. You've done your work Sybil. Bill would be so proud of you."

Sybil dropped her head and Mr Chamberlain handed her a beautifully monogrammed handkerchief. She glanced at him with a half smile and then bowed her head, covering her face. Kate watched her. She thought about her losing her husband, her son and his wife, her brother, her brother-in-law and now Bill. Kate always knew she was strong, but what she'd seen today was an example of courage that left her breathless.

A buzzer sounded and Harry pulled back her chair. Her lunch and her tea now consumed, she felt stronger and ready to take on whatever the committee threw her way as questions. As she sat, she noticed that Heller was absent. She looked behind Agnes and noticed that Malcolm was once more seated as backup. Kate tilted her head and he smiled. Looking in the other direction, she saw that Heller's wife was also among the missing. Four criminals were being questioned today because of their work and it was only one-thirty. Now if they could only find Howard.

Chairman James gaveled the session back into

session and began by calling upon himself for five minutes. His first question went to Sybil asking how we all got involved in William Salverson's investigation?

Sybil smoothly shifted the question to Agnes. She told how Bill had called her and asked her to meet him at the bank to talk about something important. When he arrived at her office, he told her about the theft and his investigation. He explained that he was being followed, and he feared that it was one of the men behind the theft. He was sure they were trying to stop him from attending this meeting. Bill handed me a box and asked me to hide it until Monday evening. Today's meeting was uppermost in his mind. I agreed to do what he asked, and he handed me the carton. As the afternoon went on, I realized that if they were after Bill and someone saw him come into her office, that I also might be in danger. So I called a good friend to meet me for coffee, and disguised the carton. Once at our favorite coffee shop, I handed him a shopping bag I'd brought with me and raising my voice, wished him Merry Christmas. He knew I'd be back on Monday to pick it up. When I returned home, it was late and my cell phone rang. When I answered, a voice told me that I would die if I didn't give them everything Bill Salverson had given me, I would die. Fearing that if they came after me, my grandmother would get hurt, I decided to become invisible. I took my bitches to my cousin's, so she could care for them. Then I disguised myself as Kate and leaving my phone behind so it couldn't be used to track me, I disappeared. What I didn't learn until I came out of hiding yesterday, was that Bill Salverson had been murdered after he left my office. He was deliberately forced off the road by a tractor-trailer while driving on Interstate 84. His car, in full view of may commuting witnesses, was pushed until it broke through the guardrail and tumbled down hill, crashing. The truck that pushed him, swerved back onto the highway and escaped at the next exit. My cousin Kate managed to figured out where I was and sent my fiancé and a friend, both police officers, to bring me back home. We ended up instead going straight from Albany to DC due to more threats.

"What threats?" Chairman James asked.

"I think I should let my cousin Kate Killoy Foyle respond to the question because she was present at the time."

Chairman James looked at Kate and repeated the question.

"I thank you of asking because some serious and

life threatening crimes have been committed since the response to initial theft was completed. Someone was determined to stop this hearing from taking place. The first I became aware that something was wrong was when Agnes' bitches turned up in my kennel unannounced. I tried calling Agnes but didn't get a response. Nobody knew where she had gone. That evening, when my husband and I were feeding my boarding kennel dogs, I heard a sound. To make a long story short, we found Agnes' phone hidden in the kennel. When we went to bring it back to the house, it rang showing an unfamiliar number. Being uncomfortable with the situation, I had him answer the call on speaker while I recorded it on my phone." Kate tapped Satu's arm, and Satu slid her tablet near Kate's microphone, opened a file on her tablet and the sound of the call filled the chamber. "Following this phone call, an attempt on Agnes' greyhound show bitches was made by a shooter. Luckily, three police dogs including the one lying at my side, were able to stop him. The shooter was arrested and none of the dogs were injured. A second call followed. The room filled with the sound of the second call. This threat was carried out when my kennel manager and I went out to feed our boarding dogs. We had almost reached the door of the kennel when a car pulled into my driveway traveling at high speed. Salvatore Mondigliani, lifted me and dove behind a concrete knee wall. I learned later he had seen a gun barrel pointing out the passenger window. Shots from an automatic rifle ripped along the wall sending chunks of concrete flying. Two Connecticut State Troopers, who were in the house at the time returned fire, taking out the tire of the car, but it escaped when it met up with an accomplice. The third threat--Kate paused for the recording to play--essentially threatened all of us. While we were preparing to appear before this committee, a young man delivered an envelope supposedly containing our passes to today's session. Dillon, my Samoyed police dog, blocked me from approaching the young man. My husband took the envelope and put it in the house. The group which now included AIC Bullock, went to my grandmother's for dinner. When we returned and entered the house. Dillon refused to let anyone near the envelope. AIC Bullock used a pair of tongs and carried the envelope out of the house and placed it on the ground outside the house. He then called the bureau's New Haven office. When investigators arrived, a sniffer drone was used and it was revealed that the envelope contained a deadly pathogen. I will say the obvious. We could all have been killed, including the law officers, FBI personnel, my family members, my dog, anyone who came to find us... and the unborn child I am carrying." Kate sat as silence filled the room.

Finally, James called to adjourn the session. Further questioning, he told the gathering, would be held in closed session at a date and time yet to be scheduled. His gavel came down, People stood and hurried to the doors. Harry leaned in and said, "You really know how to clear a room, toots."

"Let's go home." She stood and gathered her things. Dillon immediately moved into heel position and leaned into her leg giving reassurance. Harry took her hand, and they walked toward the door, only to be met by Chairman James. He reached out to take her hands and surprisingly, Dillon moved forward with his tail wagging so Kate relaxed.

"Today was an incredible hearing. I want to thank all of you for your bravery. I am terrified that these attacks on your lives have happened. I am so happy that you survived."

"So far." Satu said.

"So far?"

"There is still Howard, Congressman Heller's hit man. He was the man behind the assault rifle attack, and he's still in the wind. I wouldn't put it past him to try to kill Kate to get revenge."

"Bullock. These women need protection."

"I am aware, Congressman. We will provide protection until this man is captured."

James again thanked them and said he would be in touch, but stopped as he walked away and turned to Satu. "You are a very bright young lady. I was quite impressed today. If you are ever looking for a job in Washington, let me know. In fact, why don't you give me your card, and I will keep it on file." She looked slightly disconcerted when Harry, who was standing behind her, accidentally bumped her.

He bent over. "Sorry Satu, did you drop this?"

She looked down at her hand and then at Harry. He winked.

Opening the silver case, she pulled out one of her engraved business cards and handed it to the chairman with a smile.

He nodded to her. "Thank you. Stay in touch."

She waited until he'd left to laugh. "Harry, that was perfect."

Harry turned to Seamus. "Here is yours. I got them back from the engravers last week, but with everything that has been going on, I admit I forgot. You've got boxes with cards in them at home, but it's always good to have some on hand if an opportunity comes along."

"These are perfect. When you get that condescending career counselor in school asking you what you want to do when you grow up, you can just whip out your card and tell him, I'm already there." Kate said grinning. "I think I gave my counselor a heart attack my senior year. He looked at my name and said, 'Well this is easy.' You can imagine his expression when I said fashion designer." The light chatter continued as they walked to the waiting limo.

Once they were inside, Kate leaned into Harry and said, "Thanks."

"For what?"

"For pulling me out of the stress and tension. I needed a chuckle, or a dozen dogs."

"Isn't that the same thing? Well, you'll soon have both so hang in there." He wrapped his arm around her and watched the once familiar sight of DC pass by his window as they worked their way through the traffic.

CHAPTER 25

Tuesday afternoon

T he group had divided itself in two. Maeve, Padraig, Sybil, Agnes and Sean stayed together. They were going to spend the night with an old family friend of Sybil and Maeve's from Ireland who'd been trying to get them to visit. The woman, who had grown up with them, was married to the Deputy Head of Mission at the Irish embassy. Malcolm thought this was a good idea if they agreed to have a couple of agents with them. Until Howard was found, they were not considered safe.

Kate, Harry, Dillon, Seamus and Satu traveled home with Des. Their bags had already been taken to a small airport run by a friend of Malcolm's where a six seat Cessna, awaited them. They were hurried on board so that they'd still have the daylight to land at Oxford Airport. The small jet was comfortable and Kate, who had begun to feel exhausted due to the strain of a day with so much tension, had barely strapped herself in, lost the battle to keep her eyes open before the plane even took off. Dillon lay at her side, watching her for a few minutes and then allowing himself to sleep.

Harry and Des had been going over the events of the day speaking quietly with Seamus and Satu. He told them, "Kate handed me a note at the beginning of the session telling me that Howard was up in the gallery watching them. When I looked, he was gone. I have no idea how he will react now that his boss has been arrested."

"It depends on who his boss is." Kate mumbled softly in a sleepy voice. "Was he working for Heller, or riding herd on him for someone higher up."

Harry looked at her, but her eyes were still closed and her breathing even. It was as if she hadn't spoken at all. When he turned back to the others, he could see Satu mulling over a problem. She had obviously heard Kate.

"She's got a point. Why Heller? If this guy was working for the GRU, why choose to link him with a not that powerful congressman from the Midwest? The wife didn't look like she'd be involved in this type of thing, but it is her connection with Turchin that seemed to be the only one prior to his arrival in the US."

Seamus pointed out, "Anyone in the Kremlin could have gone on Google, found out who was a member of that committee. Then they could check their backgrounds for vulnerability. What do we know about Heller's wife? What was her maiden name? She might have connections with the corporal's family. A little pressure applied might have gained cooperation. Lazar may have been sent here for the specific purpose of becoming part of the army because Heller had been on the committee that oversaw the testing of new ordinance. From what I've read about Bill over the last few days, both friend and foe are aware of the influence of his new developments on the advancement of this style of warfare. Bill had been working on the Deflector Shield for several years. With the way this operation was carried out, and Heller's ability to influence or steer the investigation in one direction or another might have benefited the Russians or whoever is behind this. Kate is right. Howard may have been working for Heller to make sure he didn't get caught. So long as he holds his position on the committee, the plans move forward."

Satu looked at him and said, "So he may not have been Heller's fixer, but rather Heller's controller."

Des looked at Kate whose eyes were still closed almost as if she hadn't said anything. Then he looked at Harry, who frowned saying, "So the problem lies in the people doing the investigation who need to be stopped. And the one who seems to be coming after them like a heat-seeking missile, is Kate. Your wife has a target on her back, Foyle.

"My wife has had a target on her back since I first met her. Sal sent me to guard her when he realized Agnes had led her into danger at the dog show, in New York City last February. There's a reason she's on her second bullet-proof vest. I suspect that fearing for her safety will be a constant in my life."

The group became quiet. Their minds on the possibility of new dangers.

Suddenly Harry looked around and swore. "The parade. Her dog club will be marching in the parade on Friday evening. Out in the open. Exposed for anyone to take a shot at her as she walks through town or performs on the Green. This is going to be a much bigger nightmare than we could imagine."

"I'll call Malcolm tonight," Des said as a change in the sound of the engine let them know they'd be landing soon.

Harry reached over to wake Kate. "How are you doing? Do you want a cracker?"

"No, Polly doesn't want a cracker," she grumbled at being woken. "Kate needs a full night's sleep in her own bed and to have the world be rid of killers."

"We'll all vote for that one, Kate," Des said and the others murmured their agreement.

The flight only took an hour, so they'd be home and unpacked before Ann thought of supper. Looking out the window, Kate was shocked to see about a foot of snow on the ground. With all that had been going on, she hadn't followed the weather at home when they were in DC. Though it had felt like winter there, they were much further south and had been spared any part of this storm. The afternoon sun sparkled off the pristine white surface, making Kate wish she'd packed her sunglasses. A slight thump let her know they were on the ground.

Des was ready when they came to a stop and helped his friend open the door and lower the steps. He paused to take as much as he could see and waved at the driver of the black Honda Odyssey which had just cleared the gate and was heading in their direction. He nodded to Harry who took Kate's arm to hurry her down the stairs behind Seamus and Satu and Dillon, across the short distance to the car. Sal opened the doors, saying, "You kids, get in back fast. Kate and Harry in the middle with Dillon. Des, you ride with me. Harry, your extra Glock is in the glove compartment just in case. I know you aren't carrying since you came straight from having Kate testify." He dashed around to the driver's seat.

Des walked back, checked the luggage, and shut the back. Shaking hands with his friend, he jumped into the front seat as Sal began to head for the exit.

As soon as they were on the highway, Sal said, "That was quite a show you ladies put on. We watched every minute on C Span and recorded the whole thing. Satu, you looked like a lawyer assistant, slipping in the tapes of the calls with timing that rocked those politicians back on their heels. The place was frozen on you four."

"Chairman James wants her to come work for him. He was really impressed," Seamus told him. "He even asked for her business card."

"You have business cards?"

"Absolutely!" Satu and Seamus said in unison, both grinning.

"How are you doing Katie," Sal asked.

"I'm okay, but I'm sorry to say that we're not

done. Heller's fixer, Howard, is still in the wind. I spotted him in the gallery, but as soon as I passed the word, he was gone. I'd say the odds of his being on his way to Connecticut are pretty good. I don't know if Heller is the one behind him or someone higher up in either our government or Russia's. Right now they realize they are not getting the Deflector Shield, so I think that whatever is carried out is either personal or to send a message. We'll have to figure a way to smoke him out before Friday. I can't endanger all those people."

"Damn--the parade."

Silence followed.

As they got near, Kate twisted in her seat to have the first look at their new home decked out in snow. Harry locked his arms around her, their heads side by side as Sal turned the car into the driveway. Kate gasped. The entire house was decked out for Christmas. Candles were in every window, and there was a beautiful wreath on the door. A Christmas tree was showing through the living room window and lights were on all over the first floor.

Sal chuckled. "The women and your brothers have been going crazy getting the place ready. Ann had snuck all those catalogs you've been marking, home the night you left, and she's been on the phone with all the companies getting rush deliveries. Your fancy table arrived today and even I had a try opening it and closing it up. It's a smart piece of engineering. The bottom line is that supper will be served by Will at your new home tonight. Kate and Harry, welcome home."

Happy tears were streaming down Kate's cheeks as she exited the car and walked up the porch steps. Harry laughed and as soon as they reached the porch he said, "I know I've already done this once, but this is not just what our home will be, but what it is. Merry Christmas, Mrs. Foyle," he said as he swept her up in his arms.

Kate wrapped her arms around his neck and kissed him. "Merry Christmas, Mr. Foyle. I love you so much."

The door opened, and Ann with Will, Dani, Tom, Gwyn, Tim and Roger all standing behind her all shouted their welcome. Dillon dashed by them to join the other dogs who were spread out all over the living room.

Once inside, with their coats hung in the closet, Kate was able to take in the sight before her. The sofa flanked by coordinating wing chairs faced the fireplace where a cheerful fire was burning. Kate looked at Tom and asked, "A fire in the fireplace so soon?"

"Gas logs. The tank is outside beside the deck. You can turn it on and off with a remote control. It's more efficient and cleaner than a wood burning unit."

"It's nice and warm in here."

She slowly walked around the room. There were Christmas packages piled on the table behind the sofa, out of reach of curious puppies. Stepping over to the Christmas tree, she saw that all of her favorite ornaments with Sammies were all over the tree, intermixed with ornaments of reindeer, dog show jumps, dog sleds, as well as the ornaments that she and her grandmother had knit or crocheted as she'd grown up. The colorful lights reflected off all the glass balls that were hung between her special ornaments. She knew she had to find some special ornaments for Harry.

Harry came and took her hand, and they walked toward the kitchen where lively chatter and arguing was going on. It seemed the battle of the chefs continued. She hadn't chosen a dining room table yet, but she saw that the good china which had been given her as a wedding present and had remained packed away since the wedding, was on display in the glass fronted china cabinet. When she entered the kitchen, Will was standing wearing a chef's hat a wooden spoon in his hand facing Dani in an apron waving a matching wooden spoon. Kate stopped, whipped her phone from her pocket, and managed to capture the scene. As the flash went off, the two cooks realized that they were the center of attention and immediately directed everyone to find a seat at the table which was opened to it's extended form and had a dozen matching chairs surrounding it. At each place there was a festive place mat. Everyone sat and Will and Dani were about to serve the meal when a ding sounded on several phones and a car pulled into the driveway. It slowed to a crawl and then stopped in front of the house.

Kate held her breath. She knew who was in the car. Harry and Ann must also have recognized the person climbing out of the car and stamping angrily toward the house. Kate looked at her brothers, none of whom had moved. They knew what was coming.

"What is this house doing here, blocking the view from my home. Why wasn't I consulted about this. I have not intention of spending every day staring out at this eyesore whenever I get up in the morning. I supposed this Kate's doing!"

Kate drew a shuttering breath. Her mother was home from her conference.

The sound of Harry's voice came from the living room following a gasp which could only have come from Ann. "This is my home, built on my wife's land. You may be my mother-on-law, but I will tell you right now that if this is your attitude, you will not be welcome in our home. Kate is my wife, the woman I love, and I will not have your behavior spoiling our enjoyment of the home we have dreamed of, planned and had built to our specifications. If you have any complaints about it, you will take them up with me."

Everyone was looking at Kate, who had a look of wonder on her face. A smile grew as she looked around at the faces staring back at her, and she stood. Running a hand over her skirt to shake out any creases, she walked through the dining room and into the living room. "Hello, mother, I'm glad you made it home in time to join us for dinner. Harry, why don't you take her coat. I'm sure you're hungry and probably chilled after the long drive from Boston. Will has a wonderful dinner waiting. Gram, Mom, Harry, shall we go eat?"

"Ah... Yes. Thank you. I'd like that, Kate," Claire Killoy responded.

Kate took her mother's arm and Harry took Ann's as they strolled through the empty dining room and into the kitchen, where all the men stood and Will pulled out a chair next to Tom for his mother then everyone sat. Kate noticed that since there were now more than twelve for dinner, Seamus and Satu had moved to banquette and were already deep in conversation. They paused, when Tom said grace, and then the chatter began with everyone eager to tell Claire Killoy about the flying house and the excitement of a house being completed in two days. Kate let them talk and reached for Harry's hand. When her mother turned her way and congratulated her on her lovely outfit, and mentioned how the royal blue look so good with her fair hair, Kate felt Harry squeeze it. He leaned in and whispered, "Do you want to tell her your pregnant or should I?"

CHAPTER 26

Tuesday night and Wednesday early morning

As the dinner began winding down, Harry stood and asked if Will had stocked the refrigerator with any champagne. Will being Will had, and soon everyone had one in hand, except Kate. I would like everyone to join me in a toast to my wonderful wife, and to our happiness in our new home. But more importantly, I invite everyone to share our joy as I tell you that we are expecting our first child." Cheers and congratulations erupted, with nobody letting on that they already knew.

Claire stood and walked over to them, standing quiet for a minute. Then to everyone's surprise, she reached for Kate's hand saying, "Your father and grandfather would have been ecstatic over this." She paused, "I know, Kate, that I haven't been a good mother to you. I never understood my daughter as your father told me over and over again. He was right, and I was very hard on you. But I want to tell you both right now, that I will work as hard as I can to be the best grandmother this child could ever have."

Kate wrapped her arms around her mother, and hugged her. She had no memory of ever doing it before, but it felt right. Harry bent down and gave Claire a kiss on the cheek. As they all sat Kate heard her mother ask her grandmother, how hard it would be to learn to knit a baby blanket.

As people were heading out, Des stopped to talk to Harry. Then he went to get his bag and went upstairs. Apparently one of the rooms on the second floor at least had a bed in it, so he'd be staying there in case Howard paid a visit. He then went to talk to Tom about having him dig up some information. Des said he'd be back in about an hour.

Kate and Harry settled onto the couch in the living room, as each dog came looking for snuggles from the most important person in their world. They were coming to love Harry too, but Kate would always be first. She had been there when almost all of them were born. Kate watched as new favorite spots were established. She had noticed, as she left the kitchen, that Harry had left open the door connecting this house to hers through the newly constructed hallway. They'd been sitting and talking for about an hour when Kate felt something rub the back of her neck. Glancing to the right, she saw Macbeth move onto Harry's shoulder and then to his lap. Ignoring the dogs who were now focused on her, including Quinn, she curled up in Harry's lap and fell asleep. With Roger and Sal taking care of the kennel dogs, and Tom having told her that these guys had been fed, she felt free to just sit and unwind.

While they sat and talked, Harry asked her for the stories behind each Christmas ornament. When Des returned, he told them he had some sleep to catch up on, so he'd see them in the morning. Harry decided sleep was a good idea. So they stood and walked to the French doors, turning on the lights that lit not only the deck, but the dog yard as well. Tom had said, Jimmy had come yesterday and extended the fence, but suggested that come spring, she should add a run of cinder blocks on the outside, to discourage diggers. So noticing that the yard was now secured all the way to the deck, Kate opened the door and let the dogs out. Then she turned and headed for the kitchen. "It doesn't matter that we let them out from the living room, the dogs will go to the old door in the kitchen of the little house to be let in. I'm going down there to train them to come into the kitchen that way."

Kate was right. Most of the dogs stood waiting patiently at the lower door. A few were still racing around, exploring the newer part of the yard. When she opened the door to let them in, Harry called for them to run down the hall into the kitchen. Kate relaxed knowing they'd all figured out that their usual door still led to the room that held food. That was all they needed to know.

Together they made sure that everything was put away in the kitchen, but Will had already handled that. So they just walked through the house, turning off lights, and saying good night to the dogs. When they opened the bedroom door, Liam, Dillon and Quinn dashed inside. When they walked into their bedroom what they saw was a startling sight. Their suitcases were next to the closet but that wasn't it. What caught Kate's eye, and left her breathless was the bed she had circled in a catalog. It had been made up with sheets and blankets. But what had her frozen--staring, was a beautiful handmade quilt the likes of which she'd never seen. She went closer to the bed looking at the remarkable quilt before her. The quilt was made up of what looked like thousands of pieces in a landscape quilting design. The picture which grew from all the piecing was of a forest of evergreens on a snowy background with a small cluster of birch trees growing at the edge of a clearing. Emerging from the trees was a woman in a white cape, surrounded by white dogs. Peeking out from the woman's hood, Kate saw herself. Though the quilt was all pieced, layered as though painted, the face of the woman, was embroidered to look like hers. On the left, somewhat hidden in the background and peeking out of the forest, stood a reindeer with a full rack of antlers. Standing beside him wearing a dark green cape, stood a man with his hood back, wearing Harry's face. He was watching the woman, while resting one hand on the neck of the huge animal. As she got closer, she noticed small woodland creatures hidden in the design and the face of a bitch and two puppies, barely visible, peering out of the forest.

"Ann must have started this when we first met." Harry whispered. "The amount of work is mind boggling."

"I want to take a picture of it on the bed and then fold it up and put it somewhere safe until I can hang it on the wall behind the bed. It will fit because of the high windows. There is no way I will take a chance of damaging it. It is now a family treasure. She took pictures from several angles then put away her phone and went to the side of the bed to reach for the top of the quilt to fold it. A flash went off and Harry smiled. "That will be the best shot of the quilt with the enchanted Kate, and the real Kate in the same photo. Together they carefully folded it and placed it on the top shelf of their linen closet.

It was chilly in the room following the warmth from the rest of the house. Kate saw that her hope chest which Maeve had given her to hold the quilts and afghans that she made over the years had been brought to the new bedroom. These were quilts of simple design made more for warmth than beauty. She spread one on the bed and then closed the curtains, undressed and crawled into bed.

Harry finished up in the bathroom. When he came out, he saw that with the room being so large, instead of piling together, Quinn had staked out a spot in front of the French doors leading to the deck and Liam lay across the door leading to the rest of the house. Dillon, however, was in his usual spot, next to Kate's side of the bed, asleep but always on guard. He stared at the dog for a minute remembering his utter focus when at Kate's side today. He didn't get restless but remained still, leaning slightly into her leg. At the same time, he appeared to be assessing each person in the room whether they were friend or foe. Harry was sure that if anyone who had been on that floor today approached Kate, Dillon would know whether to wag his tail or go into complete Cujo mode. Harry had seen that mode in action and it was a frightening thing. But at the same time, once the situation changed, or the threat was removed, the amiable show dog returned. Tonight, with Howard still out there wanting Kate dead, he was glad that Dillon was beside them as they slept.

He crawled into bed and saw that he'd have to go search for his wife. They'd been sleeping in a double bed since their honeymoon ended, and he liked that closeness. This was a large king-size. He slid halfway across the bed and reached out to pull Kate up against him. She didn't wake. He glanced over his shoulder to double check that there were saltines on his nightstand. Then holding her tight, he let himself sleep.

***

The dings on their phones woke them. Harry grabbed his phone as he dove for his shirt and pants. Kate said, "Check the front of the kennel feed." He watched as four cars gunned their engines and drove in circles in the space in front of the kennel. They circled four times but on the final pass, the driver of a green sedan unloaded a burst of bullets into the cement wall again as the others headed back toward the highway. Though it was early, there was traffic on the highway. Truckers were taking advantage of the clear roads to speed. None of their visitors drove straight out. Each stopped for a second to make sure nothing weighing more than a ton was bearing down on them. That was all Kate needed, Her thumbs were flying, capturing and recording the faces of all the drivers. None were studio portraits, but all were clear enough to identify. When the final car pulled back onto the highway, Kate recognized Howard.

She hopped out of bed and ran to what was probably her new bureau to grab clothes. Everything was arranged exactly as it had been in the old bureau in her former bedroom. She was dressed in under a minute and ready when the knock came on the bedroom door followed by a shout from Des asking if they were all right. Harry pulled open the door and raced out followed by Kate zipping up the front of her polar fleece hoodie. Their phones were ringing, and Sal came running through the entrance to the old house and was banging on the door to the kitchen. Harry went to open it while Kate ran to the front door to let Tom in who was followed by Will, Seamus and Tim.

Kate flipped through the photos she'd saved on her phone, as she pulled her laptop from the tote she'd taken to DC. Then followed by a stream of dogs, she dashed to the kitchen and turned on the kettle and the switch for Harry's coffee maker. Plugging in the charger cord, which she'd forgotten to do last night, she opened the security app and began downloading everything from all the cameras. As each face appeared, she chose the best view and printed it out. Howard now had a team and though she may need a cup of tea to wake her brain completely, she was pretty sure she had seen these men before. She'd have to check some photos to confirm, but she thought that Howard's happy band of terror had names, ranks and serial numbers.

Will grabbed her laptop and long charger cord now stretching from the counter, and moved it to the side of the table closest to the front wall. Then he plugged her back in. Plucking her from her chair, he moved her to the new spot. You've got four out-lets right behind you, Kate. It's safer to sit there if you have a cord. This way it won't trip the chef who will be feeding you.

"Okay." She muttered, as she downloaded video files and labeled them. When a cup of tea appeared in front of her, she looked up into Harry beautiful green eyes, smiled and said, "Guess what. When you feel terror, you don't feel like throwing up. Your body doesn't have time for mourning sickness."

"See, your day is staring out on a high note."

"Funny! I've got head shots of Howard's 'band of brothers'. I'm sure I've seen them before. Once I get this tea in me and maybe some food, I'll get you some IDs."

Kate took her first sip of tea, sighed in content-ment and then began going through files.

"Kate. Malcolm's on the line He wants to know what you've got," Des asked. Kate reached her arm out for his phone without taking her eyes off the photos that were skimming across the page as she searched. "Malcolm, it's Kate. Howard brought three friends. I got head shots of all four. I'll get them-- oh wait, here we go--with photos of them in their uniforms. All are army. All are friends of Turchin, and all have been to at least one of the tests where

Turchin was lurking in the background. I'll give Des back his phone and send you this immediately. You might have the army check to see why these soldiers aren't tucked up in their beds at this hour. Here's Des."

Kate handed off the phone and began compiling a file of head shots from their nighttime circus, and shots of Turchin talking to his friends. There were enough clear shots for identification. She sent the file to Malcolm, took another sip of tea, and then decided to set the cat among the pigeons in the Army. She wrote a quick email to General Cutter and attached a copy of the photo file.

When Harry sat next to her a minute later she was staring at her computer. "What's wrong."

"I may have done something totally against protocol and the chain of command and all that stuff."

"What have you done?"

"Well, I sent the file of the men who came with Howard tonight to Malcolm. But considering the day, and what had happened, and feeling that he might own me a small favor in the way of an investigation, I sent an email, with the same photos attached, to General Cutter."

"God, Kate. You don't ever do things by halves,

do you."

"Am I in trouble? Am I going to be arrested?"

"No and no. In fact, if Cutter acts swiftly enough, we may nail these guys before they even know that we're after them. He definitely owes you and making an effort to keep you alive would go a long way with payback."

Kate's laptop dinged with an email from the general. He told her that she should stay safe and out of the line of fire. That he was ready to join her team. He'd begin working to investigate these three soldiers in right now."

"Des," Harry shouted. Everybody went quiet to listen. "Kate's just added a member to our merry band."

"Who?"

"Cutter. You'd better warn Malcolm."

CHAPTER 27

Wednesday morning

B reakfast was well under way when a knock on the door brought, Gwyn, Ann, Dani, Satu and Claire.

Claire said that she was leaving for work, but she'd seen everyone heading over here and wanted to know what was going on. Everyone went silent. Finally, Ann spoke. "I just heard from Maeve that the others will arrive at ten o'clock. I am of the belief that ignorance is not bliss in this case, it's dangerous. Claire needs to know what is going on. Though she won't be here most of the day, she will be on her own on campus in New Haven. These people have done enough research on our habits to know this. I for one, worry about her being without some sort of protection."

Des had been talking to someone when they came into the room. He picked up his conversation and explained the situation and then looked at Claire. "Will you go straight to your office before your classes?"

"Of course," she answered, though somewhat confused.

"Agent Sims will be her cover and escort her home at the end of the day. Perfect. Thanks." Looking around, he asked, "Tom. Could you drive your mother to work and explain on the way what this is all about. Escort her to her office. Introduce her to Agent Sims and then return here. The FBI will ensure her safety and see she gets home."

Tom finished his coffee, grabbed a couple of blueberry muffins and headed for the closet under the living room stairs to get his coat. Claire went with him, looking confused, but moving because it was her favorite child leading the way. When the front door closed, most of them let out the breath they hadn't realized they were holding.

Kate looked across the table. "How did you know that Tom would be the only one to get her to go without an argument?"

"I watched her at the wedding. She thinks your big brother walks on water. It was the safest choice."

Kate looked around and said, "Dani, while you are eating, could you call in the license numbers on the band of terror from this morning? I noticed that though Howard is still driving the same car, it now has a new number. I don't know about the others. I think they are last minute rushed additions, so they may have gotten their cars through traditional means rather than stealing them. I just sent the numbers to your phone."

"Will do."

They all got back to work. Moving dishes to the sink or dishwasher, and pulling out laptops. Gwyn got called out on a mysterious death, and Sal and Roger went to take care of the dogs, but Kate dove deeper and deeper into the research she had begun before going to DC. The sounds of dog food bowls being filled, pulled her attention back to the real world. Jumping up, she met Harry at the counter and then let in the dogs. Since it was a new space, they milled around until Kate walked to the end of the island and faced the banquette. Harry went to stand next to her. Each were holding bowls. In less than thirty seconds, the dogs had arranged themselves in their traditional order. When breakfast ended, Kate picked up a fistful of biscuits as did Harry. She opened the door to the hall and went to the former kitchen door and stopped. All the dogs had crowded into the hall, but then sat. Without a word from Kate, each went forward in their proper order, stood for his biscuit and raced out into the snowy yard. When it was finally Quinn's turn, he was wiggling all over with eagerness. Getting his biscuit, he was out of there like a shot, holding tight to his biscuit but checking to see if any pieces of others were lying on the ground.

Kate put her arm through Harry's. "Thanks. I'd gotten so wrapped up in research, that I forgot about feeding them."

"You forgot about feeding you as well. I checked. All you've had this morning is two cups of tea. You are not touching your laptop until you eat. I'll let you get away with some muffins and fruit, but eat before work."

"Yes sir," she said, saluting.

Once she began eating, she discovered she was hungry, so when a plate with two fried eggs and some sausage and applesauce appeared in front of her, she smiled at her husband and gobbled it up. She was deep on the trail of Heller's wife's connection to the GRU, if any, when a knock at the front door distracted her. A minute later, Maeve walked into the kitchen and set her laptop on the table and sat. "Who needs help with what? Kate. What are you working on now?"

"I'm trying to find the background on Heller's wife. It occurred to me that it was a really stupid move to bring Turchin to the session yesterday. I don't care if he was in drag, it was obvious that he didn't belong there. The other thing, that was stupid was signing her married name to his army application. It was Heller's district. Does anyone know what is happening with the arrests yesterday? Des?"

"I'll find out."

"What's her maiden name?" Maeve asked.

"According to her marriage certificate, it was Annabelle Harrington." Kate told her with her eyebrows raised.

"Got it." Maeve smiled at her. Annabelle Harrington, from Minsk. Right. Okay, I'll get to work."

Kate's phone made a sound indicating that she had a text. She looked and found it was from Cutter. Men in question were found to be AOL when checked at five hundred hours. They were back on duty at 9.25 hours. All three will be kept under surveillance until we consulted with military lawyers about protocol. Stay safe, Cutter.

She passed on the information to the others.

Agnes went out to the yard to play with her

GUARD KATE

girls, and Sean left to check in at the Barracks.

Sybil sat down next to Kate and said. "With all the rushing us off for safety purposes, I didn't have time to thank you for what you did at the session yesterday. Bill would be pleased. He worked hard to stop these criminals. It is good to know they are under arrest."

"Well, most of them are under arrest. We got a threatening visit from Howard in the wee hours. He and three soldiers drove around in front of the kennel and before he left, Howard shot up the concrete barrier again. I think he wants me to know that he can strike at any time with deadly force. The soldiers were noted as AOL when I notified the newest member of our team, General Cutter. When they returned to regular duty at nine-fifteen this morning, they were put under surveillance pending charges. There are a lot of players in this game. I don't think that Heller is at the top of the food chain. Right now Maeve and I are checking out sweet little Mrs. Heller. I suspect that there is a lot more to that lady than we first suspected."

"They shot up the area by the kennel this morning? Oh, no. Is your mother back from Boston?"

"Yes she's back. I seemed to have gained some status with her by being pregnant. She is being guarded at work by the FBI. Tom had the job of driving her to work and filling her in on what's been going on."

"Thank God it was Tom."

"Des studied our family dynamic during the wedding and knew exactly who to pick. He may start with, 'Did you know that your daughter testified to congress yesterday?' Get her to be impressed first, then bring in the threats. It will give her something to brag about with her colleagues at lunch."

They heard the door close and Tom walked into the kitchen. All talking stopped. He looked around. "Mission accomplished. I think it's the first time since you were born that Mom will be bragging about you to her colleagues. It will also be the first time they hear that she has a daughter. But, she is safe with Agent Sims. Welcome back Sybil. I saw you do a great job. We recorded the C-SPAN broadcast. I promised Mom that she could watch the recording tonight."

Kate returned to the search into the real identity of Mrs. Annabelle Heller. She went back to the statement Turchin had given the army that she had known him for a long time and that was why she was recommending him. If she had known him a long time, that would mean that she knew him when he was Konstantine Lazar so what she really needed was to learn more about the Lazar family and their neighbors, one among whom might be Mrs. Heller's family. She treated it as though she were searching for ancestors and went inch by inch. She found out when he was enrolled in school. When he graduated. Who recommended him to 'The Conservatory'. It was slow going. But by going back to primary school, she got a form which listed the names of his parents. Using that information, she went back to what was closest to a census and found where the Lazar family lived in Minsk. She also got a list of the other families on that street. She checked the families that had female children and their ages. Once the list was compiled, she had only three possibilities for Mrs. Heller.

Surfacing from having her mind buried in the research, she noticed that Will and Dani were cooking lunch. The smell had her stomach grumbling. The next thing she noticed, was that everyone else had packed up their work and the table was being set. She stood and waited for the pins and needles feeling to leave her legs. She closed her laptop and placed it in the bag by her chair along with the notebook she been using to keep track of stray facts until she needed them. Once she could walk again, she went to her bedroom to use the bathroom and splash water on her face. As she walked out into the bedroom, she paused to appreciate all that had been done for them. The bedroom set looked beautiful. Her bureau had a large mirror that gave a view out through the French doors of the woods behind the house. Harry's bureau had a coordinated cheval mirror next to it which gave a view out the front widows to the wooded space between the house she'd grown up in and her grandmother's. This gave the room an appearance of being out in nature.

She had just returned to the kitchen when Agnes' phone rang. She answered. There was talk for a minute, and then she hung up with a frown. She told them the woman said she was Richard's secretary. The woman said that Richard had told her to call Agnes to pick up the package she'd left with him last week. "We'll I guess nothing important was in that box, if it wasn't needed for the testimony. All talking stopped until Harry asked the obvious question. When does Richard want you to pick it up?"

"That's the weird thing. She wants me to come at four-thirty this afternoon."

"When does Richard's bank close?"

"Since it is primarily a trust company rather than a commercial bank, it usually closes at four o'clock."

"Let me get this straight," Kate said. "A woman called, told you that she was Richard's secretary. Was she young or old?"

"I'd say oldish."

"So this oldish woman calls and tells you to come to Richard's bank a half hour after closing to pick up a box that Richard delivered to us late Sunday. I don't see any problem with that do you. Unless you'd rather not die or be kidnapped."

"You don't think this is Richard's secretary."

"Last week at the training session Richard was telling me about his new secretary. She's only twenty-two, but she's a computer whiz and is helping with all sorts of computer safeguards for the bank. His tech department, love her because Richard doesn't even use social media."

"Well I guess that saves me a trip into the city."

"So let's have lunch."

They had only sat down to eat when Gwyn walked in followed by Tom.

"Perfect timing. Lunch is served and it smells great. How did your case go this morning. I hope it wasn't a child or anything like that."

"No it was a man. He was found in the woods behind a motel north of Waterbury by a young guy walking his dog."

"How did he die?"

"A single bullet to the heart. He was big and burly so anything other than that or between the eyes probably wouldn't have taken him down. He had no ID on him and there was no car parked in front of the unit he seemed to be renting."

"How was he registered?"

"Jason Doe."

"He had a wry sense of humor. Had he been there long."

"No, that was the creepy part. I'd say he'd been dead less than an hour. I did a preliminary autopsy this morning. I'd say he was raised outside the US because of his dental care. He had not led the most gentile life. His body was covered with scars. There were also some tattoos which were elaborate that I'll have to research. Several with eagles. One was a stylized eagle which could have been a group's logo. Interesting case, but I could use some food."

As they ate, Kate went over all she had learned about Turchin that morning. She'd get back to it, but it occurred to her that they knew practically nothing about Howard. They didn't even know his last name. She pulled out her phone and a photo of Howard and began to type herself a note when

Gwyn grabbed her wrist.

"Where did you get that photo?" She asked, pointing toward the phone."

"I got it from the security camera at the end of the driveway, during the raid this morning."

"Who is it? Do you know?"

"It's Howard, Heller's fixer. He's the one determined to kill me."

Gwyn took Kate's phone and stared at it for another minute. "I think I can tell you without fear of being contradicted that Howard is not trying to kill you."

"How do you know?"

"Because Howard is presently lying on a slab in my morgue."

CHAPTER 28

Wednesday afternoon

D es was on the phone at once to Malcolm saying they have a probable report that Howard had been murdered about an hour after he shot up Kate's place. He was getting ready to put Gwyn on the phone when Kate asked if she could speak to him first. Des handed her the phone and then began asking Gwyn questions.

"Malcolm. Right, strange morning. I have two questions. First, is everyone who was arrested yesterday still in custody? When? Is she being tailed? Second, are the other three under guard as high risk prisoners? Yes, I would suggest that." She listened for a minute. "I'm working on fitting the pieces together but I'm still missing some pieces. You might also mention to Cutter that he get his threesome into safe lock down. Let's see, charges could be material witnesses to an attempted murder. I don't know. Use any wording you like, or you may not have any witnesses to question. As soon as I know, you'll know." She handed Des back his phone and looked up to see everyone staring at her.

"What?" she asked.

"No Kate," Harry said quietly. "The question is who. Who do you think killed Howard? Who is missing? Why do all the bad guys need to be guarded?"

"I don't have proof."

"Guess, we don't care. Share your suppositions."

She looked around the room and then sat. "Beginning with the last thing I suggested to Malcolm, the bad guys need to be guarded because if not, they will die, swiftly and without any trace being left of the power behind their murders to lead back to the murderer. Cutter has the three stooges under surveillance. They know enough and have talked to enough higher up to make good witnesses and therefore also have risen to the top of the murder list. Howard had to be taken out because he was getting foolish. Two of the license plates that he stole were taken from cars that were parked at the same motel where he was staying. The joy ride he took this morning was just him flexing his muscles before taking me out. His boss obviously doesn't like showoffs."

"What else?"

"The other question I asked revealed the information that sweet little Mrs. Heller was able to convince a judge that she wasn't a threat, and she was let out on bond. She managed to slip her tail in under an hour. That was last night. I suspect that she went to Howard's motel and found him returning from his adventure here and ready to brag about how terrified he had us and how much fun he'd get taking me out... or something similar. Mrs. Heller couldn't allow this loose cannon to continue. She probably convinced Howard that they might be heard in the motel and that they should take a walk behind the building where she would give him his next assignment. You see, I've pretty much figured that Howard wasn't Congressman Heller's fixer, he was his wife's."

Kate reached for her tea cup, but saw it was empty and set it down. "Maeve, do any of the documentation you've uncovered on Mrs. Heller list her age?"

Maeve flipped through her notes and said, "She was thirty-seven as of last July. The seventeenth."

Kate opened her laptop and clicked a few keys. "Perfect. Thanks."

"Holler if you need anything else."

Kate went back to her list of families living on the same street as Turchin. There was only one female child among those families who would be age thirty-seven. Kate began to search her background. Like Turchin, she was very smart and rose quickly in school. She too attended 'The Conservatory,' and finished with high honors. She was quickly absorbed into the ranks of the GRU. One of her talents was her ability to listen to someone and be able to imitate them. It was this talent that led to a three-month immersion of study the Iowa accent and the mannerisms of the people. She was then given a new identity and Anna Chesnokov became Annabelle Harrington. When Annabelle Harrington married Heller, I'm sure the sweet congressman's wife would tell his constituents, 'just call me Anna.' The poor wife of the disgraced congressman, should have our sympathy rather than our censure.' Kate was sure that was the judge's opinion which got her bail as soon as she hit court.

She jumped when Harry slid his arms around her. The others were watching him. Would you like some tea and maybe a muffin before you tell us and

Malcolm about your murderer.

"How?"

"I've been studying you since the first moment I laid eyes on you and fell hook, line and sinker. Learning to read you is like sitting with my favorite novel, each nuance bringing richness. I can tell your moods pretty well now, but the one thing I've been most proud of learning is when you finally find the answer you seek."

Will placed a fresh cup of tea in front of her and a plate covered with Italian cookies. She reached for a cookie and it melted in her mouth. It was delicious. "The cookies are Dani's contribution. She baked them yesterday."

She sipped her tea and finished her cookie and then turned to the group. It only took about five minutes to explain what she'd learned. The association with Turchin. The fact that she was the only one in his neighborhood which fit the profile and was the right age. Heller fell for a sweet down home girl from Iowa who could help him run for congress. Instead, he got a Russian spy, who was behind the theft of the army's latest weapons. "Now that she is out on bail until Friday, and has slipped the tail which was put on her, she is free to wander around cleaning up messes. That includes both Howard and me."

"No!" The shouts came from around the table as well as the phone. "That's not going to happen."

"While Anna is roaming around free, who knows where, the danger will be constant. We can be pretty sure that Anna is somewhere in Connecticut. When I spoke yesterday, I painted a target on my back as far as this woman is concerned. She knows that just completing the Congressional session would not stop me. As I have researched her and pulled her from anonymity, I'm sure she has checked me out and has figured several ways where I am at her mercy. If I were looking for the perfect place to take me out, I'd say it would be Friday, about seven pm. That is the time my dog group will be marching in a parade through the center of town. We will be Santa, Mrs. Claus and the elves. I have been an elf since I was seven years old. Everybody in town will know where Kate Killoy will be at that time. She has only to sit and listen. People will tell her."

Malcolm shouted from the phone that Des had put on speaker. "You can't march in that parade."

"Think for a moment. If I don't show up for that parade, what do you think she will do? Thwarted of a chance to strike out at me, what do you know she would she do? When they wanted Agnes to do something, they didn't go after her, but rather the ones she cared about."

Like ice, silence settled over the room chilling everyone. A minute passed--then two. Finally, Dani asked, "What do elves wear?"

Kate looked at her, puzzled. Then she said, "Green sweat shirts, jeans, and the elf hats and boot covers that make their feet look elf-like."

"Got it." She left the room pulling out her phone.

Des picked up his phone and told Malcolm, "I'll call you when we come up with something."

Harry stood behind Kate, not saying anything. He wanted to grab her and race for anywhere safe. But the bottom line was, and he knew it, there was nowhere safe. Not from a GRU trained assassin.

Sal's phone chimed with a text. He pulled it from his pocket and stared at the phone as he slowly collapsed into his chair. He scrolled down the replies and began to smile. In a whisper, more to himself than others, he breathed, "It could work. Dammit Dani, it could work."

Will looked at him and left the room running.

Harry couldn't stand it. He stepped around the others who'd all turned in Sal's direction and grabbed his phone from his hand, and read the message.

GUARD KATE

There is a major threat against Kate's life. She and her search team members, plus some kids who train dogs must march in the town's Christmas Parade on Friday. Kate fears if she doesn't show up, the assassin who is after her will just start shooting random people and dogs to teach her a lesson. We need 'elves' to march with their dogs, armed and ready to guard Kate while others check the crowd trying to spot the killer. These elves wear green sweatshirts and jeans. If you want in--let me know and be at the barn at 7 tomorrow night.

Dani DeFelice

Harry counted the responses. There were more than twenty-five.

He turned to Ann. "How many elf hats and shoe things do you have?"

"Twenty-five I think."

"You're going to need more than twice that many. Can you make a quick pattern for the hats and shoe covers?"

"I have the patterns."

"Copy them, so that several people can cut them out of fabric at once. What about the fabric?"

"There's are two bolts of the fabric in the whelping room. This way down through the years when we made new ones, they matched the ones we had."

"Okay, trace and cut four copies of the pattern so that a team can cut out pieces. How many sewing machines do we have?"

Ann and Kate looked at each other. "I have two, one basic sewing and one a fancy embroidery machine which can also sew a straight seam." Ann said.

"I have two and there is one in the studio," Kate said, slowly understanding what was going on.

"Then we have a plan," Harry said.

Dani and Will walked back into the room to see people rushing in all directions.

Harry walked up to Dani and hugged her. "Thank you."

"What for?"

"For guarding Kate."

CHAPTER 29

Wednesday late afternoon and evening

Will, Tim and Seamus raced across the driveway and into their house, returning in a few minutes with folding tables which normally only saw use at holidays when there were crowds to feed. They set them up in the dining room. Bolts of green felt were unrolled along the tables. Kate placed a box of French chalk, skinny squares of hard chalk used to mark fabric on the table. Ann and Sybil began passing out patterns they had traced onto cardboard. "Since felt isn't directional fabric, your patterns can be placed any way which gets the most pieces from the least amount of space. Here are sewing scissors. Do not! I repeat, do not, use these scissors to cut anything but fabric.

The baskets on the third table will be labeled Hat and Shoe. Put the appropriate pieces in the basket, pinned two together, marking them with an M or an L depending on the size.

"Sewers will work at the third table. The two sections get sewn together and turned right side out. Red ribbon from the spools of ribbon, gets sewn around the brim. And a non-sewer can take the ready-made pompoms from this box and thread the trailing ends through the pointy top of the hat, using these big yarn needles, and then tie the ends in knots on the inside."

The room was quiet with all eyes on Kate.

"That, ladies and gentlemen, is why Kate was able to take the design education she got at that college in New York and turn it into a successful business." Tim said.

Since the afternoon was quickly fading, everyone got to work. Chairs were moved to the dining room for the sewers and the place became a hive of activity.

"Okay." Kate said hurrying across the living room."Let's go. Dogs out. You too Quinn and Shelagh. Twist, Thorin, I know your mom is here, but out you go." As the last dog hurried out onto the deck and raced across the now larger yard Kate turned back to the crew. "Cutters. Make sure that no scraps hit the floor. I'll put a box on each table to collect the scraps, and we'll check the floor when done. Scraps of fabric are very tempting chew toys and sometimes get caught in the gut of a puppy--meaning surgery."

"Got it." Everyone said in unison. Seamus came back in the house with the sewing machine from the studio. The five machines were arranged around the table, and plugged in to a multi-plug power strip with a surge protector. Satu pointed out that she didn't sew, so she grabbed the box of pompoms and set herself up to finish off each hat. Seamus pulled up a chair next to her and the competition for who could attach the best looking pompoms began.

Dani and Will were standing in the pantry planning dinner when Kate came up. "Dani. Thank you. My mind was so frozen with fear that I couldn't see a way around this. Your idea is brilliant."

"Actually, I've been secretly eager to try that dog dancing. It looks like so much fun." Kate leaned in and hugged her, then returned to her sewing machine, picking up pieces of a hat and getting started.

Des went into the living room. He collapsed into a wing chair and dialed Malcolm. When he answered, Des said, "You're not going to believe what's

going on around me. Project Guard Kate has begun."
Chuckling softly he filled Malcolm in on the details. A knock on the door had Harry letting Gurka in. Sal joined them and the men huddled together on the sofa and wingback chairs planning strategy. Each had copies of Anna Heller face from her mug shot that was taken when she was arrested. Harry pointed out that she may have changed her looks, but her size and structure were things that were harder to disguise. They figured that she'd be milling about in the crowd, just watching the parade like everyone else.

Seamus and Satu had been listening with half an ear to the conversation in the living room as they added pompom's to the hats. "What about Rex?" Seamus asked her. "If I were to fly him over the parade focusing on the dog group, it would give us a view of both sides of the street at the same time and with two or three people monitoring the feed, we might spot her more easily." They stopped working on hats and went to join the planning session.

"Sorry to interrupt, Boss," Seamus said to Harry, "but we've come up with an idea that may make it easier to spot the assassin before she strikes." They went on to tell the men about their idea of using Rex. Details, as to who would monitor the feed, was quickly worked out. As they talked, Satu went to get the box of pompoms and a box of hats that needed them and both she and Seamus worked while they talked.

Time flew by. Will announced that dinner was served. Everyone stopped what they were doing and headed to the kitchen where delicious smells filled the air. Des ended the call with Malcolm, saying he'd keep him posted. He chuckled when he heard his boss say that he wished he were with them.

Dinner conversation, by silent consent, stuck to plans for the Christmas holidays, what was happening in school, upcoming plans for college and more relaxing topics. Claire and the agent who was guarding her returned. Agent Sims agreed to meet her here in the morning and take her to work as well as remain with her during the day and bring her home. She thanked Claire for making the day so interesting. "I didn't know that math could be so fascinating. I'm looking forward to tomorrow."

Claire was in a good mood when she settled next to Tom and Gwyn for supper. She looked around and saw the sewing machines and wanted to know what was going on.

"It's just that time of year. The Christmas Parade is on Friday, so we've been working on elf costumes."

"Good. After all that excitement you've been experiencing, it's good for you to do something that is calm and relaxing."

"Your right." Kate replied glad that nobody filled her mother in on what was really going on.

Once dinner was done, Seamus went to drive Satu home. She wanted to finish putting all the references on the paper that she and Seamus were jointly submitting along with the graphics for their presentation to the class. They entitled the paper, Flying House. She told Kate she'd print out a separate copy, along with copies of the graphics to give to her because it would make a good entry in the archival records of the house for further generations. Their last day of school prior to the holiday vacation was Friday, and they said they couldn't wait.

Kate's dogs had been fed and were outside enjoying their biscuits. Sal and Roger had left to take care of the kennel dogs and to make a schedule for the rest of the week.

Des, Tom and Gwyn headed over to Killoy and Killoy to check on some feelers that both men had put out on Anna Heller to their sources. There hadn't been a trace of her so far. Malcolm told Des that the Bureau wasn't having much luck getting information out of Turchin, Heller or Joel. It seems obvious they feared Anna and the people behind her more than they did the law.

Suddenly alone, they curled up on the sofa, Harry drew a long breath. He was about to go over plans for Friday night again, when Kate said, "We really need more furniture in this room. We need some comfortable chairs where people who are at a gathering can hold quiet conversations with friends and not be required to focus on the main topics of conversation."

"Your grandmother put your stack of catalogs on my desk in the library. Why don't we go sit in there and look through them. There are two wing chairs in there as well as a pair of overstuffed chairs with hassocks."

"Wonderful. I can't believe that Gram got all this done while we were in DC. I know she can be a force to be reckoned with, but this is amazing."

They'd been making lists for about an hour when the sound of a knock at the door interrupted them. Des was back, and he said that he and Tom had come up with more connections that the lady had to the GRU which they would discuss with Harry in the morning. He plunked himself into one of the overstuffed leather chairs and put his feet up. "Foyle, this is heaven. If I had a library like this, I'd get nothing done. I'd try to read a report in this chair and be sound asleep in two minutes flat. And speaking of sleep, if the lady leaves us in peace tonight, we might just get some. I'll wish you two good night."

Closing the catalog she had open, Kate said, "He has a point. The munchkin needs its beauty sleep. It's got a lot of growing to do before making an appearance. I'm going to let the dogs out."

"You let them out, then head for bed. I'll put this stuff away, bring them in, then join you. Des is right. We need sleep. Tomorrow is going to be a busy day culminating in trying to teach a bunch of cops and their canine partners how to dance. Have you chosen the music to march to?"

Kate paused in the door and grinned at him. "Staying Alive, by the Bee Gees."

CHAPTER 30

Thursday morning

Kate woke and went to stretch but then thought better of it. Apparently morning sickness was quite happy to make an appearance now that there was no shooting going on. Her sigh must have woken Harry because a cracker appeared before her face. She reached out and began to nibble. Harry opened the bedroom door and headed to the French doors in the living room to let everyone out. The greyhounds were still in residence even though Agnes was back, because Ann's house didn't have a fenced yard. Once all the dogs had reached the yard, he headed for the kitchen to make tea and get the coffee going. Heading back to the bedroom with tea in hand, he passed Des.

"Coffee is ready." Harry told him.

"You're a saint." Des said as he headed for the kitchen.

Harry laughed at the number of times this week he'd been told that. He found Kate nibbling on a saltine while sitting on the edge of the bed.

"Your tea, Madam," he said handing her the cup.

"You're a saint," she mumbled.

"So I've been told," he said. When she finished her tea, he stood and taking her hand, he lifted her off the bed, and they walked into their new bathroom. Kate eyed the tub, but looking at her watch realized that the house would soon be filled with people. "Tempting as that tub is, I think I'll take a shower. We've got people coming and should hurry."

"It might be faster still if we showered together. Are you feeling up to it?"

***

They entered the kitchen a little later, much relaxed and ready for the day. Tim was apparently playing doorman, directing everyone to the kitchen where breakfast was being served. Kate looked up to see her mother walk in along with Agent Sims. She was talking to the agent over her shoulder. "You can't face a day of work without a decent breakfast. It won't take long, and we can get on the road." They headed for the kitchen and Claire settled herself next to Maeve and Padraig. She introduced everybody she knew to Agent Sims, and then they both dug into the hearty breakfasts that were placed before them. Dani and Will were working side by side at the stove and enjoying the whole process.

Kate and Harry sat at the table and dug into the food that appeared as if by magic. The magic came in the form of Sybil who passed them plates of hot food before taking her own and sitting next to them. She was looking more rested and spry than she had all week. It looked as though the rare good night's sleep had benefited everyone. "Did all the hats and shoe covers get finished last night?" she asked.

"Believe it or not, we got more than forty sets made. If that many cops and their dogs show up, we're going to be the biggest part of the parade."

"Well, your group is everyone's favorite part. People love to see all those happy dogs marching and dancing. They wait all year for it."

Kate laughed and said, "Thanks." Turning to Harry, she asked, "What was the meeting in the living room about? I noticed that Satu and Seamus were excited about something. I noticed that Satu didn't let whatever it was slow the work on the pompoms."

"The kids came up with the idea of using Rex to do overhead surveillance. Seamus thinks that if the feed is sent to multiple screens, it would mean more eyes on the crowd, and because she's a small woman, we might not spot her if we're only look-ing from street level. Gurka and Seamus figured out how to send the feed to one of the state's mobile unit that has several computers. Satu, Sal and Gurka will man it. We'll all have earpieces so that we can react as soon as she is spotted."

Kate rose to clear the table and went to talk to Sal about the kennel. Noticing that her dogs were relaxed in the yard chewing on biscuits, she real-ized they'd been fed. She told Dani that she should check in with Ellen to make sure that everything was going well there. Friday was the knitters last day until the holidays were over. When they re-turned, there would be a big push to get ready for the fashion show in February, but since tomorrow was going to be busy, she thought today would be a better day for passing out the presents. Each of her knitters would get a gift, plus a sack of presents to go under their Christmas trees at home for their children.

Harry joined the two of them as they headed out, with Dillon and Jake by their sides. They walked through the kennel on their way. Roger and Sal had polished up the lobby with two new displays of colorful winter collars and leads. The snowflakes and other designs added a festive note to the place. Kate stopped in her office to make her apologies to Hecate, her Maine Coon Cat for neglecting her. The cat was not exactly enthusiastic in her welcome, but Kate did notice that she got up to snuggle and even accepted a hug before returning to her throne on Kate's chair. Kate looked back when she left the office and mused, "I may need to buy another desk chair. I don't think she's going to let me use mine anymore."

The other's laughed as they headed out to the barn. Both Harry and Kate's phone dinged as they crossed the parking lot. Harry stepped in front of Kate as he looked up and spotted an unfamiliar car at the top of the driveway. Kate, hidden behind her husband, whipped out her phone and rapidly typed in the code to record and save all the multiple shots the camera took of the visitor. Dani looked over her shoulder and saw the license plate number appear on the display, and pulled out her phone to call it in. Looking back at Kate's phone, she added to her reporting that the female driver was a known felon, armed and dangerous. She added, approach cautiously. The car sat at the top of the driveway until Harry pulled out his phone, and then it turned back onto the highway heading south toward the interstate. Dani added the direction of travel to her report, and then they all went into the barn to get the presents.

When they got to the top of the stairs leading to the studio, Harry grabbed all the sacks and led the way with a, "Ho Ho Ho." Everyone gathered around and Kate wished them all a Merry Christmas. She told them they'd be getting their bonus' tomorrow from Ellen for all the wonderful work they've done. However, she and Harry wanted to give them each a personal present and for those with kids, a sack of presents to take home. She talked about how they had gone beyond being employees and become family. She introduced her friend Dani and her dog Jake. Kate pointed out that like Agnes' fiancé, Sean, Dani was a state trooper, as was Jake.

Dani told the women how she and her fellow officers and their dogs trained with Kate and Sal. She offered to come and talk to their kids after the holidays. "I'll bring Jake so that they can meet a cop who walks on four feet." They all laughed and said that their kids would love it.

While Kate was talking to the women who knit,

Harry went into Ellen's office, to update her on what was going on. He showed her the photo of Anna Heller's face at the end of the driveway. He told her if she saw the woman lurking about, to lock the door, call him, or Sal or 911. The troopers were already searching for her. "She may look innocent, but she's a cold-blooded murderer who wants Kate dead."

"Ann told me that Kate was pregnant," Ellen said.

Harry smiled. "Yeah, she's at the mourning sickness stage now. So far it's only mornings, but in the pregnancy book I read, almost anything could set it off."

"For me it was the smell of coffee, which both my husband and I loved first thing in the morning. During those months he had to wait until he got to the office each day to get his caffeine."

Harry looked through the glass wall and saw that Kate was getting ready to leave. He stood, but Ellen gripped his arm. "I've loved that little girl since the day she was born. She has the most wonderful heart. I know she's all grown up now and becoming a mother, but she'll always be that little golden girl Claire let me hold when she was only a few hours old. Please guard her and keep her safe."

"I will. Tomorrow is a half day for the kids. Send

all the ladies home as soon as the kids get off the bus and close up. I'll make sure that someone is here to make that go smoothly."

"You're that worried."

"Yes."

As they left, they looked up the driveway toward the highway, but saw nothing. Dani's phone buzzed, and she listened, then told them, "Gurka says that the Waterbury police notified him that they located the car parked in the Waterbury mall. It's probably abandoned. She could be anywhere in the mall, but it would be too dangerous to try to confront her there. At least we now have proof that she's in Connecticut."

Kate was quiet on the walk back to the house. When she got there, everyone was involved in some part of the project to stop Mrs. Heller. Kate told Harry she was going to lie down.

"Are you okay," he asked.

"I'm just tired." She took Dillon and went into the bedroom and closed the door.

He stood watching the door until Dani walked up and asked, "Where's Kate? Is anything wrong?"

"She went to lie down. I hope it's only that's she's tired. The schedule we've been on has been hard on us, and we're not carrying a baby. I also think she's worn out after being so cheerful for her knitters. They think the world of her, and she hates to let anyone know she's worried or frightened. I would say--right about now--she's terrified. She's in there because she's alone and can let down her cheerful, 'Kate can do anything' facade."

When lunch was ready, Harry went to see if Kate was awake. She lay on the bed, sleeping, but her face was streaked with tears, and lying next to her with her arm over him, was Dillon. He lifted his head when Harry entered, but other than that, didn't move. Harry raised his hand and signaled him to stay then closed the door and let her sleep. As he reached the kitchen Maeve was there talking to Sadie on the phone. When she hung up, she looked toward the living room and asked, "Where's Kate?"

"Sleeping."

"Is something wrong?"

"No, but I think she doesn't have the strength to smile and get on with things at the moment. She's all smiled out. She'll be fine. Dillon is sleeping beside her."

"Some men might resent that she chose her dog over her husband."

"Dillon and I are about even in the number of times we have saved Kate. He's fancier about it though. I love them both and I know that he is bringing her comfort as he did in the past when she lost her grandfather and her dad. If sleeping with an arm wrapped around a big fuzzy pup brings her even a bit of comfort today, I'll be happy."

"You're a s..."

"No, don't say it. I've run out of halo polish. I'm just a man who really loves his wife and even with all the terror surrounding us, I wouldn't change a minute of my life with her."

Kate woke slowly. Dillon was stretched out on the bed beside her, but when she moved, He stood, and jumped off the bed , then shook and trotted over to the French doors. Kate rose slowly, but felt fine. In fact, she felt better than she had in days. She walked over to the doors and let Dillon out to join the gang in the yard. Liam and Quinn saw him and raced to join him. Kate looked down at her polar fleece top and decided that it didn't show any creases, so she probably looked all right. She turned toward her bureau and saw her reflection showed some color in her cheeks. She needed to find Harry, after she used the bathroom. Kate knew that as this munchkin grew and started putting pressure on her bladder, this will be the room where she'd be spending more and more time. She stopped and looked around. It was a lovely room.

The door to the library was open and Kate spotted Harry inside. He was at his desk surrounded by furniture catalogs. The twins were stretched out in the over stuffed chairs and Des sat in one of the wing chairs. "If you make even half the basement into a man cave, you'd be a hero to the family." Seamus said.

"Provided it has a pool table." Tim added.

"They haven't seen the pool table and the games room at Lake George yet, have they?" Des said.

"Nope. They may want to spend some of this vacation at Camp, skiing during the day and playing pool at night."

Tim looked at Des and raised an eyebrow. "He's having us on, right?"

"Not even a little."

"That does it. We've got to capture this assassin fast. I've got a vacation to plan."

"I'll vote for that," Kate said from the door.

Harry rose and went to her. "Feel better?"

"Definitely. I needed that. My bed mate is out playing with his father and Quinn."

Dani stuck her head into the library and said, "Dinner is served. We need to eat. There's vital elf training on the schedule for tonight."

"Go Elves!" Tim said imitating a cheerleader.

CHAPTER 31

Thursday evening

D inner was Dani's time to shine. She served spaghetti with sauce that was her own recipe. Will did the meatballs and told them that this meal was lower on salt because he used spices instead. They'd also made several loves of garlic bread and Will had prepared a delicious spinach and mushroom casserole as a side dish. Everyone settled in to eat. Sybil asked Dani if she knew how many officers were coming tonight.

"I think thirty-six, but some others may show up. I can guarantee that these guys are going to have a ball tonight if the get to do what Kate was doing with her search group dancers. I know I am and Jake's going to love it, aren't you big guy," she said as she patted the head of the big black dog at her side. "Have you decided what we're going to do, Kate? That's going to be a lot of cops and dogs. Plus we don't want something that will distract us from searching the crowd for our killer."

"There will be only three routines which are very easy but look impressive. These you guys will learn, and they will repeat as we march. It will keep you in constant motion to make it more difficult for her to get a clean shot. I'll be marching with your group, and Kathy King and Tenney, her Newf, will be leading the Search and Rescue group which will be ahead of us, along with the junior handlers dressed as the Magi. My goal is to draw her out without her getting a clear shot at me. The most exposed I'll be will be when the Search and Rescue team does its dance at the end. Our unit annually signals the end of the parade, however, we will be performing up on the bandstand, so we'll be completely exposed. It's almost time, so we should head out to the barn." As they stood, Multiple phones began dinging announcing the arrival of their marchers.

Kate had Dillon beside her with Dani and Jake on her right. Harry fell in next to Dillon and the rest of the crowd followed behind. Canine officers and their dogs filed into the barn with some noting changes and improvements to the building. Sal pointed out that there was a fenced exercise area through the back door. Tim took over checking everyone in and Seamus and Satu handed out hats and shoe covers. Soon the room was filled with elves, laughing and ready for their assignment.

Sal called for attention. "I want to thank you all for coming. We have been working on a case that you may have heard something about. The bottom line is that Agnes, her grandmother Sybil and our Kate testified to the House of Representatives in DC this week. Kate named names of people posing a threat against our soldiers and the army in general. There have been numerous arrests, but the leader of the group, who looks like a sweet little lady but in reality, is a GRU trained assassin, is still in the wind and is coming after Kate for blowing up her plans. We caught her on camera this morning at the end of the driveway. She escaped. Kate is surrounded by protection here, but tomorrow, she and her search group, plus a bunch of kids and their dogs will be marching through the town in the parade and performing on the bandstand. This is common knowledge in town since they do it every year. Our assassin will have plenty of opportunities to shoot Kate along the parade route to say nothing of when she's exposed on the bandstand.

"The obvious answer would be for Kate not to march. However, this woman's style is if you can't get your target, go after the ones she cares about. So Kate will march. What we're hoping is that we can spot her in the crowd while she is trying to get a clear shot at Kate. What you are going to learn tonight is how to march in such a way that she will have a hard time getting that clear shot during the parade itself. If we can move her to the band-stand area, it might be easier to take her down." He stepped back and nodded to Kate.

"Okay," Kate said, "how many of you had to march in your various careers." Almost every hand came up. "Great. What I want you to do is to form two lines, with dogs in heel position. They will re-main at your side throughout, so you don't need to worry about distance control. Now at some time during the parade while the two lines are marching, you will move position but just 'follow the yellow brick road' and you'll find yourself back where you began. Let's begin by marking time, which I will mark on every other step, and left, left, left." The group moved smoothly around the barn and while marching, Kate had them, one at a time, follow her down the center of the group until they reached the end, moving back where they began. The last exercise we'll do is the cross over. In this case, I'll move down the center to the end of the line and then have each pair trade position. The marcher on the left will cross in front of the marcher on the right. When I get to the front of the line, you will have left space in front of you by shortening your step with a half step. You step with your left foot and bring your right up to meet it. On the 'All Cross' command, everyone will switch places again. If you pass in front of your partner the first time, you will pass behind him this time. Is everybody ready to begin?"

A shout went up and Harry started the music. Recognizing what the song was, had laughter filling the barn. Kate yelled, "Mark time, mark, and left," and they were moving. Kate kept the lines moving and changed from one exercise to another. As they moved, with their lines, she kept herself a blur between them. When she reached the front or back of the lines, she'd have the marchers keep going with their performance while she kept moving beside them. The marching line needed the width of the entire street. They worked until they had it cold, and then Kate had them form a single file and smiling at Dani, began the spiral. She marched the group until they formed a circle, and then she stepped to the right and passed the person ahead of her, while telling them all to follow the leader. Soon the entire group was in a spiral, when Kate did an about turn and moved back in the opposite direction while warning the marchers that the dogs would be moving nose-to-nose and to keep their focus on the handler. It worked and the applause around the room went wild.

When they finished, Sal informed them that they had just marched the same amount of distance as they will in the parade and nobody lost step. "Everyone looked great but the best part is you made a protective wall to guard Kate which should deter our shooter. We will see you tomorrow night at six-thirty at the corner of Main and Ashburton St. That's the group's designated spot."

All the elves were in good spirits as they left, assuring Kate that she needn't worry. They'd take care of her.

When they got back to the house and Kate sat, every muscle in her body told he she just marched, mostly marching backwards and facing her elves for several miles. She hadn't been working with the dogs this week, so she had begun to soften up. A soak in her new fancy tub, should take the aches out. If not, doing it again tomorrow definitely would.

Harry came in and suggested that she go soak in

the tub while he closed up. Des had gone to his room and it was almost eleven o'clock, so he'd just bring in the dogs and lock up.

Kate stood with only a slight groan. As she headed toward the bathroom, her phone buzzed with a text. It was from General Cutter.

Kate,

The three service members are in custody. Two of them lawyered up, but the third spoke with the hope it would help his case. It seemed that his family is from Minsk. He still has an aunt and uncle there as well as cousins. When he was approached, it was by someone with photos of his family members. One shot included a newspaper from the day before. He was told that he would do as he was told or his family would die. He was told, if he ever spoke of it, his family would die. It had been eating him up that he had been part of the plan to help Turchin steal the deflector. His family is very close. His father wrote to him that he was proud that his son was in the army and serving a just cause. The bottom line is, he's given us the details of the theft and the name of the person behind the whole plot. It is Mrs. Heller, the lady who is apparently out on bail. She was the one who killed the two solders and wounded the third during the theft. Be very careful.

Cutter

Harry came in while she was standing next to the tub staring at her phone. "You know it works better as a bath if you add water."

"What?" Startled, she looked around and then remembered where she was and why. "I got distracted. Kate handed Harry her phone and turned on the hot water for her bath. She went to the linen closet to get a towel and bath mat and was surprised to find a jar of bath salts. She lifted it to her nose and then shoved it back onto the shelf, reaching for the small seat beside the tub. She lowered her head and took slow breaths, fighting nausea.

"What's the matter? Are you sick?" Harry knelt beside her, slowly rubbing her back.

"The smell. What was in that jar?"

He stood and looked. "Well it's not poison, as I'm sure your stomach has told you. It's gardenia bath salts. I think you found a new morning sickness trigger."

"But it's not morning."

"Doesn't matter. It can hit you any time so long as it's one of your triggers."

"Oh, goody. At least it's winter and the likeliness of me walking near a gardenia bush isn't high."

"Why don't you crawl into your bath."

Kate stepped into the tub and then sank into the hot water with a sigh of contentment. Harry reached across and flipped a switch on the wall and suddenly the tub filled with bubbly water jets shooting out from various places under the surface. Kate squeaked, but then said, "Ahhh."

Harry looked up from his laptop as a very pink Kate, wrapped in a big fluffy bath towel entered the room.

"Better?" he asked.

"Much. I don't think I'll have any trouble sleeping tonight."

Harry glanced at the screen in front of him and then closed the laptop, stood up and went to put it onto his bureau to charge. Kate pulled on a warm flannel nightgown and crawled into bed. The dogs who had been sleeping when she got out of the bath, looked up but then, seeing no problem, just went back to sleep. She was just snuggling under the covers when she stiffened. "I forgot to feed the cats today."

"I fed them. I think that Macbeth and William McKinley will become my office cats the way Hecate is yours, living in the kennel as she does. Macbeth may venture into this part of the house sometimes, but William McKinley has made it clear that

341

he doesn't deal with change. I think that since the dogs are in here, he's enjoying being able to sleep on the sofa instead of behind it."

"So all of our family is tucked up safe. I want to remember this day."

Harry turned off the light, but didn't fall asleep right away. He had no intention of sharing the information Des' CIA friend had sent him, with Kate. Apparently Anna Heller, prior to coming to the US, was well-known in GRU circles as being a deadly assassin. But the new information was that she bragged that she liked to get close and watch the face of her victim as they died.

They needed to make sure she got nowhere near Kate.

CHAPTER 32

Friday morning

Kate reached for a cracker as soon as she opened her eyes. She was munching on it when she turned her head toward the French doors and saw Harry sitting in the chair near his bureau, staring at his laptop. The look on his face was one of grief. One of deep sorrow. Something must have happened, Why didn't he wake her? She must have made a noise because he looked up, quickly hiding behind a smile.

"How's your stomach?"

"What's happened?"

"Nothing has happened. Everything is the same as when we went to bed."

Kate looked at him and decided it wasn't worth arguing--now. Something was upsetting him. She'd wait, but she wouldn't forget.

Breakfast was held at the three houses, so for them, it was only Des, Sal and Roger joining the meal. Dani and Jake arrived just as the men were leaving to care for the kennel dogs. They were going to put up the Christmas decoration on the outside of the kennel since all their regular dogs that spent their Christmas with them would be arriving at the weekend, as the ones who'd been with them this week left for home.

Everyone was subdued. Kate was getting looks by all who passed her. The pity in their eyes had her ready to scream, but there was no argument she could give. They weren't wrong.

She finally disappeared up to the future kid's playroom with her laptop. She found a chair and a tray table, creating herself a workspace. Rather than working on finding evidence, she began to work on the album she would create of their home being built. She set up a document that would become her book. On the title page, she wrote in decorative type, 'The Journey to Create a Home for Harry and Kate Killoy Foyle.' On the next page, she began writing their story. She wrote about traveling to the Samoyed National and fighting sadness due to the death of a friend. How she and Harry were engaged, and she'd begun thinking about the house they would some day build. Her brother had installed some software on her laptop for her to play with, so she sat as they traveled to Kentucky, laying out possible rooms, and accouterments for her dream house. She slipped in a photo of them standing by 'Charlie,' their motor home. This she followed up with a description of the search for a company which could build the house quickly since her tiny house would be much too small for them once they married. The rest of the morning had her cheerfully searching among the thousands of photos for ones which covered each stage of the construction. She had almost reached the point in the story where the basement was dug and built, when her husband found her.

"So, this is where you've been hiding."

"Not hiding, just working by myself."

"What are you doing?"

"I've started the story of the house." He moved in closer and reached over her shoulder to go back to the beginning. He read what she'd written aloud as Kate leaned against him. When he reached the part where she'd left off, he closed the laptop and pulled her into his arms to hold. They stood, looking out the French doors, enjoying the view of the woods, the kennel, and the barn, bathed in snow.

The sound of footsteps on the stairs made them turn as Agnes made an appearance. "This is where you're hiding. The house is wonderful. I came to ask why I just got an email from some girl named Carisa Amaya thanking me for letting her work with Thorin."

"Oh, I forgot to mention it. The kids in my Junior Handling class are involved in the parade. Carisa's Borzoi bitch came in season this week, so she can't be part of the parade because it would disturb the other dogs. She was devastated until I came up with the idea of her using Thorin instead. She's a good handler and has bonded nicely with your bitch. You might want to talk to her about showing her for you in the special's ring."

"Boy, Killoy, you do like to arrange my life with consulting me."

"You had disappeared."

"At least when she manages your life, she doesn't invite killers into the mix making you a target for the villain," Harry muttered, glaring at Agnes.

"Harry." Kate set her hand on his arm.

"No, he's right. Both times I didn't take into consideration what would happen to you. You were

Kate. You would manage."

Kate looked between them and decided on a change of topic. "I don't know about you two, but I'm starving."

The rest of the day passed quietly. When it came time to leave, Kate went to dress. She put on her thermal long johns, a warm shirt, and her bullet-proof vest. Then she went to pull on her sweatshirt only to realize that with all the layers, it didn't fit. Harry walked into the room to find her going through his bureau in search of a green sweatshirt. "Need something?"

"My sweatshirt doesn't fit over all these layers."

"Sweatshirts are on the third shelf in my closet. The green one is on the bottom of the pile."

Kate raced to the closet area and emerged dressed in a sweatshirt that was way too big for her, and made her look like a little kid.

"Now I know why everyone thought of you as a kid before I met you."

She stepped in front of his mirror and frowned. Then snapping her fingers, she dashed to her bureau and pulled out a large Christmas pin from her jewelry drawer. Grabbing the sweatshirt, and pulling the hem to just below her waist, she gave the excess fabric a twist and pinned it.

"You designers really do have an answer for everything," he said as he spun her around. "You look beautiful."

When the cars reached the corner where they were to line up, They saw the place was teaming with elves. It was a sight to behold. Not only elves, but elves with dogs, many of which were sporting bows or holly on their collars. Dani met them with Jake, wearing a wreath around his neck. The massive charcoal gray dog managed to carry off the large decoration with style. Agnes appeared with Carisa and Thorin. Carisa was truly a queen in her flowing robes, and Thorin now not only had matching robes draped over her body, but the snood she wore over her head sported a tiny crown. The two of them were talking about the show schedule for January, so Kate could check off another good deed to get her into heaven. She just hoped she wouldn't need to use it soon.

Once everyone was in place, Tom drove into place, the all-terrain vehicle which the search and rescue team used. It had been converted into a jazzy sleigh for Santa. He had the boom-box with massive speakers which would supply the music for the marchers in the back. Tom was dressed as Santa and Gwyn was this year's Mrs. Claus.

Kate walked down the center of the double line of elves thanking them all. Then nodding to Kathy to begin the march with Tenney, and they all began moving. They were the last group in the parade, so they didn't have to worry about marchers behind them. Instead, there were three police cars, with their lights flashing, bringing up the rear.

Kate's earpiece buzzed for a second, and then Satu's voice came in clearly. "Kate, Rex is overhead and scanning the crowds. He has spotted a man on the roof of the Carter Building on Main closer to the Green. He may just be watching the parade, but we're going in for a look. The marchers look fabulous and I think you should do this every year. I can't wait for you to see your formations from this angle. Sal and Gurka are monitoring the feeds with me."

Kate moved to the back of the line and signaled Gwyn to watch her for the signal to start the dancer's music. Because she'd marched in this parade since she was seven-years-old, she knew how many steps it took to get to the bandstand. That meant she knew when to begin the first set of maneuvers. She signaled Gwyn and the Bee Gee's burst forth with their strong beat and with a "Mark time, March!" they were on their way.

The cheering crowd went crazy. Kate grinned,

strutting between the lines, keeping everyone in step while at the same time the marchers were scanning the crowds to either side. She had just finished the 'cross-over and back' maneuver, when Satu spoke into her ear. "Don't get startled, Kate, and keep smiling, but Rex has discovered that the man on the roof is a sniper. He doesn't seem to be focused on you--yet. He is positioned to shoot at the bandstand. Gurka thinks it's where Anna is hiding. She probably plans to use the sniper as backup or to go after the crowd if she doesn't succeed.

"Kate, we got a close up. It's your ghost, Charlie. He's setting up to cover the area around the bandstand. Um, Kate, he said not to tell you--but I must. Sal has gone after him. He and Liam. Gurka couldn't stop him."

Kate missed a step but then got back into the pattern. Sal! Sal was putting himself in danger. At least Liam was with him. She remembered Liam's reaction to 'Charlie' when he came to get the box If Sal hadn't stopped him, he would have taken him down then and there. Liam, even more than Dillon, could spot a person's intentions and quickly react to them. He'd been her first 'police' dog to train since, at the time, she wanted to keep Dillon's head in the show ring. When she noticed Liam's prey drive might not be best for situations needing more subtlety, she trained Dillon. He was her biggest success so far. But if she had to choose which dog to put up against a cold-blooded killer positioned to shoot people from the top of a building, she, like Sal, would choose Liam hands down.

"Kate," The feed sounded in her ear. "I'm watching. The door to the roof just opened. 'Charlie' is still focused on the street. Sal just waved his hand at the man and Liam is--well he's creeping up on him. Damn! He nailed him. The guy has dropped his gun is biting his arm and dragging him toward the middle of the roof. Wait. He's stopped. He's gone to sit by Sal and his tail is wagging. Sal has the rifle. Two troopers just got there and have taken over."

Kate let out the breath she hadn't realized she was holding. "Thanks, Satu, I'll let my elves know. We could all use some good news about now."

Marching back through the line with a fancy strut that had her taking longer to get to the end of the line when she took two steps back for each step forward, she told everyone what had just happened. She told them that since Liam, Sal and Gurka were covering their part of the job, they should to get ready to repeat the three patterns as soon as she got to the front of the line. It took all her concentration to call the signals for the marchers to change sides, and do a 'four step double reverse.' She marched up to where Billy, one of the troopers, was when he whispered, "I saw our guys up on the roof. Thanks to Sal and Liam we can strut our stuff without worry." Kate encouraged the marchers clapping in time to the music. Sal must be feeling he's forty again. He and Liam make a great pair--retired cops but still able to fight the fight. Then she noticed movement beside the line and realized that it was Agnes, dressed as a much more feminine elf, passing out fliers. Sybil had been right. She was back and doing her job.

They finished the final run through of their marches, as they approached the bandstand. Kate noticed a space had been cleared around the bandstand, so as the Search and Rescue dance troop mounted the bandstand steps, and the Magi and their dogs moved off to the side, Kate had the double line split in two moving around it and forming a circle facing out, with their dogs at their sides, eyes searching the crowd and hands behind their back resting on their guns. When the last one she marched up onto the bandstand and turned to face the crowd.

This was the part where every year they ask for

a child to volunteer to hold the flag for their final number. Kate's mind froze. She'd forgotten about this part. There was no way she was inviting a child up onto the stage and into possible danger. But before she could open her mouth to speak, Agnes walked up onto the platform, waved the flag and bowed. Turning her back on the crowd, she looked at Kate, raised her chin and nodded and with a flick of her finger, their music began and the dancers worked through almost a dozen routines. When the final one came, Agnes was ready for the music to change to the National Anthem. The dogs went through their routine and then right on the beat, Kate said, 'stick' and Dillon broke from the line, leaped into the air to grab the flag from Agnes, circled the whole group and then wove between the dancer/dog pairs and came to stand by Kate. At her command, salute, all the dogs sat, rocking back on their hind quarters and raised their right front paw in a salute as Dillon lifted his head to wave the flag. The crowd cheered.

Kate signaled the troop to leave the bandstand, waiting as they passed and scanning the crowd. She saw nobody who looked like the assassin. Taking a breath, she walked slowly down the steps. When she reached the bottom, a hand shot out from the shrubbery that surrounded the bandstand and grabbed her right arm.

A woman's voice said, "The dog is dead if he moves."

CHAPTER 33

Friday night

"Dillon, hold.!" Kate commanded.

The woman emerged from between the bushes. She was dressed in a lush dark brown mink coat with matching hat and was wearing knee-high boots. To Kate, she looked like a witch from a fairy tale--beautiful but venomous. The gun she held glowed in the lights surrounding the bandstand. Kate took this all in as her head and body began to react all too familiarly. Oh no, not now. Her stomach muscles were moving, slight movements were starting to grow. Kate could barely focus on what Anna Heller was saying. The woman was yelling something about a sniper on the buildings if anyone moved. Kate struggled to focus, opened her mouth to breathe and suddenly realized what was happening. The woman was drenched in perfume--Gardenia perfume.

She struggled to lean away from the smell--breathing only through her mouth. The woman pulled her arm, forcing her closer and face-to-face she screamed, "You have ruined all that I worked for and brought me into disgrace. You will die and I will watch you. I will watch your face as the bullet steals the last breath from your body Mrs. Kate Killoy Foyle."

"The smell," Kate cried out. 'I can't take the smell."

"What are you babbling about you crazy woman," Anna screamed, and she shook Kate's arm forcing her to stand right in front of her.

Kate's concentration broke and in the next second, she heaved the contents of her stomach, Will's delicious dinner, all over Mrs. Heller's mink, and knee-high boots.

What happened next Kate didn't notice. The first heave was just the start. Heave after heave rapidly followed one-after-another. Anna was screaming as though attacked by zombies. As she becoming more aware of the smell, she might have preferred the zombies. Thing began happening around her, but Kate's awareness was totally on her stomach.

Kate later found out that when Mrs. Heller reared back from Kate's onslaught, she raised her arm. Dani grabbed the gun out of her hand while in unison, Dillon and Jake knocked her to the ground and held her, their mouths inches from her throat, growling and daring her to move. Des and Sean were there instantly. Dani called Jake to hold then shouted to Kate to pull Dillon back. Kate gave the command between her struggles for breath. He moved to her side as the men picked the screaming assassin off the ground and handcuffed her. What she screamed was probably filthy and all focused on Kate, but since Kate didn't speak Russian, it had no effect. Anna Heller's mid-western accent was gone, and she reverted to her native tongue.

A hand appeared in front of her face as she finally managed to stand up straight. It held a saltine. She took it and began to nibble as she let Harry wrap his arms around her and hold her close. As soon as she finished the cracker, everyone began asking her questions. 'Was she alright?' 'Was the threat really over?' 'Did she know they'd captured the sniper?' On and on it went. She had just begun her second saltine when her favorite question came.

Billy stepped up and smiled at her. "That was

the most unusual takedown of a killer he'd every heard of," he said. "But what I really want to ask is Kate, can we do this again every year? Rosco and I had a ball." A crowd of cops had formed behind him echoed the question. They thought that if they had extra members working the crowd as they walked they could raise money for a bunch of charities. Plus it was fun.

Kate had finished her cracker and felt good enough to grin. "Consider yourselves signed up for next year. We'll even add some more complicated steps to keep you guys and gals on your toes."

They cheered and headed out.

Harry looked at her and said, "Your color is coming back. Are you ready to head home?"

"Definitely."

"My question is how did you come up with the idea to distract her by throwing up?"

"I didn't. She was drenched in perfume."

"Let me guess. Gardenia."

"My baby does not like the smell of those fancy flowers."

They drove home only to find their house filled with people. Apparently her brothers invited everybody back to Kate and Harry's house for a Christmas party. People were everywhere. For the first time, Kate didn't feel that the house was huge. With all their friends and their dogs, it felt positively snug. Someone had lined up the three folding tables in the dining room and put table clothes on them. Will and Dani were sending out platters of finger foods, as quickly as they could get them out of the ovens. For once all the ovens were going in the kitchen, She and Harry moved from group to group, chatting mostly about the house and how it came together in just two days. As they walked around, Kate heard Tim tell a group, "Who but Kate would think to take out a Russian assassin who had a string of kills as long as your arm, with a barf. She's unreal."

Then her phone beeped with a text. Kate opened it and laughed.

Harry asked, "What?"

She showed him the phone. When he laughed, Tim reached past him and grabbed the phone. He took one look and read the message aloud.

Kate,

I have just finished having an amazing talk with Malcolm Bullock. My mind is still spinning over everything he told me about what you went through today. I am proud to be on your team. I can't wait to tell my daughter, who is also pregnant, that I am part of an army where our General takes out an enemy--with a barf.

*If you are ever in need of help, you have only to call,
soldier.*

Cutter

The crowd laughed. The party lasted only a
couple of hours. The cops left with smiles on their
faces saying that this was the new Christmas tradition. Des came by to say that he was flying back to
DC to be debriefed by Malcolm and the army. He'd
keep them posted. Dani and Will got the kitchen in
pristine order and then headed out. Following Satu
and her other brothers.

Ann approached them. Kate thanked her for the
most beautiful quilt in the world.

"I began it the day you returned from New York.
I knew that my little Katie had fallen in love. The
design grew as I got to know Harry, and I finished it
while you were on your honeymoon. Harry told me
you wanted it hung over your bed so that you could
see it every day. That's what makes every stitch
worthwhile." She hugged Kate and then joined
Maeve, Padraig, Sybil, Tom and Gwyn. Sal and Roger
said they check on the boarders and then settle in.

Kate reached up and kissed Sal on the cheek.
"You and Liam are my heroes. Satu gave me an on-
going description of the two of you in action on

that roof. You two may be retired cops, but you've still got it and are a tough as they come. I'm proud of you." Sal hugged her. "I love you as if you were my own daughter and I love that dog." Then he and Roger left.

Harry took her hand and together walked through the house, locking doors and making sure all the lights were out. Harry let in the dogs who loved having company but were absolutely worn out. The pups settled in their new favorite spots and settled down for the night. Heading into their bedroom, with Liam, Dillon and Quinn in the lead they stopped in surprise. The bedspread now hung on the wall over their bed looking perfect. Ann must have had someone do it while they were getting ready for the parade.

Kate stood looking at the quilt and asked, "Do you think we'll ever live the kind of nice quiet lives that other people live?"

"Do you want a reassuring answer, or the truth?"

"I'm tempted to say reassuring, but I want the truth."

"Then I'd say no. Kate, if one of our friends is in trouble, or if we see something that's really wrong, I don't think that turning away and leaving it as someone else's problem, is in our DNA. I just hope that next year is a little less exciting than this one was. But look on the bright side."

"The bright side?"

"Trouble brought us together, and we went from being strangers to being engaged. The rest of the year trouble tested our love many times. Even our wedding and honeymoon presented deadly threats. So if you want the truth, I'd say that living quiet lives is not our style. But, with you as my partner, I'll take whatever comes."

Kate reached out and held him, her head resting on his chest, and felt safe. She'd take whatever comes, too.

A WORD FROM THE AUTHOR.

I hope you enjoyed the latest adventure of Kate and Harry. If you haven't read the earlier books in the series, check out the sample that follows of the first book, Fashion Goes to the Dogs. Learn how Kate and Harry met, and how this unusual pair of misfits, found each other and built a life filled with dogs and mathematics all while fighting crime.

I'm often asked what my books are about. The best way I can describe them for those who love movies is to ask you to think DIE HARD meets BEST IN SHOW.

FASHION GOES TO THE DOGS

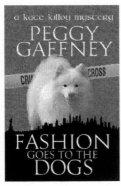

A Kate Killoy Mystery - Suspense for the Dog Lover

Book 1
Chapter One

"**K**ate, we need to leave now." My cousin Agnes charged past me out of the pre-dawn darkness, grabbed my shoes from the shelf where they lived safely out of puppy reach, and tossed them at me. While I was still struggling to tie my shoes, she pulled my coat off the rack, shoved me out the door and into Henry, her Ford Explorer. Before I could even ask where we were going, we were headed south on the Yankee Expressway, known to the locals as Connecticut Route 6, toward the interstate. She reached between the seats and grabbed a large Dunkin' Donuts bag which she plopped onto my lap.

"There's two cups of tea and croissants with orange marmalade. It was the best I could do on short notice."

Having grown up with four brothers, my first instinct was to argue, but the smell of those buttery croissants on my still sleep befuddled brain was too tempting to ignore. In half the time it normally took, we turned up the ramp onto I-84 and were heading west.

Once the bag's contents, including both cups of tea, were history, I felt awake enough to speak. "Where the hell are we going?"

"Into the city."

"I hate to inform you, Rambo, but taking someone across state lines against their will is kidnapping, a federal offense. I've got two businesses to run in Connecticut and don't have time to watch the sunrise over the Hudson with you."

"It's all taken care of. Sal is getting coverage. You were smart to bring him on as kennel manager. He told me he could manage without you in the boarding kennel this weekend. This week's numbers are low because, next week, everyone and his brother will be boarding their dogs, when they go away for the long Thanksgiving weekend. Since it's Saturday you're not scheduled to teach training classes. Also, I checked, and you don't have any entries in the dog show at the Big E this weekend so that's not an issue. Lastly, according to Ellen Martin, you could take the month off from your knitting studio and still submit the number of new designs you've created for the business since summer. Your studio manager is about to start kicking your butt."

I stared ahead, silent. I had to admit, I'd hit a dry spell. Following the second funeral, I'd just stopped, thinking, doing or caring. If it didn't happen by rote, it didn't get done.

In the Killoy family, I was not only the sole girl of the five children, but the only offspring who possessed a passion for the world of dog breeding and showing, especially Samoyeds. My mother and all four of my brothers lived and breathed mathematics. That was Dad and Gramps' field too, but their true passion was the dogs.

I, meanwhile, showed no aptitude, let alone genius, for numbers and it absolutely appalled everyone when I snubbed MIT to study fashion design. But Dad and Gramps stepped up to the plate and supported me, turning the second floor of the dog-training barn into a design studio for my business. The fact that my designs were aimed at people who showed dogs, also helped.

Losing Gramps to cancer had been heartbreaking, but I'd seen it coming and I still had Dad. Sharing our love of dogs, the three of us had been a team all my life. Since I was seven, we'd spent weekends together at dog shows. They had taught me my craft the way no one else ever could. Always together, we became "The Three Amigos" of the dog-show world. With Gramps gone, Dad and I had just begun to build a new connection, working as a pair. We had even begun taking an interest in the new litter of puppies and their show potential.

We'd actually been in the puppy pen, laughing at their antics, when the aneurysm hit him. They told me later there was nothing I could have done. Dad was dead before he reached the hospital. My world caved in as though the ground had been cut out from under me. I stood at his graveside, oblivious of the crowds that had gathered. I was alone and, after that, nothing seemed worth the effort.

We'd driven for about half an hour when I finally roused myself. "Why?"

Agnes didn't take her eyes off the road. "So, I can

help a friend. As for why you're going, I need someone who looks like you."

"Looks like me how?"

"I need someone who looks like a kid. You've got to pretend to be a kid who likes dogs but knows nothing about them. Act like you're very shy so you won't have to talk, your voice would give you away."

Her eyes were glancing at the clock every few minutes.

"I'm twenty-four." "You look twelve." "Bitch."

"Agreed. Though I think I qualify as veteran bitch. Look Kate, you've been trading on that 'little-girl' look in the ring for years. I just thought I'd take advantage of it for once. You run around the ring with your braid flying and your cute innocent expression and all the judges think it cool to put up the young handler with the great dog. Tell the truth. Don't you think it's about time to start playing on a level field with the grown-ups?"

"Any more advice, Dear Abby? What else can't you stand?"

"Well someone's got to tell you this stuff. Your mother doesn't notice you exist, Ann is too sweet to criticize her granddaughter, and everyone else thinks it but likes you too much to say anything.

It needed saying. You adored your dad and grand-dad, but they kept you frozen in amber and didn't let you grow up. If they'd tried this type of control with your brothers, there would have been war, but you were their sweet little girl. They could keep you young and play with you in the dog show world forever."

"They didn't..." I began what I knew was a flimsy protest.

"You haven't changed a thing about yourself since you were twelve.

Even in design school, people thought you were some young kid in a special program. People didn't take you seriously."

I moved as far from her as possible. Pressing up against the door I stared out the window. I wanted to scream and shout that she was wrong. She wasn't. What's more I'd known it for a long time but just didn't want to admit it because the thought of change scared the hell out of me.

With work everything was fine. I could run the kennel and teach the classes, no problem. And my design business was done online. No challenge there. No, I knew she meant that I should have a so-cial life as a woman. Truth was that terrified me. The world of sex, drugs and rock n' roll was not even in my solar system. I glanced at her determined expression and knew I was about to be ripped from my protective cocoon and thrown into the cold cruel world. After more miles of silence, Agnes sighed and glanced my way.

"Remember when we were kids and I'd ask you to do things and not ask why?" I nodded. "This operation is like that. I'm involved in something I can't discuss, but I need your help."

The words "Go to hell," popped into my head, but "fine," came out of my mouth.

We were making excellent time. She crossed onto I-684 heading into White Plains. It was good we'd gotten this far so early because the sun was coming up—and that meant a gazillion cars would be flooding the highway any minute traveling the same direction we were. I twisted in my seat to look at Agnes. She was biting her lower lip as her thumb twisted the Claddagh ring she always wore. She was nervous which was unheard of for her. She could handle any situation with style and aplomb. Hell, her photo was on a billboard in Time Square. I'd never seen her stressed. I went back to staring out the window. We ate up the miles as we transitioned from the Saw Mill River Parkway to the Henry Hudson Parkway which ran along the Hudson River as both the city and the sun rose before us.

Before I knew it, we were swinging into the parking garage of Agnes' condo. I headed toward the elevator, but she yelled, "Come on," and ran for the street.

Five minutes later we slowed to a stop at the entrance to Central Park nearest Strawberry Fields, an area named in memory of John Lennon. Agnes grabbed a gaudy scarf from her pocket tying it around her head like a turban, and turned her reversible white coat inside out so, the white fake-fur collar stood out against a now bright-purple coat. Then she put on the ugliest pair of glasses ever designed and slipped the strap of a camera over her head.

We'd barely gone forty feet into the park when I noticed a group of men moving toward us. "Don't speak and follow my lead," she whispered.

Then in a voice that dripped of a supposed Georgia birth, she ordered me to pose in front of a statue as she morphed into the quintessential obnoxious touristzilla. My eyes focused immediately on a gorgeous Afghan Hound walking at the side of Bill Trumbull, a handler I'd known all my life. "Oh my God, darlin', will you look at that pretty doggie!" Agnes gushed. "Oh, I've got to get a photo of that.

People back home won't believe that you can see something that beautiful just walkin' in the park."

The men had all stopped because we were blocking the walkway. I automatically moved toward the dog which was an exceptional blue-gray color with a white blaze. "I just know that you gentlemen won't mind if my baby sister poses for a picture with your magnificent doggie. Step a little closer sweetie. Stand right behind the—excuse me, what kind of dog is this?" Agnes raised her camera and waved me into position. I stood beside Bill, but he didn't show any recognition.

"It's an Afghan Hound, madam. You may touch the coat young lady." He reached out to stroke the dog. "Feel how sleek it is—like your own beautiful long hair." He reached out and stroked my hair, giving it a slight yank partway down.

"Oh, thank you so much." Agnes gushed. "Come on, darlin' we don't want to be late meeting Cheryl for breakfast." I turned and waved shyly at Bill then hurried to join Agnes. As soon as we were out of sight, we exited the park. She waved down a cab and gave the cabbie an address I didn't know. As we started forward, she looked back to make sure we hadn't

been observed. Once we were in traffic, Agnes

grabbed my shoulders. "Turn around and let me see your braid." Her hands worked their way down to the spot where Bill had yanked it. "Ouch."

She pulled something out of the braid along with a clump of hair that had recently been attached to my head. Turning, I saw her slip a mini memory card into her bag.

"What the hell is going on?" I was now getting worried. "Bill acted as if he'd never seen me."

Agnes didn't answer; she just looked out the window.

We pulled up in front of a brownstone building with a plaque on the door that read Marcel. As we got out of the cab, I looked at her. "Those men with Bill were not the kind I'd like to meet in a dark alley. Are they a danger to Bill or to us?"

"Neither, they're bodyguards."

I looked at her in surprise as we climbed the front steps, but her frown told me the subject was off limits. When we neared the top, she turned to me, grasping my shoulders to hold my attention. "Since you were twelve years old, what has been your one goal in life?"

I laughed because this had been the family joke forever. "You mean my fantasy, to have my own fashion show here in the city during Fashion Week?"

"Well, what if it weren't a fantasy? What if it were a challenge? What if I told you that since we were coming into the city today, I thought it might be a good time to kill two birds with... well, you get the picture? Kate, it's about time you show the world that you really are a serious designer.

Fashion Week is in February right before the Westerland Kennel Club show. I pulled some strings —well a lot of strings—and you'd better be ready to put your ass on the line, kiddo, because your fashion show is in the works. I suggested it at the board meeting of the Canine Genetics Foundation. They were looking for something to use as charity event to raise research money during show week. It will happen the last evening of Fashion Week. You'll meet with the sponsors later today to finalize the plans and sign the contracts."

My foot slipped on the top step and I grabbed the railing to keep from falling flat on my butt. Her words slowly sank in and began to have meaning. "I get a fashion show of my designs...here?"

"Actually, I think Marcel might object to that use of his front steps, but the ballroom of the host hotel should do. It's scheduled for the Saturday of their show week, which, as I said, happens to be the last day of Fashion Week so all the buyers will still be in town. You'd better close your mouth or Marcel will think you're an idiot."

"Marcel who?"

"There is only one Marcel. He's my step one in the plan to pull you out of your cocoon and turn you from a frumpy, dog-enrapture child into a sophisticated fashion designer. That has got to happen before you sit at the grown-up table today to sign the contracts for the show."

Agnes pulled me inside to meet Marcel and in a flurry of activity my transformation began.

Like Alice after falling down the rabbit hole, I felt disoriented. Each successive change was tearing me farther away from the only Kate Killoy I had ever known. Saying goodbye to my braid broke my heart since my hair had never been cut. The resulting stylish hair-do, clothes, and make-up created an entirely new person. As she stared back at me from the mirror, I didn't recognize her. She was beautiful. She scared me to death.

Agnes and her agent, Arden, supervised all the contracts for my show.

The deal guaranteed a winning result for all. The Agnes & Arden show took over the room, charming everyone while they pointed to the many places I, and everyone else involved should sign.

Once the stack of contracts was complete, they left, pulling me in their wake. Each gave me a high-five and welcomed me to the world of high fashion. I had ceased thinking hours ago and was running on autopilot. All I could do was smile and mutter my thanks. Reality began forcing its nasty way into my brain and I questioned whether thanks were premature. Had I just signed contracts that could be the death knell for my career?

We'd spent so much time today in Agnes' fairy-tale world that I was surprised when we arrived at a place I actually recognized.

Reilly's was my great-aunt and -uncle's favorite pub. We pushed open the door, and there they were. I was so happy to see familiar faces I almost burst into tears trying to hug them both.

Maeve, held me at arm's length, just staring at me, but Padraig leaned over me to whisper in my ear. "You are the spitting image of Maeve the day I fell in love with her. John and Tom would be thrilled speechless if they could see you now. In fact, they're probably doing a jig up in heaven now, knowing their little girl has grown up."

I wanted to cry but was afraid the tears would turn my newly applied makeup into a horror mask.

Supper turned out to be a noisy affair with

friends of Maeve and Padraig coming over to our table to be introduced to Agnes and me. For some reason, many thought I was a model too. Only their oldest friends recognized me right off.

Reilly's attracted mostly retired members of what I called 'The long arm of the law club.' Patrons tended to be both active and retired NYPD, FBI, CIA and MI-5. Maeve had been working for MI-5 when she met Padraig. They moved to New York where Padraig's family business was, but Maeve had kept her hand in, on an informal basis.

Partway through dinner, a man whose name wasn't mentioned joined us at the table pulling up a chair next to Agnes. As I watched, she slipped him the memory card. He apparently knew everyone there, because he jumped right into the conversation. After about five minutes he said his goodbyes and disappeared. Agnes leaned back, relaxed and ordered a cocktail, the signal, I guess, for a job done.

I wasn't sure if I was just overly conscious of my new appearance, but I was aware that we were being watched. The watchers sat at a table to our left. At first, I didn't pay much attention. I know the effect Agnes had on the world's male population. However, as one hour passed into two, this began to feel creepy. The younger one, who was dressed much more formally than any of the other men in the place, neither spoke nor ate. Every time I glanced in his direction, his eyes—his beautiful green eyes, I noticed—were focused on me. He didn't look like the men shadowing Bill, but...

When we stood to leave, I took Agnes' arm. "Those two guys at the table on the left have been watching us since we arrived. The guy in the double-breasted suit hasn't taken his eyes off me since we came in. Could he have recognized us from the park? Should we be worried?"

She glanced casually in their direction. "No, you needn't worry. Nobody could recognize you as that little girl in the park this morning." She grinned at me. "Brace yourself, Kate, I'd say it's a case of you having your first admirer."

When we turned to go out, I frowned and glanced back at the table. Both men were still watching. From where I stood, I couldn't read the expression on the younger guy's face, but when I looked at his older friend who had focused all evening entirely on Agnes, what I saw wasn't admiration. His look was pure, unmistakable hatred.

ABOUT THE AUTHOR

Peggy Gaffney

 Peggy Gaffney, like our protagonists, Kate Killoy, spent years raising Samoyed dogs and as a designer of knit clothing for dog lovers. For more than fifty years Peggy has bred and shown her line of Westernesse Samoyeds.

She studied writing in college, however that career got put on hold for more practical careers such as being a teacher and a librarian, as well as for time to raise a talented son with a killer sense of humor. When the writing finally returned, it came in the form of a series of suspense novels involving, a knitting designer, the world of show dogs, and a large Irish family.

Peggy lives in Connecticut with her family, plus two cats, and two Samoyeds whose names are Dillon and Quinn.

For those interested in being the first to know when

the new books will be available as well as follow the adventures of Dillon and Quinn, sign up for my newsletter by visiting the peggygaffney.com web-page.

Made in the USA
Middletown, DE
19 November 2020